love

is all you need.

THIA FINN

Half sac

Thia Finn

Disclaimer: The material in this book contains graphic language and sexual content and is intended for mature audiences, ages 18 and older.

Edited by Nicki Kuzn Swish Design & Editing
Proofreading by Kaylene Osborn Swish Design & Editing
Book designed and formatted by Swish Design & Editing
Cover design by Jason's Photography
Cover photo model: Jamie Walker
Cover photographer: Wander Aguiar Photography

ISBN 13: 978-0997340792

This book is dedicated to my readers who have stuck by me since the beginning. Without you, I would be nowhere. Thank you.

HALF
sac

PROLOGUE
BLUE

"Open the door, Blue." My dad could easily break it down if he wanted.

"Nooo." The long moan that followed the word came all the way from my toes.

"Son, we can't help you if you won't let us in."

"Just call an ambulance like I asked." The pain caused my body to bend in half. "Did you call them yet? Owww. Hurry, Dad."

"We aren't calling an ambulance until we decide you need one." I heard him talking to my mom.

"Your mom's getting a screwdriver so I can get in there. Just open the door."

"I can't get to the door. It hurts too bad to move. Shit. What did I do to myself?"

Mom's footsteps sounded on the wood floor, and then the knob started turning.

"You can come in here but not Mom. Do you hear me?"

She whispered through the door as my dad twisted the tool. "Blue, please let me in. I might be able to help you."

"No, Mom. You can't come in here. Just Dad," I yelled as loud as I could without causing more pain. The last thing I wanted was my mom coming in here and seeing this.

Dad spoke through the door, "Okay, Blue. I'm opening the door, and it's only me. Your mom's going to wait outside."

"I don't want to wait outside. Something's wrong with him if he needs an ambulance."

She didn't understand.

"Mom... just let Dad in, please. I'm hurting so call 9-1-1." I heard her footsteps retreat from behind the closed door.

Dad opened it slowly and peeked around. I don't know what he expected to find, but me balled up in the middle of the floor probably wasn't it.

He dropped down beside me. "Blue, what's wrong, son?"

"God, Dad, this is so embarrassing. It's my balls. They're swollen up, like big time."

"Well, let me see them."

"Shit." Showing my junk to my dad wasn't high on my list, but right now I didn't care.

"Son, talking like that's not going to make it better."

"Yeah, it kinda does."

"Roll over and let me see what's going on. I'm sure it's going to be okay."

"No, it's not. Something's bad wrong." I rolled over, and he looked down. His eyes said everything I felt. I balled back up on my side.

"It's bad. I knew it, Dad. What's wrong with me? Am I gonna die? Ohhh. It hurts bad, Dad.

"I don't think you're going to die from it, but there is a problem, Blue. We have to get you to the doctor."

"I've been telling you that. Call an ambulance, please Dad." The pain got worse each time I took a breath.

"Let me talk to your mom first."

"No, don't tell her and don't let her in here. I'm not showing her my nuts. Owww."

"Right. I'll step out, but I have to tell her, Blue. The doctor will anyway so I might as well."

"Just hurry. I'm hurting badly." I wrapped my arms around my legs and balled up as much as I could without squishing them more.

"I know you are, son. I know."

MR. MYERS

"Please take a seat, Mr. and Mrs. Myers." My worry meter set off from the grim look on the doctor's face, and he hadn't said a word. Not a good sign. Gina's strength surfaced in times like this, but she knew catastrophic news for Blue hung in the air.

"So, Doc, what do you think?" The day Gina delivered our son this man took over his care and had cured him of all kinds of normal childhood maladies. This problem topped them all, though.

"I called in Dr. Richards, a urologist who specializes in testicular problems so we would get the best diagnosis."

Specialist ticked my meter up another notch. I glanced at Gina whose face said everything I thought.

"He reviewed the scan on Blue and came to the same conclusions I have..." he looked up from his paperwork and directly into my eyes, "... one of the cords to his left testicle twisted, testicular torsion is the medical term. Unfortunately, Blue failed to mention it until the pain became so bad he couldn't put it off. When caught early, this can usually be repaired, but in his case, he put it off for too long. The testicle's blood supply cut off from the twist and is no longer viable. We will need to remove it. Bottom line, it's dead and if not removed, will become gangrenous which could infect the other testicle. It's imperative we get on this immediately." He leaned forward and folded his hands on this desk. Dr. Richards's told us devastating information and now wanted a fast decision.

"There's no decision, Doctor. Do it. Do it now." I didn't bother to consult Gina. The results could be catastrophic if we didn't act quickly. I finally looked at Gina grabbing her trembling hand in the process.

"Right, Gina?" Her nod was the only reply as tears welled in her eyes. Her strength once again pushing forward.

"One question, Dr. Richards." He dipped his head. He had to know the information I sought.

"He will be able to have children. Most men produce more than enough sperm with one testicle to father all the children they want. The surgeon I've called in to perform the surgery is also a specialist. There should be no damage to the nerves from the operation."

"Thanks, Doctor." I stood and shook his hand and turned back to Gina. "Do you have any questions, honey?"

She first shook her head no, and then looked up at the doctor. "Yes, I do have one. How's it going to look with one gone? Will others know by looking? Is this going to give him some psychological problems from looking abnormal?"

A brief, nervous laugh popped out of me. "That was more than one question, honey." I couldn't care less how it looked. Save my son's future children was my only priority.

"I know it was more than one, but I'm thinking about Blue. Kids can be so cruel these days. Anyone who has something different about them is made fun of and ridiculed. They look for reasons to bully each other. I don't want him to develop any complex over only having one." Her tone told me how serious she was about this. I never thought about it. Blue's self-confidence never ceased to amaze me. Could this cause it to wane?

"Mrs. Myers, I assure you if we get this taken care of, he'll be fine. Your son's a big kid with a great self-image, but if you think we need to consult with him, then, by all means, we will. We need to tell him ahead of time what's going to happen anyway. We could listen to him, but I have to impress upon you the importance of having the dead testicle removed quickly. There's always the possibility that we could have the surgeon replace it with a prosthesis during the surgery."

BLUE

"A fake nut in my junk? *No way,"* I yelled. "I'll just be nutless. I'll be half a nut. No, I'll be half sac. Yeah, that's it. Just call me Half sac."

BLUE

I loved the start of football season. My dad always told me football was a fall sport, but it was year round here in Texas—spring training, summer six-man leagues, sweaty two-a-days in August before the first day of college classes, and finally, the first big fucking game. Some guys lived for the opening day of deer hunting season, but not me, I lived for the season opener on that sacred hundred yards, one white line at a time. Nothing said a perfect day like running through the smoke in the tunnel to the roar of the crowd on the other side.

"What are you smiling at, dumbass? It's already hot as hell out there on the field," Jenko spoke as he pulled his shoulder pads over his head and settled them into place.

"Just thinking about the start of the season. Damn, I do love the first day." The two of us got lucky as high school seniors and were offered scholarships to the same university to play ball. We'd played together since Pee-Wee football back in Payton, Texas, home of the Fighting Jaguars. Now we were both Rams for Texas Agricultural University, TAU. The mascot got a lot of laughs with jokes about guys and sheep, but we didn't care as long as we beat the other team to a pulp on the field and added another 'W' to our stats. That's all that counted anyway, winning.

"Half sac, you're doing it again. Dude, you gotta stop. The new guys all think you're checking them out and liking what you see."

"Like I give a fuck what they think?" I leaned down, tying my cleats.

"Well, I know that, and the rest of the team knows that, but the dumb-fuck freshmen don't."

"You worry like a little bitch over stupid shit, Jenko. The freshmen are here to watch and learn from those of us who know how to play football on our field." I stood and slid my jersey over my pads. "This is our house."

"It will be next year when we're the seniors. Right now, we still have the douche bags lording over us."

"No one's lorded over me since I left my mom's tit, and you know it." He gave me a grin as I grabbed my helmet leaving him behind.

My parents begged me not to play a sport after my surgery in ninth grade. There's no way I could live without playing football. My mom tried her best to put her size six foot down, but Dad and I pecked at her like cocks in the yard. She knew how much I loved to play the game.

I even agreed to go to a sperm bank and leave a few of my swimmers to freeze so she'd get to see her grandchildren. What a fucking hilarious day in my life. Nothing like having a sixty-year-old nurse telling me what I needed to do while I sat alone in a room with porn and my phone. I didn't know they even made magazines with pictures like that anymore. Now that I think about it, they were probably leftover from *Playboy's* better days. I wouldn't touch them without rubber gloves on. Stuck-together pages told me all I needed to know. Besides, my brain had more than enough spank bank material from the dot com sites out there to take care of this business.

With my jizz tucked away in subzero for safekeeping, my parents finally agreed to let me play. I prayed the day would never come when the doctor undeniably determined my condition occurred from a hit I took in football a couple of weeks before surgery. My mom quietly informed me I'd never step foot on a field of any kind again.

I wanted to understand her decision, but I couldn't accept it, so I worked hard to find people to be in my corner for my plea bargaining. Dr. Richards became my all-time hero when he suggested freezing my boys for future use. I still send him tickets to all the home games I play.

Jenko caught up, and we jogged to the middle of the field to take our places for stretching and warming up for the brutal morning ahead. That first day of practice always kicked our asses no matter how good of shape we stayed in over the summer.

Close to noon, we made our way back to the locker room. We walked in laughing at something one of the freshmen said about being hurt from all the hits he took. Didn't he know tomorrow would be worse?

"Yo, Half sac. You coming to the house tonight?" Timms asked. I'd never joined a frat. Why join when half the team belonged to one? I had the best of all the Greek life without having to do all the craziness required that went along with belonging to a frat. I got an invitation to everything they did for fun, so joining one made no sense.

"I don't know. I haven't spent much time at my place since I got back to campus. It's been a long day, so I might just hang there tonight."

Timms' roommate threw his big-ass arm over my shoulder pads. "Dude, the chicks are hot for us. It's been a long, dry summer for most of them. They're willing and ready."

"Yeah, I'm sure they're ready for you." Gerrod's three-hundred-pound lineman's body kept most of the girls running the other way. If they only knew he was all talk and no action when it came to getting down to the deed. We harassed him all the time over how long he could go with only self-love.

"Dude, this is going to be my year. I'm going to have a girlfriend. I've already made up my mind."

Timms almost fell off the bench laughing. "What the hell, Gerrod? Why wait until your senior year to decide you need a girlfriend? You've done without all these years."

"Yeah, I know." The bench moaned under Gerrod as he sat. "I decided I might want to find one who'll stick around once I graduate."

"Dude, you know you're gonna get in the draft this year, and then you can have your pick of the pussy, banking all that cash." Timms loved giving him hell about going professional. Gerrod hadn't made the decision to keep playing yet.

"Whatever, dickwad. I want a girlfriend. If she sticks around for the season, I'll consider taking her with me on that millionaire gravy train."

"That's crazy thinking. The last thing I want is one girl when I go pro... I want a harem all to myself." If I made it into the draft, I didn't want to be saddled down with a woman.

"That'll get old fast," Jenko spoke as he removed the last of his uniform heading for the showers.

I always tried to be the last to the showers. Jenko knew my back story and the details of my surgery. I didn't try to hide it because I didn't give a royal fuck what anyone thought about me. I came to this field to do a job and as long as I did it, what the others thought didn't mean shit to me.

"Hey, Half sac, let's go eat before the party. I'm starving," Jenko called out.

A round of players all joined in. Damn, we'll take over any place we go. "Sure, let's do it. Hey, any of you freshmen rejects want to go?" I asked, remembering what it was like when we were the new kids and were treated like a loser both on and off the field. Several nodded in response.

"You do know how to talk, right? They didn't let you out of high school without speaking, did they?" Jenko and I laughed, and it caused some to look up. We weren't that intimidating. The coach wanted us to mix it up with the new guys. We always got the lecture at some point.

"I do," one big kid finally said out loud. "I'm starving. Can we go some place that serves real food? I'm sick of the cafeteria, and classes haven't even started yet." A few around him made noises and grunts affirming what we already knew.

"Dude, you gotta know where to go on campus to get the best food. Otherwise, you'll be eating shit all semester, and we can't have that. Y'all need to put muscle on, not lose it. Come with us, and we'll set you straight on the right cafeterias."

I'd done my good deed for the season.

Loud laughter and screams shouted from the pool area at the back of the Chi Omega Chi (XOX) house, typical for a preseason party. Music blared throughout the field surrounding the house. XOX had moved way off campus our freshmen year because they got tired of paying fines for noise violations. Out here on the prairie, only field rats ran from the noise.

"Hey, Blue," a short, little blonde haired, blue-eyed chick sidled up to me before I made it past the front door.

"Hello, yourself." I pulled her in for a hug to avoid having to call her by name. So many girls assumed because I'd met them once or twice that I would remember their names. Hell, the group that hung around here all looked alike. I could never go by hair color since they seemed to change it with the wind direction. At this minute, all I knew was this one smelled delicious. When I took an interest in a girl, I loved it when she smelled like I could eat her up because sometimes I did.

"Are you here with someone special tonight?" she whispered in my ear before letting me go.

"No, just hanging around for a while. The long practice whipped our asses today in the heat."

She wrapped one arm around the back of my waist and put her other on my chest before she started slowly working her way down my abs. "I know something else we can make long and hot."

"Damn, girl. That's some opening line." I gave a little laugh before grabbing the hand that had made its way to the top of my bathing suit.

"When I know what I want, I go for it. What about you?" She batted her eyelashes at me.

If she only knew how much this made me want to get the hell out of her sight. The only way I'd be touching this girl was if she managed to get me so drunk I didn't know what I was doing, or she drugged me. Neither of those would be happening tonight nor would she. I peeled her off me and smiled. "Maybe another time."

The door outside to the pool called my name loud and clear. I couldn't get out of it fast enough taking two full cups of beer to last a while.

"Dammit, why do I have to go to a fucking frat party at douche central? Daddy's money will have the booze flowing, and their sense of entitlement will be at maximum height." I shoved clothes back in the dresser of my furnished apartment bedroom. "How long am I stuck here again?"

"What's your problem, Noelle? I thought you wanted to transfer to TAU? That's all we heard about last year at Roberts." Quinn confronted my bad attitude.

Quinn and I met our freshmen year at the junior college where we attended our first two years away from home. Now we'd moved on to TAU, and I was already over this whole college thing. The idea of going back to classes and cheering after working all summer killed me. The internship I'd landed at the television station for the summer, gave me a taste of being in front of the camera reporting news, a taste which solidified my decision as to what I wanted to do with the rest of my life. Being stuck for two more years here in the school's Radio, Television and Communications Department doing lame-ass work did nothing for me.

"I'm just ready to be done with school. I went to the RTC Department yesterday and spoke with the director. All she could say was I would get my time like all the other students. She didn't seem impressed at all that I worked my ass off at KTKR all summer."

"You're going to have to prove yourself to her, Noelle. She's got students who've been in that department paying their dues since they walked in the doors their freshmen year. You're the new kid, and she probably wants to see what you're capable of doing."

"Sorry, you're right. I don't mean to take my shitty attitude out on you. The idea of cheering one more year is so far down the list of what I want to do. I can hardly stand to be around myself from acting like Negative Nancy." I pulled my short jean cutoffs over my bikini bottoms and turned to the mirror attached to the back of my closet door. "Are these too short? They make my ass look fat."

"Oh my God, Noelle. There is nothing fat-looking about your ass. Why would you even say something like that?"

"Sorry, again. I'm just in a mood. The head bitch told me I needed to watch making a pig of myself. Her words, not mine." I looked at my ass again and tugged down the bottom of the shorts as much as I could before sliding on my sleeveless button-down. "Honestly, I don't give a flying fuck what she thinks."

"Now that's the smartest thing you've said since I walked in here. You ready to face the lion's den?" Quinn laughed at her own joke, but in reality, it felt like the truth.

Once ready, we took off and a short time later pulled up to this house in a field, I had my doubts.

"Well, Quinn, what do you think? Should we head back to our apartment pool or get a beer and blend in with everyone? It's your call?"

"No, it's not either. She told you to be here. New squad members need to meet the guys on the team. Head bitch demanded your presence, not requested it."

I glared at her. I wasn't good at taking directives from someone my age. I liked cheering, and the school paid for my classes, but someone telling me what I had to do that wasn't part of cheering had always caused a problem.

"I guess meeting the guys I'll be cheering for is a good thing, but it doesn't mean I like being forced to come or risk making HB angry."

We both laughed at my shortened version of her name as we got out of my Jeep. The typical huge frat house looked like something out of *Neighbors* with lots of Zac Efron types everywhere. Easy on the eyes, short on everything else.

"Well, shit, this should be interesting." Quinn walked around the front of XOX not able to take her eyes off the candy displayed before us. "If I find one who's not heavily intoxicated, looks like any of these, and fucks like a madman, I'll see you tomorrow. Have I told you how much I fucking love you?"

"That list might make your dream a no-go."

"I'll settle for two out of three," she replied, and I swore she wiped the drool off her chin.

"Put your tongue back in your mouth before we get any closer. They'll have 'blowjob' on their minds the entire time you're trying to find the one," I laughed as I said it, but I knew it was sound advice.

"If it's reciprocal, I'm down."

"Don't you wish. Guys like this are only into sex for themselves. Hell, they're only into everything for themselves. We've walked this road before, Quinn."

We'd both had our fair share of short relationships in high school and college. From the looks of things, this would be no different. Hot guys, money to burn, and booze to consume all spelled nothing long-term for either of us.

"Now you're moving over to the Debbie Downer stage. Why don't you be Noelle today? She plays a lot nicer."

"Oh, yeah, right. I forgot I gotta play my bright, shiny cheerleader self today."

"It'd be nice to see only one of your many charming personalities in one afternoon. Try to keep that in mind for the next twelve hours, please."

"Right. Maybe I should've written it on my hand as a reminder."

"You don't need that. You're capable of being the Noelle everyone knows and loves. Just be yourself."

"Okay, okay. I hear you, Mom."

We reached the front steps and wound our way through a group spilling out the front door to reach the air-conditioned inside. Didn't seem to matter that it worked overtime to keep the place cool. Doors never closed during parties.

A couple of girls stood on the hearth talking to the audience of guys in front of them. They looked as though they conducted a choir the way they swayed their arms and hands around, but I decided clothes were about to be removed when I heard the music. It was still early, too. Some would have a long night and a bad hangover in the morning.

"Let's get a beer and head outside. I don't want to watch this," I said in Quinn's ear over the loud suggestive music.

"Good plan. I'm not ready for 'all shout for boobs out' yet." We laughed and walked through to the kitchen.

"And what would a frat party be without a few kegs standing by?" Quinn offered pointing to the six metal barrels before us cooling in garbage cans.

"Red solo cup, it is." I pulled two clean ones off the stack and ran the cold liquid down the side as any good bartender did. I handed the first one off when I finally got Quinn's attention. She couldn't concentrate for all the tanned abs on clear display around us.

After filling mine, I dragged her out the back door. "There's a lot more where that came from, Quinn."

People in various stages of dress filled the huge pool. It seemed like some didn't come prepared to get in but were there anyway. Partiers didn't care. Everyone eventually ended up in a pool if one was available. Summer Texas scorching heat meant keeping cool however possible.

I made a sweep around the pool standing at one end a safe distance away. Someone had to be going live on one of the social media sites. Too many possibilities for a YouTube hit waiting to happen.

"Let's walk around it first. I want to see some of this up close and personal before we find ourselves in the water today." Quinn pulled my hand in a forward direction. We held hands a lot when we were out for three reasons. One, it offered a little comfort in the unknown. Two, guys might avoid us thinking we were into each other, which was not the case. Three, guys might flock to us because they thought a threesome might be on the table, which was a 'hell no' and not an option. It was a win/win for both of us.

Making our way down one side, I spotted HB sitting in the lap of a massive hunk of man meat. "Hey, Madelyn." I gave her a little wave. She only needed to notice it was me, I didn't expect any recognition. Her cheerleading at TAU started her freshman year on a scholarship, too. She loved parading her seniority over the squad.

I couldn't have been any more shocked when she jumped up from muscle boy and squealed like she'd seen her BFF from third grade or something.

"Noelle, I'm so glad you came. You are going to love it here at the Chi Omega Chi house. The guys are the greatest, and they are the AZ's match fraternity for the first quarter." Whatever that meant, I had no clue. Trying to wrap my head around why she almost had me in a chokehold, I didn't have time to decipher her Greek language.

"You have to meet all the guys. They're going to love you, girl." She blared this out as if she were making a loud speaker announcement to the frat guys to head her direction for introductions, and that's what happened. Guys suddenly surrounded Quinn and me.

"Chi Omega's, this is our newest cheerleader, Noelle." She looked down her nose at Quinn. "And who might this little thing be?" she asked.

I spoke up as loud as she did. She would not make Quinn feel anything other than welcome if I had my way. "This is Quinn, and she's even more thrilled to be here than me." I turned to Quinn and gave her my best fake smile. The look she returned said how badly she would murder me later before she raised her hand and did a little sprinkle with her fingers to the crowd.

The guys liked what they saw if the crowd gathered around her was an indicator. They moved off a little, allowing me to talk to Madelyn.

"That was very nice of you to make introductions, Maddie. I appreciate you calling us out that way."

"It's Madelyn, hon. No one calls me Maddie but my parents." And just like that, she was back to her usual HB self now that only I could hear her. Tattooed forearms wrapped around her and pulled her back into his lap.

"Now, Maddie, don't lie. I call you that, too, when I'm about to nut." She whipped her head around and even though I couldn't see her face, I knew the look she gave him. It was a crude comment, but she deserved it. I snickered, but only Mr. Tattoo could see me.

"Hi, I'm Noelle Jeffries. It's nice to meet you." Honestly, I took great pleasure in meeting anyone who could put Madelyn in her place. I stuck my hand out to him.

"I'm Theo Timms, but everyone just calls me Timms." He shook my hand and held on an inappropriate amount of time considering his girlfriend still glared at him. I pulled my hand free forcing him to finally let go.

"You can't be a freshman. You a transfer student?" he asked.

"Yeah, from Roberts." He had beautiful brown eyes to go with the drop-dead gorgeous face, but all I could sense was 'player' like it should be glowing in neon on his forehead for any girl with half a brain. He never took his eyes off me while I spoke even with Madelyn facing him.

"That's good. We need lots of beautiful new faces on campus. Keeps things fresh, you know?"

Yeah, I knew all right with big caution lights blinking behind my eyes.

Keep away. Keep away. Keep away.

"Okay, well, I think I'll grab a chair with Quinn." This caught Madelyn's attention.

"Good idea." She left little doubt about how she felt about her boyfriend eye-fucking me while holding her in his lap. If she only could see those caution lights in my head, she would know that'd never happen.

I turned to look across the pool hoping to spot a place to sit down but instead ran into a hard body of abs and pecs smacking me in the face. This sent beer all over both of us before his impressive biceps wrapped around me to keep me from falling over or into the pool. Unfortunately, his maneuver to keep from hitting me put him too close to the edge, and we both fell in wrapped together, beer and all.

BLUE

I immediately stood up bringing the brown-blonde with me. Her hair was half and half, top and bottom. What color did she call this? I still had my arms encasing hers down by her sides when we came out of the water. At least we could breathe now.

"I'm so sorry, I didn't realize I was that close to the edge when I tried to pass behind you." When I knew she was stable, I moved my arms away from her sides.

"No, no. It was my fault. I didn't know you were there." She looked up at me blinking away the chlorine water. Damn, this girl had height on her. I expected her to be mad and tear me a new one, but instead, she pulled her hair out of her face and smiled one of those smiles that I thought glowed 'interested.'

Nope, not happening, girl, I thought to myself. I'd left one of those behind already in the house.

"I'm sorry you spilled your beer. I guess mine's gone, too." She held her cup upside down with the chlorine-blue water pouring from it. I should have offered to get her another, but that would only encourage her to continue with the fake grin.

"Yeah, I guess it is. Uh, you want me to help you out, or do you want to stay in?" It was the least I could do since I'd been responsible for putting her there.

She turned to the edge and popped right up on the side, turning and sitting down. "No, I got it. Benefits of having long legs."

"Well, okay. I'll see ya later then." I turned and swam to the other side and climbed out. It was rude. I didn't even introduce myself, but I didn't want to get caught up in a girl I already knew was not the one for the night. Her cute and normal act told me to keep looking elsewhere. Not what I anticipated considering she talked to Madelyn and Timms. I expected one of Madelyn's clones, but she seemed okay and didn't take me up on my offer to help. Most of the clones would've jumped at the chance to have me put my hands on them anytime, anywhere, but not this one. When I looked across the pool, she stood looking at me, so I hurried to the house for more beer.

Gerrod leaned against the counter by the kegs holding some dumbshit upside down doing a stand. "Dude, you've already drunk two beers?"

"No, spilled them both in the pool."

"You fell in and haven't even been drinking?" He laughed at me putting the kid's feet back on the ground before turning my way with the spigot in his hand to fill my new cup.

"Some chick took us both in." I never looked at him.

"Where is she, then?"

"How should I know?"

"Was she that ugly?" he questioned.

"Nope, she was fucking gorgeous, even if she had two-toned hair."

"Oh, so pink and blue or something?" He knew I didn't care for girls with that free spirit.

"No, brown and blonde."

"Let me get this straight. You get taken down by a gorgeous, blonde-haired girl, spilled both beers, and you don't bring her with you?" He looked at me with a disbelieving face.

"Yeah, so?"

"What are we here for, dickhead?"

"I'm here because you guys all seemed to think I needed to be here. So, I'm going to drink, look around, maybe take one to my room, get laid, and send her home."

"Wasn't this one a good start?" He wouldn't let it go.

"No, sure as hell wasn't. I'll know when I find the one I'm taking home and until then, fuck off and find your girl for the night."

"Oh, right. You have that certain type you can only fuck while the rest of us love 'em all."

"Damn right I do. You know I don't do sweet, caring, looking for the MRS degree girl. And from the looks of her, she could be on that mission."

"You're way too picky. Were you TTAG?"

"What? Have you been studying *Urban Dictionary* again?" This got a laugh from a few of the football team who'd joined our conversation."

"Toilet Trained at Gunpoint."

"Yep, just what I thought." I looked at the other guys taking their minds off me. "These guys, right here, is why you don't read *Urban Dictionary* on the throne." The comment gained loud laughter.

"You're avoiding the question. What is it with you and this filter you have to women?"

"I know what I want in my bed, and I'm not settling for anything less." I pushed off the wall and went back out to sit by the pool to try to enjoy it this time.

I liked to watch the girls interact with people before I considered choosing one. No one knew my preferences in the bedroom. Jenko had his suspicions since he'd been with me forever. He knew better than to ask. What I did in my bedroom was no one else's business but mine. I picked and chose the girl carefully who would be into the kind of kink I wanted without question. Today would not be the day for me to tell the world what I needed when it came to sex.

A few beers later, I looked up to see Timms and Madelyn, his flavor of the month, headed my way. He'd keep his girls around long enough to get close to that 'L' word and then cut them loose. I thought he enjoyed hurting them, but it seemed to work for him. He always had a beautiful girl on his arm when he wanted it.

"Enjoy sitting over here alone, Blue?" He sat down pulling Madelyn in his lap again.

"Sure do. I like people watching when I'm relaxing."

"Why would you want to be alone when there are so many pretty girls who showed up to meet the team?" Madelyn asked looking directly at me.

"I can learn a lot about people by watching them, like watching game films. I watch one specific person to see how he reacts to his teammates. It tells me how to prepare for his moves on the field. I might watch that film ten times, a different person each time. I know where they are going depending on who's on the field with them or where he lines up."

"What does that have to do with watching girls?" She didn't get it at all.

"When those girls are alone with me, I know how they'll probably react. I say probably because women are tricky creatures. Just when you think you have their moves figured out, they up and do something completely out of character. It's as though they don't have regular tells for me to follow. The more I watch them, the more I learn but not always."

Timms spoke up. "Dude, you think way too much about hooking up with women. Most of them I take home want one thing, to please me. If I do a few things right, I get what I want out of them in the end."

Madelyn looked at him with her mouth twisted in an ugly way. "Is that what you think? If you play me a little, I'll give you what you want?"

"Sure do, babe. I know exactly how to play this hot, perfect body to get it to return the favor." He chose that minute to kiss her. When they pulled apart, she looked out over the pool, and he looked at me and winked. He's no different from me. He paid her with body compliments he knew would make her respond. Damn, some people's shallowness amazed me.

He pulled her back to him, so she put her head on his chest to one side, then started rubbing circles on her stomach with his middle finger. At first, he went closer to her boobs, which both peeked out the bottom of the small bikini top she had tied around her. When he reached that soft skin, he lightly rubbed little circles on it. There was no doubt what he was doing to her if the perky nipples I could now see were any indicator. He looked at me and gave a slight head tip. He wanted me to watch him get her excited. I might be picky in bed, but watching some light porn was always on the table.

Once he had her wiggling on his lap, he started moving his hand down her body in the same slow circular motions, taking care to move across the sensitive skin over her ribs. He'd also started nibbling on her neck. If someone glanced over without paying real attention, they would never realize how he affected her.

He reached a shiny ring on her navel and started flipping it with one finger while his others slid around the barely-there indentation of her stomach. This caused her to rub on him even more, no doubt making him hard with his dick right at her crease hidden behind a small cut of material covering her ass.

Timms took that as a sign she enjoyed it, so he pulled the beach towel from around his neck and draped it down the two of them covering her from most prying eyes. He placed it long ways with her body purposely leaving my side exposed so I could continue the peep show.

She wrapped one arm over the towel just below her breasts but left one hand under the towel. She didn't keep it resting on her body for long, though. She wiggled forward enough to run her hand between them pulling the Velcro open on his swimsuit to reach inside and mold her fingers around his erection. This caused Timms a momentary halt as he squeezed his eyes shut to keep a grip on not blowing his load too soon. Her soft hand pumped up and down his now slightly exposed cock.

As he calmed himself, he began moving down under, closer to her bottoms. He used one hand to untie the little string on the side of her suit, exposing smooth flesh. I couldn't see it all from the side, but it was enough for me to know exactly what he now had in his hands.

He whispered something in her ear and then bit her neck just below it. She moved her legs, so they were on the outside of each side of his. He had control of the width she spread open to him. I watched her face as he dipped his hand between her legs further. The more his hand moved in circles, the more expressive her face became until she closed her eyes shutting out everything going on around them.

When his hand started moving in more of an up and down motion, I knew he had found his way inside her maybe with more than one finger. Her face flushed, and her bottom lip moved between her teeth biting back her sounds. Only I heard the soft moans from both of them.

I tore my eyes away long enough to look around the pool area. No one paid them any attention. So much went on in and out of the pool that even people who walked by were watching the water and not the two lovers. I turned back to see her looking at me which shocked me at first. I figured if she knew I could see, she'd put a stop to the visible sex they indulged in. She didn't. As she gazed at me through hooded eyes, I knew it excited her even more.

Who knew Maddie had some exhibitionism in her?

Timms' hand dipped lower as he parted her wider, and he shoved hard between her legs while sucking hard on the soft curve of her neck causing her to come as she arched her back. I knew it happened from the fire in her eyes as she stared me down. Her need to cry out looked painful, but she held in the sound like a champ. Before she could come down from the orgasm, he shot a stream of cum up her back while she continued squeezing him to drain him dry. He laid his head over on her shoulder while she put hers back on his chest.

The hot sex scene they played out for my pleasure made me realize the passenger seat of my car would now hold a female on the way home, or self-love would be my only outlet tonight. Timms spoke to her softly, and she tied the bathing suit back just before he picked her up, and they jumped into the pool.

I reached over and got the towel she was under and draped it across my raging hard on until I could coax it back down. When I looked around to see if anyone else witnessed what I had, my eyes landed on the tall beauty I took swimming earlier. I knew she'd seen it. Even hiding behind the big sunglasses, I understood she'd viewed the openly displayed sex. Her cheeks flared a reddened color, but not from the sun or embarrassment. The scene turned her on as much as it did me. I'd simply viewed it from a better angle.

Damn, I might need to pursue her a little more. Was she into public displays? Would she consider my ideas too much for her? This required more time on my part, more checking her out to find out what others knew about her.

I wanted to jump in the pool causing instant dick deflation, but I knew what the two lovers inconspicuously cleaned off Maddie's back. I'd rather face the crowd hard than get in with that knowledge. The two climbed the steps at the corner and made their way back into the house, arm in arm, leaving me to wonder how often they engaged in public sex. Everyone had their kink, not just me, and maybe my earlier swim partner did too.

"*Where's my friend when I need her*?" I said it out loud sitting on the chaise lounge nursing the drink I replaced. I hadn't seen Quinn since we talked to HB, and I took my dip with Mr. Muscles. Climbing out of that pool and then having him blow me off with only a few words of apology had stung. My bruised ego and I spent the next hour or so licking my wounds huddled in the chair. I needed to dry off anyway but sitting alone sucked. All these hunky football guys running around the pool dressed in board shorts strained my eyes behind dark sunglasses.

My need to watch what he did after his hasty departure spiked when I saw him return with another glass of beer and sit alone at a table. He looked like he enjoyed people watching as much as I did. Too bad we weren't doing it sitting side by side. He looked lickable with that long, dark blond hair pulled back in a perfect man bun. Between that and the thick scruff on his face, I had a difficult time not staring. Thank God for sunglasses. His tanned skin, and sweet mother of all holiness, that perfect body could make any girl drool and most guys jealous. The perfect cheekbones on that drop-dead gorgeous face didn't hurt either. I couldn't wait to see him in his form-fitting football pants. I felt sure he filled them out to be every girl's nighttime fantasy.

Before I could get my fill of watching him relaxing, HB and Timms joined him. They laughed it up before a scene unfolded before my prying eyes. I tried not to watch but couldn't help myself. I realized what was happening when Timms draped an extra-large beach towel over Madelyn. She closed her eyes and leaned into him giving him an all-access pass to her body only covered by her tiny Brazilian-cut bikini. As his hands slowly roamed down her body, I felt my own react to the look on her face imagining what she felt. She moved her arm behind her, no doubt to free him from the discomfort he felt from his swimsuit keeping his aroused flesh confined.

Their faces told the entire story as she leaned into him, so her back arched. With her eyes shut tight, a flush appeared on her cheeks with her mouth barely open. She ran her tongue around her lips before sucking in a breath. A movement to their right caught my attention, and I realized from Mr. Muscles' position, he witnessed what was taking place under the towel. Timms treated him to a private showing by purposely laying the towel askew and open in Mr. Muscles' direction. The real-life porn affected him as much as my obstructed view did me.

A bead of sweat formed on my face as I watched him viewing the scene. The two lovers became unaware of anyone around them. As his hands plunged further down, Madelyn's body rocked with the movement. When she sucked her lower lip in her mouth and her back arched, I fought my body to prevent an orgasm while she rocked through hers. All the while, Mr. Muscles seemed mesmerized by the scene, but when the two reached their pinnacle of desire, he looked around and caught me watching.

I looked down, but I knew it was too late—I'd been busted. I pulled my phone from my bag beside me pretending something of great importance scrolled across the empty screen. I typed in a message to Quinn hoping she would return one. I needed to get out of there, fast. I'd had enough of this party.

My eyes darted quickly over to see if he was still watching me and was relieved he wasn't. He'd moved the lovers' towel onto his lap. Ha! No surprise he found the scene undeniably hot, too. One benefit of being a woman.

Quinn's response came indicating she wanted to stay a lot longer, like maybe until tomorrow. Ugh. Guess I would be going home alone—no big shocker there.

I gathered my few things from my chair and crammed them back in my bag to make a quick escape. I kept an eye on Mr. Muscles to make sure he wasn't going to confront me and walked around the side of the pool to the house. Duty fulfilled, I could make a fast exit with no one knowing any difference.

That lasted until I reached the back door. Long fingers wrapped around my arm before I stepped inside. I knew who it was without even looking. He couldn't let it go.

"Hey, wait." Mr. Muscles loosened his grip but didn't let go.

I glanced over my shoulder. "Yeah?"

"Where are you going?"

"Home. I have some things I need to do this evening before classes start tomorrow." I stepped outside to let a guy holding two handfuls of red cups pass. I didn't want to wear beer today.

"Oh, well. I wanted to apologize again for taking you in the pool with me. I didn't bother to introduce myself either. It caught me off guard. I'm not usually rude that way. Sorry." He put his hand out to shake. "I'm Blue Myers."

I looked down at the huge hand and extended mine. "Hello, I'm Noelle Jeffries."

"I guess you're on the cheer squad if you know Madelyn, right?"

"Yeah, she expected us to be here." I rolled my eyes thinking about her mandatory appearance policy. I witnessed all I needed to know in the short time I was here, though.

"You didn't want to come meet the team?" He said it like I'd hurt the team's feelings for not being thrilled at making their acquaintances.

"Well, I expected to meet most of the team at the football mixer or something like that."

"We don't have a mixer for that. Only the Greeks do mixers."

"You're not a frat boy?" I realized how it sounded as soon as it left my mouth, so I smiled hoping to lessen the blow of my thoughts about frat boys. He started laughing.

"Uh, no. I'm not a frat boy as you put it. I play on the team, and a lot of the team's in a frat but not me. I don't need someone telling me how to dress and when to be somewhere. I have a coach for that, and he's great at barking orders." It was my turn to laugh.

"Sorry. I don't have anything against fraternities, but the guys do put themselves up on a pedestal to be noticed." I glanced around to where a few were holding court. "See what I mean?" I nodded in the direction of two circles of guys all listening to one particular person.

"If I had to guess, those are new pledges. They take shit just to be a part of something. See that group at the other end of the pool playing water polo?" She nodded. "Those are my teammates. They may be joining one of the fraternities, but football or sports comes first. Their personalities aren't exactly conducive to letting someone else tell them what to do. The frats know the players listen to the coach first and them second, so they don't put them through all the stupid shit they make the other pledges do."

"Good to know some of you guys think for yourselves."

"What about you? You listen to Madelyn." He came back fast with the comment.

"Only because I'm here on a scholarship. My parents could've sent me, but I hated to ask them to pay for school when I could do it this way."

"Makes sense."

"I'd have gone to college one way or another. My parents wouldn't have it any other way. They preached college to me from day one. I think I had orange TAU onesies." We both laughed.

"I know what you mean. My parents were adamant about me going, too. They wanted me to go here but would have been happy anywhere I chose."

Our conversation died down when a loud whoop came from the pool followed by a request for Blue to join.

"Guess I'll go rescue their sorry asses. The losers are calling."

"Oh yeah. You better go then. They need the captain to show them the way."

"I'm not the captain yet. Only a junior," he spoke as he started moving toward the pool. "Nice to meet you, Noelle. Talk soon." He pointed his finger at me like it was a gun going off.

I had to laugh. Who did that? Oh yeah, football jocks. Damn, he looked good doing it, too, like he naturally did it all the time. He dove into the water and joined the game. My first instinct said I should drop my stuff and sit in the nearest chair to watch all the testosterone in the pool as they worked to outdo each other. If I hadn't told him I was leaving, I probably would've, but since I did, I decided I'd better follow through.

I'd hoped Quinn would change her mind, but I spotted her engrossed in a conversation with a huge guy at the kitchen table. From his looks, he had to be on the team. Probably the entire offensive line fell on his shoulders. Quinn looked like a pixie up against this massive ball of muscle. I smiled to myself thinking of them having sex. He'd kill her if he laid on her.

I shook my head needing to get sex off my mind. The live porn I'd watched out back resurfaced and made me think Bob, and I might have an appointment tonight. Good thing she wasn't coming home.

It took me ten minutes before I could get to the front door wading through the writhing bodies who decided dancing was far more fun than killing each other in a game in the pool. Before I could open it, Madelyn appeared with two of her minions in tow.

"Where are you going so soon, Noelle?" Her haughty tone called to me.

"Home. I have some things I need to take care of before classes start tomorrow."

"You need to check in with me before you leave events we decide the squad attends."

"Why?"

"Why? Because we might want you for something, that's why. Why are you questioning my authority? You know it's my job to make sure everything flows smoothly."

"I'll keep that in mind." I opened the door and turned to her. "Oh, by the way, Madelyn. I'm leaving now." I wanted so badly to say something about the porn movie she provided but decided against it.

"I'm not through talking to you yet. I saw you talking to Blue."

"Yeah, he pulled me in the pool with him earlier and was apologizing for it."

She turned to the sidekicks. "Sounds like our Blue, huh, girls?"

My mind thought back to high school. Were these three stuck in the mean-girl movie or something? I left that drama behind years ago. I'd lived through it already, especially being on the cheer squad, and had no intention of living it again.

"Blue is off limits to you. We love that guy, and he's different than most of the guys on the team."

"You mean he thinks for himself instead of being lead around like the rest of the frat pack, unlike some of the people here?" I glared at the two behind her.

"A couple of the girls on the squad have already spoken for him, and you need to keep away until they change their minds. We realize you're new to TAU and don't know exactly how things go with the cheer squad, so I'm doing the right thing by telling you." She smiled a sickening smile at me.

"That is ever so kind of you, Madelyn. I do appreciate you informing me of all the 'rules' I need to observe because God knows how important rules are at the college level." I poured the most syrupy, southern of accents on I could manage. "I'll try ever so hard to keep those *rules* in mind when I'm fucking him behind the bleachers tonight after the hot dog supper the parents are supplying for the team." I walked through the door and slammed it behind me.

"What a bitch," I said to myself as I walked to my car. I glanced over my shoulder a few times halfway expecting her to follow me out screaming and yelling. I had no intention of having sex with him or anyone else behind the bleachers, but damn, it felt good to paint a high school scene where she obviously still lived.

BLUE

"Five, green, hut hut." The center hiked the ball, and I ran the down-and-out pattern we practiced a thousand times catching it at the one-yard line, stepping in untouched for a touchdown. I passed off the ball to the ref standing on the sideline and made my way back to our quarterback in a dead run. We jumped off the ground and slammed chests, which never hurt in our pads but was more for show.

"Great job, Blue."

"Back at ya. Perfect timing."

My first touchdown of the season felt good, and I prayed it was the beginning of a perfect season ahead of us. Of course, our first games were exhibition play since they didn't count in the conference. Every school wanted to win all their games with hopes of making it to a bowl. A bowl led to the two teams playing for the national championship. A loss would look bad to the guys who voted on those teams, especially to a team from a smaller school. I played to win no matter what.

By the end of the game, I'd scored two more touchdowns before Coach pulled me so the underclassmen could have some field time too. Winning the season opener always made for starting off right. Now we could party and savor the win in style, not that we would discuss that kind of thing with our coaches, though. It fell under the 'don't ask, don't tell' unwritten clause.

"Blue," Jenko called from his locker behind me. "You gonna make it to the house tonight?"

"Hell, yeah. This win deserves celebrating." I turned, and we bumped fists.

"Lots of women gonna be there, too. We put out the all-call for the first game party."

"Looking forward to it," I responded heading to the showers with my towel. I usually didn't shower when the whole team was in there. But this year I decided, fuck it. I don't care who knows about my issues. I was a grown-ass man, and if they had a problem, they could damn sure ask me about it. I wasn't ashamed of the way I looked. The women didn't mind when I went without a shirt or when I wore my uniform. Naked was another story.

Guys were going in and out of the showers when I took my spot at the wall letting hot water spray me in the face. Damn, it felt good. I'd been hit hard a few times in the game, which had left me sore all over. When I turned around and put my head under the nozzle, the hot water ran through the long hair I'd become known for both on and off the field. The females loved running their fingers through the strands. Hell, I did nothing to it. I washed my hair with body soap half the time, but it always looked like I took care of it and used good products. The hell with that—if I had to do something special for my hair, I'd shave it to the scalp.

I opened my eyes to grab the soap and saw one of the freshmen looking at my junk. "Dude, like what you see?" I grabbed my junk and gave it a little shake.

He immediately looked away. "No, man, sorry."

Timms was standing at the next showerhead. "Didn't you know that's why we call him Half sac? But don't worry your little shit for brains about it. He does more with one fucking sac than the rest of us can do with the normally required two. Ain't that right, Half sac?"

I laughed it off. "What we don't do is discuss it in the shower. That just ain't right."

The kid looked like we were going to hang him up by his dick and take turns punching him, but we were just playing around.

"That's right, Blue. Staring isn't right in the shower, dude," Jenko added. "It is what it is. It's been that way forever. Does it bother you, 'cause it doesn't bother Half sac."

"Uh, no... no man. It's fine. I mean, it doesn't bother me at all." The three of us made the kid uncomfortable.

"It's all cool, man. No problems." I turned off the water, ran the towel through my hair and wrapped it around my hips. "They're all used to it, and it's not like we spend time talking about each other's junk. Don't sweat it." I slapped him on the back on my way out. He gave me a brief smile like he understood.

I heard Jenko in the shower still talking to the kid. "What'd you think we called him Half sac for?"

"I don't know. Maybe he holds the record for assists in sacking the quarterback or something."

I started laughing. A lot of people thought that. They'd never guess the real reason in a million years. I suppose I should be grateful that we didn't have women doing interviews in our locker room. Not that they couldn't, they could, but so far we hadn't had any since I started playing. If we did, I'd have to start making an attempt at keeping my package covered lest the info makes its way out to the women.

"So now that we've cleared that up, I'm gonna run by my house and grab a bite to eat and come over," I told anyone around who was listening. "Later," I called and headed out to my truck.

Typical party with hot chicks everywhere. I could spend some quality time with one this evening. There were a few that I'd been with before. I picked my ladies carefully. They had to be into my personal style of sex, or it was a no go.

I passed through to the back where packed-to-the-rim coolers filled with beer waited. Popping the top on one fresh from the ice, I glanced around the room.

"There's the man," Gerrod greeted me. "I heard you were coming out tonight."

"Hell, yeah. We need to celebrate the game and first of many wins."

"Fuck, yeah, we do." We clicked cans and proceeded to both guzzle them down.

"Where you been, dude? Other than on the field, I haven't seen you at all," I asked as I looked across the backyard where various groups of people stood talking under haphazardly strung white bulbs provided some lighting.

"You remember that little girl we met at the first party at the XOX house?" His eyes told the entire story before he even started on the description. He'd finally met someone.

"That five foot nothing one?"

"Yeah, that's her."

"Dude, you could squash her like a bug. What does she go about a buck?"

"I don't know. I'd never ask her, but yeah, you're probably right. About yea tall." He held up his hand to show maybe five feet. "Her name's Quinn, and we've been spending a lot of time together. She likes me." A goofy grin formed on his face.

"That's great, Gerrod. You said you were going to have a girl this year."

"Yeah, it just kinda happened, though. I didn't go looking for her. She found me at that party, and we've been together ever since." Again, with the smile.

"Happy for you, dude. Really. You've had a long dry spell since I've been here at TAU. Glad you found someone to make you happy."

The little fairy herself blew in with the wind and jumped right up in his arms and laid a big sloppy kiss on him like they hadn't seen each other in years. When they finally let go, he stood her back up but never took his hand off her.

"This is Quinn. Quinn this is—" she cut him off.

"Blue Fucking Myers," she interjected and stuck out her hand.

"Yeah. I'm Blue, but I don't think my parents added that middle name on my birth certificate." I smiled and shook her tiny hand gently.

"I don't break that damn easily." She squeezed my hand hard.

"Nice to meet you, Quinn. Apparently, my rep precedes me," I laughed as I said it, knowing it did.

"Sure as hell does, Blue Myers. Gerrod sings your fucking praises all the damn time, and I know he's a good judge of character." I had to laugh again. I liked this girl. She obviously didn't lack self-confidence. Forget Gerrod being pussy-whipped, this girl would lead him around by a ring in his nose. But, hey, if he was happy, maybe it was the best thing for him.

"I think you might've met my roommate, too."

"Oh yeah? I meet lots of girls. Would I remember this one?"

"Noelle Jefferies. She's part of the pussy posse otherwise known as the cheer squad."

I had to laugh at her title for those girls. I'd seen them practicing. They usually worked hard. "Yeah, I met her. She's coming tonight, isn't she?" I hoped she would at least make an appearance.

"If that head bitch in charge has anything to do with it, she will. I swear that twat waffle makes me want to puke when I hear her voice. She grates on my every fucking nerve."

Gerrod and I laughed so hard, we had tears in our eyes over her description of Madelyn. Of course, Quinn was spot on, but hearing it come out of this little pixie's sailor mouth made it even funnier.

When we finally got it together, she stood with her hand on her hip sporting an indignant look at the two of us.

"What, babe? That was so damn funny, the way you said it." Gerrod tried to stop laughing not wanting to piss his girl off.

"I damn sure got it right, though, didn't I?"

He pulled her closer to him and kissed her forehead. "Hell, yeah, you did." He looked over at me. "See what I mean? She's perfect."

I smiled at him, patting his back. "Yeah, and she calls it as she sees it. I like her already."

"Well, Mr. Muscles, I'm damn glad you do 'cause I'm going to be around a while with this one here." She hugged Gerrod around the waist and gave him a look like she might climb him like a tree. Gerrod's year just got a whole lot more interesting than the last one.

"Okay, I leave y'all to that." They didn't even realize I'd left when I looked back over my shoulder. In the kitchen, I stood watching two freshmen shot-gunning beer. Waste of a good brew. Most of the time, they threw it all back up. From the looks of these two, I would take a bet on it right now.

Something caught my eye coming through the doorway. Noelle breezed by and grabbed a can on her way out the back door. Guess she didn't appreciate the fine art of stupidity of kids' first days away from home like some did. Walking to the door, I looked out to see her talking to some of the other cheerleaders. I suppose they were required to make an appearance like last time.

I made my way out to the pool area not wanting to make a repeat performance in the pool with her. I stood far enough back that I could watch her interact with Madelyn's minions. Her body language quickly told me she didn't care for any of the shit these girls constantly provided. Nothing but drama, and I preferred to stay out of it. I wasn't looking for a relationship like any of them had to offer. Hell, I wasn't looking for a relationship at all. I had school to finish and hopefully make it to the draft. My plan had always been to play pro ball if possible.

She walked away from the group with a small grin on her lips. I watched her from across the patio as she made her way back to the house. The girl had a lot going for her—beauty, grace, and obvious intelligence. I didn't know what she did that intrigued me, but I decided I needed to find out.

She had stepped onto the patio before she noticed me standing there watching.

"Oh, hey." Her gray eyes looked almost iridescent from the miniature lights offering a small amount of glow to catch her irises.

"Yeah, hello. Surprised to see you join the party after the last time you came out."

"You know us cheerleaders." She raised her hands in a cheer move. "Always here to support the team. After parties are a necessity with a win." Her sarcastic tone said it all.

"We did have a great game. You can't take that away from us." I wanted her to be proud of our win like we were.

"Yeah, you're right. Sorry. Once again, I hate being told what to do by someone I have no respect for." She glanced back to the girls. "I might have shown with Quinn all on my own."

"Good to know. It's important for team morale to have support from the school."

"True." She stopped there looking as if she wanted to say more.

"What's going on?" I needed to know what she left out of her little tirade.

"I was told you are off limits. How do you feel about that?" With her face looking down, she raised those long eyelashes and met my eyes. Damn, this girl was beautiful. This innocent look quickly told me she was off limits to a guy like me.

"Who told you that?" Again, she glanced over Madelyn's way.

"That girl has no idea what she's talking about, and I'm not into that little petty shit she tries to portray as knowing the territory. I make my mind up on who and when." I shook my head at the audacity of the bitch. Maybe Noelle was right to keep her distance from her.

"I think I'm about to head out anyway." She glanced toward the opening into the house almost like planning her escape.

"You should hang around longer. Never know what's going to happen around here with all the freshmen trying their first kegger."

"Yeah, that doesn't interest me. I saw enough of that shit in high school. She told us to make an appearance, and this is me, appearing." She pointed to herself.

"You're not a freshman then?"

"No, I'm a transfer from Roberts. I did my first two years there and then got a cheer scholarship here."

"Sounds good."

"You said you're a junior, too?" She looked at me knowing this was right. She probably remembered everything I'd said at our first meeting like most of these girls did.

"I'm a true junior, but then I figured you'd do your homework on the team and know that." She ignored my blatant smart-ass comment.

"So no redshirting for you?"

"No, I came to play football not sit around and vegetate for a year while others played my game." I meant what I said. I knew some guys needed that year for a few good reasons like gaining some muscle mass, wait for their spot to open from a senior graduating or some shit like that. Not me, though. I wanted to play from day one.

"No time wasted then," she nodded as she said it.

"Nope." A cute little redhead came up behind me and wound her way around me looping an arm and encircling my waist. I'd seen her around a few times, but I'd never taken any initiative to make a move. Why would she jump into this conversation?

"Hey, Blue."

I looked down at her large green eyes. She was a beauty but so was the one in my line of sight.

"I don't think we've met," I told her.

"I'm Laurin, with an 'i.'" She batted her long dark lashes at me making me think the red wasn't her true color. Who could tell these days, though?

"Oh, yeah. One of the fifty on campus, huh?" I looked back at Noelle who studied the clingy thing still wrapped around me.

"I'm the only Laurin you need to meet this season." The purr of her voice told me exactly what I needed to know about this particular one. I pulled her arms from around me and stepped back.

"I'm kinda busy here, Laurin... with an 'i.'" I nodded at Noelle.

"No, no. Don't mind me, I'm going to make an appearance and mingle for a short time, and then I'm out." She moved toward the back door and glanced back one more time. "You two have fun."

BLUE

What the fuck was that? I told Laurin I wasn't interested, but Noelle ditched me anyway?

"Looks like that leaves just you and me for some fun, Blue. I hear you're kinda bossy in the bedroom and that's so on point in my opinion." Once again, she glued her arms around my waist. This time I didn't bother to peel her off me. If she wanted it, I was down, especially after being kicked to the curb. That was a first for me, and it'd be the last, too. Fuck her. Plenty of women wanted a piece of me.

I looked down at the red hair spread around her shoulders. "Let's take this party to a more private place, right? You down for some fun and games in my room?"

She feigned an innocent look, but I knew girls like her. They wanted me for the rep it would give them. I didn't care at the moment. If she wanted to see the real Blue in action, she'd see it.

"Let's get this party started, Laurin with an 'i.'"

Her laugh told me all I needed to hear. I may not have a room in this house, but I always had a spot to put on my brand of sex. The guys all knew what I was into and didn't give me shit about it. Some wanted to ask questions but didn't. Only Gerrod, Timms, and Jenko knew the truth.

I took her by the hand and led her inside to the common area where the steps loomed like a stairway to heaven. Maybe Robert Plant and Jimmy Page spent some time in this house instead of Wales in the 70's. God knows the house is older than that.

I couldn't stop myself from looking around. I had to know if Noelle would see me pick another over her. Not that I cared what she thought. I never cared what a female thought. Absolutely no one tied us together.

My eyes landed on her standing by the fireplace watching some of the hilarious dancing that never stops during these parties. As her face lit up with her gorgeous smile, a small part of me felt guilty about what would ensue. I couldn't help myself, though. She'd blown me off like a nobody, and I refused to allow that to happen.

I slid my arm around Laurin's waist and pulled her tightly to my side as we rounded the bottom of the stairs and started up them. I glanced back over to where Noelle stood. Our gazes met, and I couldn't decipher the look on her face, but I didn't care. I gave her the best smirk I could muster under the circumstances and then whispered something filthy into Laurin's ear causing her to turn red and give a small laugh. I knew it was wrong when I did it, but I had never been treated like that before, and I damn sure wasn't going to go down without a fight.

When we entered Timm's empty extra room, I spun her around and pushed her face first, roughly against the door. I was pissed, and at first, I was willing to take it out on Laurin. Luckily, I realized the signs and took a step back, holding her firmly in place.

"Look, if you want to go, I'll understand. I'm not sure I'm feeling it," I spoke calmly now.

"Oh no, you don't. I've waited a long time to get my chance at you. There's no backing out now."

Guess she wasn't afraid of me. Good thing.

I leaned into Laurin pushing her harder against the wood thinking I'd just have her here and send her on her way. I could do this, fast and furiously. I pulled her mouth around enough to kiss her first while I ground my semi-hard length against her sweet ass trying to think how good she'd feel in a few minutes coming on my dick.

"Are you good with here or you want the bed?" I asked in a low voice over her ear.

"I'm good wherever."

Why did girls debase themselves this way? Laurin was pretty, creamy skin, a sweet smile. She didn't need this kind of meaningless sex. I couldn't do this to her this way. I pulled her around and kissed her hard again pressing her back to the door. I picked up her legs and wrapped them around me. She immediately began grinding on the wood now between us.

I walked over to the bed and crawled up the middle of it to the headboard with her still attached. Her nails roamed up and down my back. I knew she felt my full length against herself from the groans coming out of her hot mouth. I pulled Laurin's hands from my back and moved them over her head, holding them with one of my big ones as I continued to kiss down the soft skin of her neck toward a nice rack hiding under a sweater.

My other hand slid under the hem and pushed the bra up for access to the perfect globes. She began wiggling when I twisted her hardened nipple with my thumb and index finger. I needed a taste of this, so I sat up between her legs letting her hands go.

"Keep your hands on the headboard." I didn't ask. I told her, and she gave me a short nod. I pulled the sweater up and tied her wrists with the arms of it and then fastened it to the slats above her. With her arms twisted in the material and it tied, there was no way she'd get loose. That's the way I needed it to be.

I stared down at the rosy pink nipples that were hardened nubs begging for attention, so I leaned in and gave it to them. Circling the crests with my wet tongue and slightly biting them caused her to writhe under me and grind on my now brick-hard dick. I reached over and opened the nightstand. I know she thought I was getting a condom, but that would come later. I pulled out a blindfold.

"Does this bother you? I need to hear you say it, Laurin."

"Uh, no. I've been blindfolded and tied before. It's hot." I smiled at her as I pulled the elastic out and behind her head. "So I'm not going to see or touch you?"

"Nope. I don't do looking and touching. Are you good with that?"

"Sure. Anything for you, Blue." No floundering in her words made me believe she was into it this way. Good. I liked a willing participant. I never wanted to scare the girls I took to bed. If they hesitated, I might try a little persuasion but nothing harsh and demanding. They either wanted it, or we didn't continue.

"That's great darlin', I like to hear that. If it gets too much, you say stop, and we're done. You understand what I'm saying?"

"Just stop? I don't need a safe word or something?"

A small laugh escaped. I loved these girls who read BDSM—not that I practiced it, but I had my limits. I never had sex with women touching or watching me. I tried a few times and couldn't do it. I didn't have sex until I got to college for that reason. I figured my bedroom habits would get around in our town because people liked to talk. The last thing I wanted them talking about was my sex life.

"No, babe, stop is enough for me. I won't let things get so out of hand that I can't do that. Also, since you can't see it, I'll be wearing a condom. Don't want or need surprises of any kind."

"I'm on the pill anyway."

"Good to know we are double covered then." I slid up her body until I was eye level with the luscious pink tits calling to me and ran my tongue around the nipple causing her to gasp.

"You like that?"

"Yes, it just feels so different not being able to see what you're doing."

"Your other senses become heightened when one or more are removed," I told her as I took the whole nipple into my mouth and sucked hard down on it. She groaned loudly. I liked to hear my partners moan in pleasure, and my dick responded to her sounds.

"That's it, babe. Tell me what you want."

"I want it all, Blue. All of you." She wrapped her long legs around me, and I realized we both had our jeans on still.

"Let's make that happen then." I eased down her body leaving kisses and nips on her white skin. Each time I bit a little, she arched off the bed, and I would soothe the spot with my tongue lingering over the redness. When I reached the top of her jeans, I undid them and stood pulling them off her body, panties and all.

"Really a redhead, I see." She nodded, and her cheeks turned a dark shade of pink. She'd shaved but left a little up top. I could live with that.

"I suppose you know that when you get embarrassed, you glow all over with a delicious shade of red skin."

"Yes, it's a curse, especially in a bikini."

I laughed, and she did, too, calming her down some. I dropped my jeans beside hers and crawled back over her, kissing my way up from her knees. Parting her legs for me, I slid my hand up to her mound and ground down some with my palm as I bit the skin of her inner thigh. I worked my way up to her hip bone.

I slid my finger down her slit and circled her swollen bud a few times. I wasn't shy going down on a girl at all, but I didn't know about doing it the first time I'd met her. That wouldn't stop me from making sure she had several orgasms before I claimed my own.

My tongue slipped up her body back to her breasts, and I worshiped them as I slid a wet finger into her slick channel and pushed inside her. When I added the second finger and bit down on the hard peak in my mouth, she started clamping down on my fingers.

"Oh yes, yes, right there. Please. Please. Please."

I moved to the other nipple and did the same thing again, knowing it would push her over the edge. When I curled my fingers up and found the spot I searched for, it did the trick. It surprised me she came so fast, but when her whole body gave a shudder and her inner walls contracted hard on my fingers, I knew she was gone.

"That, Laurin, was beautiful." I kissed up her neck, and I moved back over her. When I got to her lips, she finally started breathing somewhat normal again. "You good?"

"Better than good. That was amazing. I think I love this blindfold thing."

I sat back on my calves and grabbed her hips flipping her over. "We haven't even gotten to the good parts yet."

She gave me a little laugh. "I know. I can't wait."

"No more waiting, babe." I ripped open the condom and rolled it on before I slid my dick from top to bottom of her dripping channel. I circled her clit a few times again before I pulled her hips off the bed even more. The gorgeous peach stared at me, all pink and soft and beautiful. I couldn't keep my hands off her ass, as I kneaded the plump cheeks. I leaned down and bit one leaving a nice red love bite that would be there tomorrow. She squealed when I did it.

"That's for you to see in the morning to remind you of our night." With the last word, I pushed in some which earned me a moan as she pushed back against me, so I plunged in balls deep. I loved that first thrust to be hard and if the sounds she made were any clue, so did she.

"Do you like it hard and rough, Laurin?"

"Yes, don't be easy with me. The harder, the better."

Whoa. I hadn't heard this from a female in a long time. Damn, who was I to hold back if that was how she wanted it?

I grabbed her hips, and she grabbed the headboard. I fucked her like a champ. If I stopped at all, Laurin whined aloud, "No." Man, this girl had potential as a partner that could kill me. She met me stroke for stroke for a good while.

I flipped her over, knowing she couldn't see me and pulled her legs over my shoulder. It offered a whole new reach inside her, and she rolled up and down with my strokes. She knew what she wanted and where, so she took her initiative to get it.

"Damn, that feels fucking great," I told her as I hit the spot she seemed to like, but she didn't come again.

I moved her legs to one side causing her channel to tighten and kept pumping in hard. This did the trick.

"Oh, Blue, Blue. Yes, just like that. Yes. Yes." I felt the first ripple of her walls latch onto my cock trying to keep me from moving inside her. This feeling quickly caused me to join her in the shuddered orgasm that felt so damn good.

I rolled over spent, but I didn't take my eyes off her. I removed and tied off the condom tossing it in the garbage can by the bed.

"Laurin, you okay?"

"Better than okay. I'm fantastic. That was awesome like I knew it would be from what I'd been told."

I hated these words.

Why couldn't people not talk about their sex lives with others?

"I'm not into kissing and telling, but I guess you have some friends who are." Her admitting this told me she only agreed to fuck me for the notoriety, and that pissed me off.

I climbed off the bed and pulled my jeans back on without the underwear. I wanted her out now. So much for after bliss and cuddling and all that women usually desired. I leaned over and untied her arms but didn't bother with the mask.

She peeled the mask off and stared at me as I stepped into my flip flops and ran my fingers through my hair without so much as looking at her getting dressed. Normally, I would have at least offered to help but not tonight. One girl pissing me off a night was enough. I needed to leave.

"Did I make you mad?" She pulled the sweater over her bra and crawled to the end of the bed picking up her jeans.

"No. You got it from here?" I knew I was acting like a douche, but her words right after sex were not what I wanted to hear.

"Uh, yeah. I guess. I'm sorry."

Her eyes followed me around to the bathroom door. I opened it and turned on the light. "You can use this if you need to."

"Thanks, I guess." My reactions upset her. I felt it with every word now from her mouth, but it didn't stop me.

"No problem. See you around." If she wanted a quickie to brag with, she got it. The door slammed behind me. By the time I got to the stairs, I needed to get the hell out of this house. I was done for the night, but two gray eyes caught me.

Noelle looked up from the hearth where she sat and watched me intently. I couldn't do this now. I took the stairs two at a time and made it to the open front door in two long strides. I popped the locks on my truck on my way to it and climbed in shutting the door harder than necessary. Starting the engine, I yanked down the gear shift into D and did a U-turn in front of the house. There Noelle stood on the steps watching me.

I didn't care. Let her watch me. Her loss.

NOELLE

"Nope... not doing it."

I woke the next morning drooling on my pillow but refused to leave my bed. My soft comforter and sheets were a huge splurge from my graduation money. Sleeping well if nothing else, while I was in college, made a lot of sense to me. Azure blue skies peeked in where my curtains slightly parted. Fall held off in Texas, and sometimes we didn't have it all. With the temps hitting ninety again today, I guess this would be one of those years. I swear shorts and sandals would work for class until next semester.

I rolled over and stared at the huge calendar on the wall. Bright colored highlights adorned every square with something. I liked color coding. Kept my life straight.

Hot pink meant cheer practice tomorrow but a meeting this afternoon held the bright yellow square for today.

"Dammit. I can't escape a day without seeing that crazy bitch." No one hung around to appreciate my bitching.

The football team would be on the field when we practiced. If God were answering prayers tomorrow, they would be in the weight room. I hoped so. After what I witnessed last night, I wasn't ready to look most of those guys in the eye.

When Blue stomped past me with that red-haired sleazebag in tow last night, it was time for me to leave. My eyes followed them as they made their way up the tall staircase to the bedrooms on the second floor. Curiosity got the better of me, so I sat down on the hearth. The occasional random guy came by to ask me to dance, but I wasn't in the mood to be hunched on, and from where I was sitting, that's all that was happening on the dance floor.

Not too much time passed when he came flying down the steps, which caught my attention. I would've never noticed him if he'd calmly walked down them with so many coming and going, and I told myself I wasn't watching for him. When he took the steps two at a time in a race to the bottom, it happened to catch my eye.

Blue's green eyes stalked mine, and I knew something was wrong. Maybe he didn't get what he wanted. Maybe she wasn't what he was after. Maybe she said no after the big show she put on in the backyard. Whatever happened, anger flared from his face. He broke eye contact before crossing the threshold. I jumped up and slipped past the grinding bodies in time to get to the front porch as he spun a quick turn and left tire tracks on the street. I knew he saw me on the steps, but he didn't need me, and I didn't want him. At least not then.

My phone buzzed, and I looked down to see a text from Quinn.

Quinn: *Awake, sunshine*
Me: *Unfortunately*
Quinn: *Be home soon. Let's do brunch*
Me: *And by brunch, you mean pizza and mimosas*
Quinn: *You read me like a book ;)*

"Ugh." I put my feet on the floor and padded to the bathroom to shower. After the party debacle, I was too tired to do anything else, but when I laid in my bed, all I thought about was what could have happened in that room upstairs to make him so angry.

She wore the proud look of a woman about to parade her good fortune before the multitudes when she descended those same steps. And by multitudes, I mean her entire group of friends who waited to hear her tale.

The last thing I wanted to know involved him fucking her in an upstairs room at a frat house. By the time her foot hit the bottom step, her little clique looked at her with a new respect. What a misguided group of females if all they wanted was a play-by-play action report of the mind-bending sex she'd had with Blue.

I walked out the front door. "Sick, sick, sick." I thought I'd mumbled the words to myself.

"If you're going to be sick, at least get off the porch," Timms yelled from a lawn chair he sat in at the edge of the darkness.

"Not going to be sick."

"Not what you said, Rah Rah." His speech said intoxicated.

"You know my name is Noelle, Timms." I glared at him.

"Hmm. Yeah, I think I remember the dumbass who just left a bunch of tire marks on my street tell me that." He didn't slur his words, but he spoke them at an awkward pace. Maybe drinking slowed him down. I wanted to smile at that thought.

"Where's your girl tonight?" I hadn't seen him and Madelyn together since the last party now that I thought about it.

"Don't have one girl. Got a whole harem of them." He smiled a big smile, then resumed his little speech. "Didn't feel like picking one out tonight. Too tired."

"All that quarterbacking too much for you?" I tried to make it sound sarcastic but couldn't pull it off.

"Awe, hell no. That's my game, right there. Gonna play till I'm too old to hold the ball." His head flopped back against the headrest. "What about you and my boy Blue there?" He started laughing hysterically. "Little boy blue, get it?"

"Uh yeah." Not that funny. "Nothing with Blue and me. Why?"

Had Blue talked about me?

"He needs a good woman. Someone trustworthy to keep his secrets. He keeps 'em bottled up. Gonna bust wide open one of these days. Not gonna be a pretty sight to see."

"What's that supposed to mean?" I never got an answer, but I did hear a soft snore from his lips. Guess he was done for the night.

I climbed into my car and headed home alone.

As I stepped into the shower, the warm water ran down my body, but my mind still tried to make sense of Blue's anger. He had it all—looks, personality, football, friends, women. What more could he need to make him a happy man?

I turned the water off and wrapped one of my few big fluffy towels around me. I needed to get my mind off Blue and onto more important events in my life—

things I needed to focus on. College had to be a continuous balance of classes, study, cheer, and social life. It seemed to me social life took up way too much of my brain these days.

"Sit down, bitch. I brought it all. Pepperoni and pineapple. Cheap champagne and OJ. We're good for a while." Quinn knew me so well.

"Good. I've got a lot to do today. Need to get my Sunday off right."

We clinked glasses and took long sips of the sweet morning nectar.

"Fucking perfect. Now for the good shit."

I thought she was talking about pizza. I opened the box to a wonderful aroma and pulled a huge piece onto my paper plate. After generously applying the cheap sprinkle cheese from the paper package, I dipped it in the ranch dressing and took a huge bite. It never occurred to me she was talking about anything else until I looked up and she was watching me.

"What?" I said between chews. "Did I get it all over my face?"

"Hell, no, chickadee. I'm dying to hear what happened last night at the party."

"Uh, nothing happened. I drank a couple of beers while I sat on the hearth, watching basic sex with clothes on happening at eye level with me. Too bad it didn't do a thing for me."

"What happened with Blue, dumbass? That's what I want to know. Who cares about dry fucking?"

"We didn't happen if that's what you're asking. He took his time with a redhead that I've seen stalking around there before. They made it upstairs in record-breaking time. Guess she got what she was after." I took another drink of my mimosa. I didn't want to talk about Blue's sexcapades.

"How do you know? You gotta give me more, babe." I knew she'd never rest with the questions now.

"A redhead wrapped around him and offered herself up on a silver platter for his enjoyment. Who was I to stand in their way, especially since I'd been told to keep away."

Quinn's head jerked up almost upending the dressing everywhere. "What the fuck? A little ginger ho warned you off Blue while you stood talking to him?"

"No, drama mama, calm down before we're wearing ranch. The cheer queen told me to stay away, because he was already spoken for. Then ruby red came up and wrapped around him. He tried to look innocent and peel her off, but she wasn't having it, so I let the two of them go at each other. Didn't take long before they ascended the steps to sexdom."

"And you stood by and watched it all? Why didn't you tell her to fuck off?"

"Because I wasn't going there with him so why should I be the cockblocker? If he wants her, I say do it, and he did."

She finished her first flute and starting pouring another before she spoke. "You get the hell out of there after that?"

"No, I sat down on the hearth and watched what was going on. If MTV was doing a documentary on teens, drinking, and sex, they've recorded enough clips for an entire season in one night. And that would be only on the dance floor." We both laughed because we knew it was true at most frat-house parties after a big win.

"And you never saw them again?"

"Blue and Laurin, with an 'i'?" She nodded at me. "Yes, I did. Funny thing, too. He left there about thirty minutes later pissed off about something. I watched him from the doorway."

"He knew you saw?"

"Yeah, looked right at me as he drove off."

"Oh, babe. I'm sorry. I know the two of you would get along. He seems like a helluva nice guy when he's around Gerrod and me."

"Maybe I bring out the worst in him. Who knows?" I got another slice and leaned back in my chair. Why'd I keep thinking about the look on his face when he passed me? It's not as if he acknowledged me in any way.

"Hey, that Timms guy asked me some weird questions, too."

"Oh, yeah, like what?"

I hadn't thought too much about what he'd said in his drunken haze until now. What was he talking about?

"Gerrod knows him well, right?"

"Yeah, sounds like they've been friends forever."

"Timms said Blue had secrets, and he needed to find a woman he could trust. What's that supposed to mean?"

"Hell if I know. Gerrod thinks Blue hung the moon, though. Maybe it was the damn drunk in Timms talking." I watched Quinn for a second. I knew those wheels were turning on how to get the info from Gerrod. She wasn't the kind to leave stuff alone, especially when it involved a friend.

"I gotta go to a cheer meeting today. What y'all got going for the afternoon?"

"We're going to study together."

"Is that code for sex or something? You never study with a guy.

"Hell, yeah, it is. I'm thinking about breaking the cherry on the third-floor study room. We hear sex hasn't ever happened there."

"You guys are crazy. You could get caught so fast."

"That's the fucking fun of it, Noelle. It's the risk involved."

I rolled my eyes and tipped my flute to catch the last drops of juice. This semester just got longer if I had to hear about all the places they had sex on campus every week.

When Quinn's phone rang, she saw it was her mom. "I gotta take this." She walked out onto the back deck of the apartment and spoke. It didn't take long before she came back in with a strange look on her face.

"What's going on, Quinn?"

"Oh, uh, nothing. My mom's going on a cruise with a girlfriend for the week."

"Is that a problem?"

"No. Except as long as I've known my mom and dad, they've never gone anywhere without each other."

"I'm sure it's fine, Quinn. Don't read into it something it's not."

"You're absofuckinglutely right, chickee. I'm not going to worry about it at all."

We both knew what a huge lie that was. Quinn always worried about her family.

BLUE

Sitting through my boring as fuck stats class always got my Monday off to a bad start. Since practice happened in the afternoon, our classes had to be in the morning.

"Blah blah blah blah blah," the professor droned on like Ben Stein in the Ferris Buehler movie. Why couldn't I get a Cameron Diaz from *Bad Teacher* or a hot little TA to stare at?

Jenko leaned over and made a snoring noise causing me to laugh. I knew where this would lead if we caused trouble. The coaches would hear about it, and then tire pulls would be in the lineup for practice.

A smaller university could do this because the team was well known around campus.

I shoved him with my elbow, and Jenko sat up straight. "Sorry."

The class finally dismissed, and we walked out the side door onto the campus.

"Where you headed?" he asked me.

"I've got an hour break. You?"

"Yeah, me too. Not long enough to go home. I gotta grab some coffee. I need something to keep me awake after that damn snore fest."

We walked down to the Coffee Bean in the quad and sat.

"So, Quinn said—"

"Stop."

"What?" His mouth hung open.

"I don't care what she said. I already know I'm not going to want to hear this shit." I knew what was coming. Quinn and Noelle probably shared everything, and Saturday night's disaster would be at the top of that damn list.

"You can't know what I was going to say, shithead." For someone who said he couldn't hold his eyes open, he seemed fully awake to me now.

"Is it about the shit that went down Saturday night?" From the look on his face, I knew where he was going with this.

"Well, yeah, now that you've brought Saturday night up."

"I didn't bring it up, dumbass."

"Just tell me what happened. Quinn will drive me fucking insane until she knows what went down. Did you spend time with Noelle?"

"If you call five minutes time, then yes, but nothing else. She shut me down and walked off." I didn't want to think about that night again, ever.

"Did you piss her off or something?"

"No, we had some interference, and apparently Noelle didn't think I was worth sticking around for."

"Really? Quinn thinks differently."

I was glad I had my sunglasses on because I didn't want him to know his comment caused me to take notice. If she's interested, why did she leave me to deal with Laurin? Noelle had to know I wanted nothing to do with Laurin.

"What did Noelle say?"

"Nope, not saying shit. Remember you don't want to talk about this." He liked giving me trouble when it came to women.

"Fine. I'll give you the *Cliff's Notes* version." I told him the story leaving out the part of me leaving behind a good chunk of my tires on the road.

"So you're talking to Noelle. Laurin propositions you. You choose the sure thing. Noelle leaves you to it."

"Pretty much."

"Why did you leave mad then?"

I'd left this part off, too. I didn't want to talk about women using me. Jenko knew my proclivities for ropes and blindfolds, but we didn't discuss it. I let out a deep breath before speaking again.

"Red was only into it to spread around she'd slept with me. You know I hate that, and she had the balls to say it to my face. What kind of girl does that?"

"One you chose to take to bed. Why'd you go for that douche move?"

Shit, this conversation sounded like something my dad and I would have had. "Because Noelle blew me off like she didn't need to spend her damn time wasting it on me, and Laurin was more than willing to do whatever I wanted to do."

He looked at me like I'd grown a third nipple or something. "Dude, of all people. You know better than that. Please tell me there were no handcuffs involved. She'll be broadcasting that all over campus before the day's out."

"Too late."

"You know for someone who likes to keep his fucking sex life private, you need to learn more from damn past mistakes."

"Don't I know it." I stood and shot my cup at the garbage can clearing the rim. "Later."

"Yeah. See ya." He rambled off in the opposite direction I needed to go.

When I thought the day couldn't get any worse, I looked up to see Noelle headed in my direction. At least we'd only have to pass each other on the sidewalk and keep going. She typed into her phone as we got closer but looked up at the last minute spotting me.

"Hey, Noelle." She didn't return the greeting but kept her eyes on me. "Are you going to ignore me?"

"No. I don't have anything to say to you, Blue."

"A simple hello would work."

"That would imply I care enough to address you."

I couldn't stop myself. I grabbed her elbow and led her off the sidewalk into the grass away from those rushing by to class.

"Look. I didn't ask for Laurin to come over and talk to me, and I sure didn't ask for her to offer herself up like that."

"You also didn't turn her down, so I think I made the right call to leave the two of you to go at it."

I let go of her arm. She was right. I ran my hand through my hair, pulling it back from my face.

"I was wrong, and I'm sorry."

"What were you wrong about Blue? Wrong that she wanted a quick fuck? I think we both know she got what she wanted."

"No, I was wrong to let her take over our conversation. I would've preferred spending my evening with you."

Noele looked up and stared me in the eyes with intent. "Are you sure about that because from where I stood, it looked like you were completely happy with the outcome. Oh, wait, maybe not, since you left mad. What happened? She back out and not let you do the deed?"

I wanted to shout at her just how great we did the deed but knew that would only make this worse than it already was, so I kept my mouth shut.

"No kissing and telling on your part, Mr. Muscles?" The little minx smirked at me.

"You're damn right. I don't kiss and tell, which is more than I can say for her. What I do with a woman is no one else's business. But the bed wasn't even warm, and she was ready to shout it from the rooftops. That pissed me off, so I left. You just happened to witness me expressing my anger in a childish way."

The shocked look on her face said it all. She didn't come back with the smart-ass remarks I expected. "Regardless what you think of me, Noelle, I'm not a bad guy. Yes, I like women. Yes, I like sex, but I like a lot of other things, too. I'd like to spend some time with you doing other things."

"Yeah and that's all?"

From her tone, I couldn't decide if she was glad or mad at my confession. "I mean, well, it's not that I don't want to have sex with you, too. I want to do other things also. I, uh…" I completely blew up this entire speech with that line.

"Stop talking, Blue." I felt like she was seeing me for the first time. She stared at me with a look that said she might be trying to make up her mind about me.

"Right. I can do that." I smiled at her and surprisingly, she smiled back. We were making progress. Thank God.

"I gotta get to class now, and then I have practice." She looked down at her phone.

"Yeah, me, too. Can we hang out sometime? You know, grab a coffee or eat or something?"

"Probably. We'll see." She smiled again.

Definite progress. "Okay. We'll talk later."

"Yeah, later." She turned and walked away with me watching her move down the sidewalk. She had on a killer short jean skirt. God, I loved a skirt. Her legs were lean and long with the summer tan still glowing on them. I could watch her walk away all day, but I didn't want to look like a total perv, so I turned and made my way to my next class.

This day felt better as I walked away and by the time I made it to practice, nothing could bring me down from the high I floated on. The field burned from how good my plays came off. I caught passes that I should've dropped, ran some sprints faster than ever, and smiled while doing it all. Damn, I loved football.

"What's got that stupid shit-eating grin on your face, Blue?" Timms asked as we made our way into the locker room. You've worn it since you walked on the field. Keep that up, and the coaches will think they aren't working us hard enough."

"You maybe. I gave a hundred and ten percent today, dude." I peeled off my jersey bringing my pads with it.

Coach walked in when I sat down to remove my shoes.

"Listen up, men. This week we'll be playing a team that's on a whole other level than last week. They take winning seriously. It's going to require everyone to step up their game. Blue, come here, kid." I stood and walked to him. "The effort I saw out there today from this guy is what I need from y'all every single day. Blue came to play ball today, and some of you looked like you were returning from a weekend of drunken debauchery. Now, I know you like to celebrate with a good win like Saturday's, but if we're going to be able to beat a team like Dallas, we need for each one of you to get off the drinking and treat your bodies like the temples they are. Alcohol has no place on or off the football field, especially during the season. I want you all to think about what I'm saying.

"I've been getting some reports from my coaches that the majority of the team's hanging out at the frat house out of town. I need my leaders to step up and shut this problem down. Summer's over, class is in session, and football is king. Treat it that way."

He let go of me and walked to his office shutting the door behind him. He'd said all he needed to say and expected us to fill in the gaps. Stop drinking. Stop going to the frat house. Get our heads in the game.

Timms walked up behind me. "Sounds like the coach wants us to shut down the parties."

"Yeah, sounded that way to me, too."

"You coming to the house this evening?"

"Wasn't planning to."

"You are now. We should talk about investing in the team." He never took his eyes off me while he said it. I knew he meant business.

"Okay. I'll come out after supper."

"Good idea." He went back to his locker area in a slow move. For someone who could scramble like a rabbit being chased by a wolf, Timms moved at a snail's pace all the other times.

Chicken and vegetables sizzled in the oven while I studied notes from today's chemistry class. If I couldn't play professional ball when I graduated, I wanted a degree in something competitive. Chemistry excited me, but I didn't want to be a chemist, so it only made sense to get a marketing degree with a chem minor. Working as a pharm rep had to be a great job because I knew some who did it and loved it. Talking came naturally to me. I could sell a snowplow to a beach dweller, and the chemistry background would help with all the drugs involved. Win/win in my book.

Alexa's timer sounded just as Gerrod and Quinn walked through the front door laughing about something.

"Alexa, turn off timer." That device and I were BFFs.

"Oh, hey, Blue boy. Your AI taking care of you again?" Quinn said laughing.

"Hey, baby Quinn, you know it," I replied to the nickname I'd heard all my life.

"That's fucking Miss Baby Quinn to you," she said with all the dignity she could muster.

"True that Miss." I laughed and placed my plate on the table.

"Smells good. You cook?"

I looked at her like she was stuck in a bad Bill Engvall redneck joke. "I want to say here's your sign so badly right now. Yes, I cooked, and it's some good shit, too. Just like Momma made it."

Gerrod came around the corner into the kitchen. "Did you make enough?"

"Of course, I knew you'd smell it over in the quad and come running."

"Hell, yeah. Did you make the rice, too?"

I glared at him. He knew I liked my chicken cooked this way.

"Quinn can eat, too, right? I hate eating in front of her and not offering her some."

"No thanks, I don't pay for y'alls' damn grocery bill."

"No, please, there's plenty. We've gotta watch our food intake. You know how the females love to rub their hand over my six-pack, and too much of anything good will cause that to go away." I raised my shirt and rubbed my hands down my stomach crunching just enough to make the abs pop. Showing off those abs was always fun, and the women loved it.

"Stop, dude. You're making me look bad in front of my woman." He leaned in and kissed her on top of the head.

"Really? Do I look like someone's bitch to you, Blue?" I knew she was kidding with Gerrod, but he loved going all caveman by claiming to have a girlfriend.

"Oh, let him have his fun. He can't get past the idea that someone as pretty as you agreed to go out with him." I winked at her and noticed her cheeks turning light pink. Did I embarrass Quinn?

"When you put it like that, Blue, how can I not allow my main man meat to call me his woman?"

I threw my head back and laughed. These two made a perfect pair. They joined me for dinner making our lives seem more like family than usual. Jenko was family for a long time, and Gerrod added to it since we started college. Sharing a meal together around a table felt real. I could get onboard with his foul-mouthed girl.

BLUE

The frat house's huge den area allowed for the starters and upperclassmen on the team to all gather in the same place. A few well-placed texts and the team came running so we could have a meeting without involving the coaches. Too bad it happened at the spot they wanted us to steer clear of. Guess we need to show that some activities here could be productive. Tonight's begged to be.

Timms climbed out of the recliner he brought with him to the house when he moved in. No one was allowed to sit in it without invitation, and those only went out to females sitting in his lap.

"I know y'all have an idea why we called this meeting." A general mumble spread across the room. "The coach needs for our team to step up this week. We gotta show the suits what we came to this university to do. Some of us are proving ourselves week after week to the scouts sneaking in to judge us. The whole team gives that hundred and ten percent every single game. That's only gonna happen if the team gives that effort every day at practice. Now I know we're all tired from this weekend, so I'm not holding you here long but guys, let's face it. The time to step up is now. I'm not the only man on this team. It takes all of us to make a perfect season and right now, I'm looking at you all to pull this off this fall. We need a championship and can't do it unless we play like a team all the time."

Timm's voice grew a little louder with each sentence he spoke. He knew how to fire up these guys, knew the words to use to make it happen. That's one reason why he was team captain. He could rally this bunch of muscle and brain like no one else. By the end of his football diatribe, they were all standing and chanting with a mob mentality.

Now I go in for the kill. I stepped up on the coffee table so I could look down on the huge group of fired-up testosterone.

"Y'all know this is the last real exhibition game, but this game, *this one game*, is as important as any conference game. Beating Dallas isn't just some state rivalry shit… it's *the* state rivalry. All the other teams in the state and the conference will send scouts to watch the players and dissect the plays. They'll chalk up stats on both sides on each and every person perceived as a threat to their game. The scouts will shoot their videos of people they need to watch all season. They'll be watching performance, endurance, and improvement. We, *the entire team*, need to show them that hundred and ten percent on Saturday. *The entire team* needs to outperform to the best of our ability, and *the entire team* better show up ready to *ram* some kick ass down their throats on that field."

I stated each of my sentences with more force and a little quicker than the one before it. Timms and I knew how to get this job done. When he was gone next year, a junior would take my place and do the same thing. The traditions never die in football on winning teams. This tradition was no exception. The guys were pumped and headed out chanting… Rams, Rams, Rams.

We'd done our job for this week. No doubt we'd be doing it again several times before the season ended. Timms, Jenko, Gerrod, and I headed to the front door. I had notes to get back to, but Timms lived here full-time, so he stopped on the front porch and sat down in the lawn chair he kept there.

The other three of us stepped off before he said anything to me.

"You and that Rah Rah got something going on?"

"Who?" Turning to face him, I didn't know who he was referring to.

"That pretty new one that questions Maddie when she's barking her damn orders."

"Oh, Noelle." I scratched down the side of my scruff. "No, not really. She barely speaks to me in a civil way. Why?"

"She ran out here at the party when you were throwing your little temper tantrum as you left. Thought I detected some emotion over your hasty departure. Didn't look too happy about it."

"Yeah, she was pissed that another chick wormed her way into my bed that night." I knew that wasn't exactly the truth but close enough.

"So, you saying you don't want her in your bed?"

His interest in Noelle caused the hair on my neck to stand up. Timms' record with women glowed big neon flags of caution. While he never agreed with her, Madelyn claimed they were together to anyone who would ask. Timms never used the word commitment to anyone except the team.

"I didn't say that, but she's not like the rest of the girls I normally spend my time with. It's going to take more time and effort with her. Why do you ask?" I wanted to know where he was going with this. The last thing I wanted was to compete with a teammate over a woman, especially Timms.

Where I exhausted all efforts to be a nice guy, Timms had the whole dark, brooding thing going for him. He stood six foot four towering over many of the players, which made him intimidating as fuck in the quarterback position. He rarely ever laughed out loud but was quick with a brief smile. For some reason, the women loved him. If we all went out, he attracted the most attention. At the frat house, the women flocked to him unless Madelyn showed. The two of them made an impressive pair.

"I'd keep my eye on her if I were you… just saying." It didn't sound like a warning, but I decided to file that tidbit away and take his advice.

"Will do, captain." I mockingly saluted him and walked to my Jeep. I waved at him as I drove off, and he nodded his head in response.

On the way back to my apartment, I decided maybe I needed to step up my game with Noelle. Damn, I had a lot going on in my life that I never planned for, but I wouldn't let her slip through my fingers until I made up my mind if I wanted more of her. Hell, who was I kidding, *if* she would let me more in her life was more like it. Nothing about this girl would be easy. The battle to win her would be fought before she gave into to my charms.

As I walked into my apartment, I spotted Gerrod and Quinn first thing.

"Shit guys, take it to your room, please." Quinn was riding him reverse cowgirl style, so I only caught her attention when she looked over her shoulder before I turned around. "I'm not into watching, dude, please."

"Awe, poor little boy Blue. Are we burning your eyes?" She made no movement like she was stopping her ride.

"Hey, Blue, this is what real sex looks like. Not that shit you like," Gerrod, the king of no woman ever, had the balls to yell.

"Just go to your room, guys. I have to study, and my notes are on the table in front of you. Or cover up, and I'll get it and leave." I walked backward toward them.

"Give us a sec, and we'll go," Gerrod growled, and some movement sounded before I heard bare feet slapping on the tiles.

"Okay, Blue balls, we're gone now," Quinn yelled down the hall before slamming Gerrod's door. I heard them both laughing before the banging resumed. At least one of us was getting laid.

I banged on the door where I think sex went on nonstop last night. "Quinn, you still here?"

"What?" It was her voice, but she wasn't awake.

"Tell me Noelle's number."

"Dammit, you woke me up for that? Use my fucking phone on the coffee table."

I opened her messages at the same time one came in from Noelle.

Noelle: *You coming home today?*

Hmm. Did I answer for Quinn or tell her it's me? Oh, I could so cause problems this way.

Quinn (Me): *This is Blue*

Yeah. I'm a nice guy like that.

Noelle: *Why do you have Quinn's phone?*

Should I tell her the truth? What would Quinn do?

Quinn (Me): *They were fucking on the couch when I got home, and I asked them to go to his room. They never stopped once they got there*
Noelle: *Sounds about right for them... gets annoying*
Quinn (Me): *I wanted to see if you'd like to meet for coffee today*
Noelle: *I don't know. What time?*
Quinn (Me): *10 at Coffee Bean*
Noelle: *I could prob make that*
Quinn (Me): *What's your pleasure, and I'll buy*
Noelle: *My pleasure is more sleep, but I would like a tall caramel macchiato*
Quinn (Me): *See you then*

A step in the right direction, finally. My morning already looked better. As I sat through my first two classes, I thought about what Timms said to me as I was leaving. Maybe he was simply giving me some advice instead of checking her out for himself. I needed to look into this without seeming too concerned. He'd spot it first thing.

"Mr. Myers, would you like to weigh in on this idea?" Busted. I had no clue what my prof had asked. I looked around as others stared in my direction.

"Sorry, sir. Would you repeat that? I'm not quite sure I understand."

"Mr. King, what about you? Were you paying better attention to my lecture than Mr. Myers?"

"Uh. No. I wasn't. Sorry."

"Was anyone in this class paying attention to what I asked?" the professor elevated his voice. Thank God one girl raised her hand and stated the answer to the question. I knew the answer right away. I'd done the reading. This was right out of last night's assignment. When she finished, I raised my hand and added to what she had to say. I needed to gain all the points I could with this guy. I wanted that 'A' on my transcript.

Class ended, and I made my way out with the crowd to head to my second class, but not before I ran into Laurin.

"Hey Blue. Thinking about me when the prof called on you?" She batted her eyelashes at me.

Who does that?

"Uh, no, Laurin. I was thinking about football plays. See ya later." I took off around the crowd just outside the door. The last thing I wanted was to get into a conversation with Laurin and chance Noelle walking up. Besides, I didn't want to encourage anything with her, but when she got out, I heard her call to me over the group.

"You didn't seem to have your mind on football when you tied me up." I stopped dead in my tracks and turned to her. She'd said that loud enough for everyone to hear, and the snickers and looks I received were a mixed bag of reactions.

I calmly walked back to her so I could speak loud enough for her ears only. "You didn't reject the idea either, so what does that say about you to all of these people you've enlightened?"

"It says you're a freak, and I like to have fun. Why'd you leave so angry, Blue?"

I looked down at her. She didn't get it. I knew she wouldn't. "Let me ask you this. Why did you agree to go to bed with me?"

"Because you're hot." She stopped and tried to run her hand down my shirt, so I backed up enough so she couldn't touch me. "I figured you'd know what you were doing instead of fumbling around like so many guys do." She ended her comment with a smile.

"Thank you. I'm sure that's a compliment, but honestly, I'm not really into the whole fuck'em and brag thing."

"Your reactions after we were done said otherwise, Blue. Are you sure you know what you want?" Again, she stepped toward me with her hand out, and I backed up. "I can help you figure it out. From what I've been told, you've spent plenty of time figuring it out your first two years here."

"Right. I did do that." I ran my hand down my face. I was done with this whole situation. I'd worked hard in the first two years, and now I suppose I'd be working harder for the next two undoing the damage. "But I'm thinking my one and done days are over. You taught me a good lesson, Laurin. Thanks." I turned and walked away leaving her staring at my retreating form.

NOELLE

Why did I agree to meet him today? I have so many other things I need to be doing like straightening my sock drawer. I'd just noticed how messy it was this morning. I looked up as I opened the door of the Coffee Bean to see this gorgeous smile aimed at me. How did girls resist all that long hair and beautiful face? Damn him.

"Hey, babe," he greeted me.

"Babe?" Nicknames already? We weren't dating. "Forgotten my name already?"

"No. You know what I mean. I'm happy to see you're not glaring at me for a change." He reached in, wrapped his arm around my neck, and pulled me to him for a brief hug. Not the full touching kind that my body secretly yearned.

"Oh." I couldn't come up with better words after that. He smelled divine, woodsy and all male. This fragrance could come home with me, and I'd be happy for days.

He pointed to the table. "One caramel macchiato as ordered."

I lifted one eyebrow at him. I did say that, didn't I? I'd never actually splurged and ordered one, but when he asked, it's the first thing that popped into my mind.

Who went to a specialty coffee place and just got regular coffee? This girl.

"Thank you. You didn't need to get it. I would have taken care of it when I got here. Let me pay you for it."

"Hell, no. It's just coffee, Noelle. I wanted to do something to make it up to you for being such an ass all the other times we've been together."

I looked down into the cup trying to decide if he was sincere and then raised my eyes back to his. God, I could climb over this table and kiss that panty-dropping smile off his face.

"Well, thank you. That was uh, sweet of you." He liked that answer because his smile grew even deeper with some dimples making a brief appearance. I wondered if he could make them happen on demand. It was hard to tell, though, when he let the scruff on his face get much longer. Between that and his long, dark blond hair, I'd rarely seen all of his face at once.

"So do you ever wear all that hair pulled back?"

He laughed a little. "Yeah, I got that whole man bun thing I do when it gets in the way. I usually put it up when I'm in the gym. Can't do weights and watch it in the mirror for form if I have it all in my face."

Oh my God. I'd love to see his hair that way while he lifted causing those big biceps to expand to full capacity. I wonder if he wore spandex when he did this? Or a shirt? Some guys didn't wear shirts in the gym, and even if they did, it was probably sleeveless. "Is the gym open to everyone on a team or for football only?"

"Why, you want to come see me lift? I think I could arrange that for you." My eyes popped up from my cup, and I looked at him hard. Was he trying to be cute or serious?

"What makes you think I'd only be there to see you? I bet lots of guys lift while you're there. I'm sure the rest of the team is required to go as well." I liked this playful verbiage between us. It felt easy and right. "You know like Timms and Jenko. I'll ask Gerrod about it."

His hand reached over and covered mine on the table top. "You can come anytime you want, but please, only when I can meet you there. The last thing you want to do is go in the weight room when the team's in training. Believe me." He never took his eyes off mine or his hand away. The seriousness of his expression told me all I needed to know.

"Oh, okay. Well, maybe sometime. Lifting weights would be good for me." I had to cover up the way my breath picked up from his protective comment and touch. He didn't want me in there with a bunch of meatheads gawking at a female.

He entertained me with crazy stories until we had to go to class. One thing we did figure out about each other was that we had lots in common. We came from smaller towns, our parents were both still married, and we hated missing classes—normal things and normal conversation two people would have when they were getting to know each other. I don't remember visiting like this with a guy since I'd been in college.

Real conversation was a breath of fresh air considering most of the guys who spoke to me made it seem like one of two things. One, they needed me for something or two, they were hitting on me. I felt neither after we spoke.

He opened the door, and we both stepped out in the fall air. "Thank you for the delicious coffee."

"Anytime, babe." He pulled me in for another hug, and this time I responded by wrapping around his waist. His warmth spread all over making me feel all sorts of things inside.

Before he let go, he leaned in. "Noelle, I honestly meant what I said about going to that weight room. Please listen when I say it's not a place for you to go alone. Mostly guys hang out there. The talk is rough, and they don't cut females any slack for invading their territory."

"Okay, I won't. Promise."

"Thank you."

He dropped a kiss on the top of my head before he let me go. I felt the tingle down to my toes. Pulling my backpack tighter on my shoulder, I turned and walked away. When I glanced back, he stood watching me. I gave him a little wave and spun back around to go to class. There would be no more grouchy looks from me for Blue.

A bounce in my step hadn't happened in a while. Guess I needed some hot male attention to get it back. Hopefully, he felt a little of the same tingles I felt when he touched me.

Cheer practice began with a lecture. *What's new?* Madelyn had several new things she wanted executed for the next game and a couple of ideas to carry through as the week went on to help excite the student body. They all involved being around the players, and I decided I could quickly climb on board that bus.

"I've given each of you a list of players you are to touch base with tonight. Call them, see them, text them, whatever. Just do it. Make a plan to hang out with as many as you can somewhere out in public. There is also a schedule of clothing that needs to be worn daily from now until Saturday. We need to support this team in every way possible. Go the extra mile this week. They want a win, and we want to help them."

I opened my list to see names, phone numbers, addresses, and email addresses along with their daily schedules. How did she get all this information?

"You have all you need, and it's private info so guard it with your life. There's not another copy."

I shot several pics of mine with my phone. Being responsible for keeping up with that didn't appeal to me. The clothes consisted of jerseys and tees we already owned. As I scanned the list of guys, I didn't recognize a single name. Couldn't she see clear to give me one guy I'd already met? She probably had the captains.

We spent the remainder of the time going through the new moves she wanted us to learn. I liked that there were several strong guys on our squad to do all the lifting. I wasn't a flyer, though. My long legs and weight made it difficult for guys to keep me on top for very long.

As practice came to a close, I took a long drink from my water bottle.

"Noelle, a moment please?" I loved the formality she used to make herself seem so important.

"Yeah?" I refused to buy into her power party.

"I heard you spent the morning with Blue. Do you not remember me telling you about him? I didn't think you were drunk when I told you that, but I might have been mistaken."

"No, Madelyn, I wasn't drunk. I heard you. He's the one who asked me to meet up with him. I didn't arrange it." I picked up my bag slinging it over my shoulder. I didn't plan to hold this conversation with her.

"I spoke to Timms about it, and he assured me you facilitated this."

"How would Timms know? I've only spoken to him once, and he was intoxicated."

"Blue must have told him, but it doesn't matter. I've told you what you need to know. Please adhere to the rules." Her nose stuck so far up in the air, she'd drown if it rained.

"I'm not aware of rules that you can tell me who to see, Madelyn. If he asks me out, I'm going. Not you or anyone else will stop me from seeing a guy who wants to spend time with me. I suggest if you have a problem with it, you need to tell him not to ask me." I spun around and walked away before my inner bitch came out and attacked her.

All the way back to my apartment, I steamed from the nerve of this girl. And what was Timms' deal? Was he stalking Blue or me to know who we were spending time with? I found it hard to believe he even cared enough about the two of us to do any spying.

My phone chimed with a text as I walked through the door.

Quinn: *At Gerrod's. You should join*
Me: *Sorry, got an HB assignment*
Quinn: *Do it here*
Me: *Is there food involved?*
Quinn: *Yeah, we'll order Pho*
Me: *Yummy*
Me: *Who's there?*

I didn't want Blue to think I was stalking him in his house.

Quinn: *Just us, come on*
Me: *K, be there in a few*

I stood in the shower and tried to think of fun things I could do for my list. God, this was getting so old. It seemed like I'd been baking, buying, and making stuff for football players forever. My patience ran thin on cutesy. I bet the guys didn't even like it, except if it was food. Those guys eat anything.

When I transferred here, my parents told me I didn't have to keep my scholarship. They were more than willing to pay for my last two years, but if the money was there, why would I ask that of them? Maybe this would be my last year. They could cover my senior year, and I could get a job or something. I needed to file this idea and come back to it after football season ended.

I walked into the guys' apartment. For three football players to live there, the smell didn't overwhelm me when I walked in like it did in some apartments. Guess they didn't like living like animals any longer.

"Hey cheer bitch," Quinn accosted me.

"Don't call me that. You know I'm not a bitch."

She shot me a look. "It does when it comes to doing cheer shit."

I looked up and smiled as I thought about her comment. "Yeah, maybe you're right this time."

We both laughed.

"So what's on this list of HB's?" Gerrod came in the room with his phone out.

"I'm calling Pho Sure. What do you want?" We both gave him our order before I pulled up my list on my phone.

"How damn many pages did the bully give y'all?" Quinn leaned over my shoulder to scan the information.

"It's like four pages. I think we each got five guys to work with. The funny thing is, I don't recognize a single name, so she must have searched hard to find players for me."

Gerrod finished the order and looked up. "Who would be on the team you didn't know? Let me see that list."

He took my phone and scrolled through the pages. "I don't even know these guys. Where'd she get 'em?"

"I don't know, but I'm supposed to talk or see them this evening and make plans to do stuff with and for them the rest of the week." I started reading the information on the list. They each had school email addresses so at least they were enrolled in TAU.

I texted the first guy on the list, Bradley Summers.

> **Me:** *Hey, this is Noelle from the university's cheer squad. You busy this evening? We need to meet up if we can arrange it.*

A text came back immediately.

> **Brad:** *Sure, I can meet you now. I'll come to you. Where are you?*

"Overeager much?" It sounded worse out loud.

"What'd he say?" Gerrod looked over my shoulder trying to read it.

"I don't think you should meet these guys alone, Noelle."

"Meet who alone?" The door opened, and Blue stood there looking over my shoulder at Gerrod. "You gotta big date or something?"

The puzzled look on his face said all I needed to know. After our time this morning, he was confused. It was only coffee, though. Did he expect more already?

"No, not a date. We have an assignment from Madelyn." I rolled my eyes at the stupidity of that comment. "She's given us team members to do stuff for or with this week. She wants us to keep you guys motivated for the game."

"Nothing about you hanging out with another guy motivates me to play better ball. If anything, it pisses me off, and that's not where my head needs to be before a game."

"Right." I didn't know what to say. "So, I texted this guy about meeting up."

"Yeah, and he shot a text right back. Wants to meet up now." Gerrod supplied Blue with the information before I could repeat it. Not that I needed to filter the guy's response, but I probably would have worded it differently than Gerrod.

"Who's the guy?" Blue looked at me as he asked. "I know all the people on the team."

"Bradley Summers. Never heard of him." Once again, Gerrod jumped in with the answer.

"Bradley Summers? He's not a player. He's a freshman water boy. Do you have more people on this list?" Blue took my phone.

The more names he read, the angrier he grew. "I can't believe she did this. These are all freshmen, and they are only allowed to bring water and supplies to the field. They can't even drive golf carts yet. Coach doesn't trust them to do it without screwing something up."

Quinn's comment came fast on his heels. "That sticky cum queen. She had to work fucking hard to find you guys like that."

I couldn't hold back my laughter at her creative name for Madelyn, but when we all stopped laughing, I agreed with her.

"You're right. She wanted me to have leftovers. Hell, she might have started with these guys just to make sure they landed on my list. Technically, they are part of the team, right?"

"Yeah, and probably harmless but damn, y'all didn't have to include them, and it would've given the girls fewer players," Gerrod added sliding in beside Quinn on the love seat pulling her closer to him.

"Right. So let's go meet Bradley. I'll drive." Blue picked up his keys. "Where we going?"

"Nowhere. You need to eat and relax. I'll go alone. I'm not exactly afraid to meet up with the guy. I could take him in a dark alley." I smiled.

"I damn sure don't like the idea of you meeting a stranger alone even if he is on the team."

I stood straight and leveled my eyes on Blue. "Mr. Muscles, I'm a big girl. I think I can handle this task. Besides, I've got to contact all of them before I agree to meet one. Let me text him back." I sent a text saying I'd contact him later if we were going to meet. "I'd prefer to meet them all at once since they're not players. It'd be a helluva lot faster in a group."

"If you're meeting a group of fucking guys, then I'm going to be there, too." Blue's face told me his stance was non-negotiable.

I'd never had a guy be all possessive, and we hadn't even had a date yet. "We'll see. Like I said, I need to contact them first."

"Just keep me in the loop on your meeting, please, babe." The second those words left his mouth, I saw Quinn's drop open. She cut her eyes to me and smiled. Quinn would put far more worth on the nickname than I did. He probably called all girls babe, so he didn't have to remember their names. "I'm gonna hit the shower. You'll be here when I get out?"

"Uh, I don't know. I guess. If you want."

"Yeah, I want. Don't leave." It wasn't a request this time.

"Sure. I'll hang out a while." Did I like him telling me what to do? He'd said please on keeping him informed. Was that more important to him than me hanging around, or did he like the idea that our time together be at his demand?

BLUE

I stood under the hot water as it eased my tight muscles. Thinking about Noelle meeting up with a bunch of strange guys didn't play well with me. I knew Madelyn schemed plans with everything she did. She'd warned Noelle to stay away. Girls sure liked doing things the hard way. If Madelyn wanted to be with me, she sure had a strange way of going about it. Besides, she's with Timms most of the time, so what would ever give her the impression I would take his sloppy seconds.

Noelle's take on hanging out with the team made her one in a million when it came to most of the women on campus. She acted as though she wanted nothing to do with the players. Didn't she enjoy hanging out this morning? It seemed like she did. I enjoyed coming home to find her in my apartment, but it was way too soon to be having those thoughts.

Thinking about her in the shower was a bad idea. Warm water, soap suds sliding down and dripping off the end of my dick only led me to think about having her in here with me. Would she enjoy being in here? And just like that, my dick started thinking with its head.

Rubbing one out with my mind on having her in here to lather up and run my hands over those tits of hers, made me harder in seconds. I fisted the length at the base now coated in soap and precum. The fully expanded shaft throbbed with sensation as I quickly pumped on it forming the friction needed to explode. Images of her naked up against the tile etched itself in my mind. Her hard nipples waiting to be tasted and teased caused my half sac to draw up tight, and a simple lick of her slick passage waiting for me had me squeezing tighter. A few pumps later, I bit my lip to keep from calling out her name or groaning out obscenities that usually followed shooting my load.

It took me a little time to come down, but once I had, I stepped out of the shower and dressed. Walking out into the living room, I found the three of them laughing. I prayed I wasn't loud in the shower. The TV played *The Water Boy,* and I knew better.

"Hey, dude. Look what Quinn pulled up. We thought it fit the bill for tonight. Wanted to give Noelle something to laugh about while she entertained her new friends." Gerrod laughed at his joke. I didn't find it all that funny.

"You ready to go?" Noelle stood. "I got them all while I waited. We're going to meet at the Ram's Horn. I figured it would be a safe spot." She moved toward the door.

"You intend to go through with this all week?" I hoped her reply would be no. No such luck.

"Yes, and I'm surprised you haven't gotten a text or call, too. You're on someone's list."

I hadn't looked at my phone since before practice, so I picked it up. "Dammit."

"What or should I say, who? Who got your name?"

"Aubry." This girl personified airhead Barbie. "You know the one I'm talking about?" I looked at Gerrod. She decided Gerrod was 'The One' when we got to campus as freshmen. She's a year ahead of us, but it didn't stop her from trying to climb Gerrod the first time they met. Of course, he immediately liked the idea of the older woman showing him so much attention. After a few dates, he figured out she was majoring in an MRS degree and wanted nothing to do with that. She'd planned their wedding, their kids' lives, and the mansion they would live in off his pro career. He got out of that as fast as he could run the other way.

Quinn spoke up. "Should I be making a shank for this nasty ho?"

"No, sweetheart, no need for blood. She knows there's not a chance in hell that would happen." Gerrod had shut Aubry down fast, and she didn't try again after the ugly scene she caused.

"I guess you need to make plans with Aubry's group then?" Noelle spoke up.

"No. I said I'm going with you, and I still intend to. They can change me to your group. Hell, I can be your whole group."

She shook her head no. "Not gonna happen. These boys were assigned to me, and I'll do what needs to be done. You can join or not, but I'm going to take care of my assignment. Who knows, these guys could be fun."

Noelle picked up her phone and slung her purse strap across her body. "You going or not?"

I grabbed my phone and caught up with her at the door. "I said I was, babe. Let's do this."

I heard Quinn and Gerrod laughing, and I knew I looked pussy-whipped already.

The Ram's Horn sat across from campus and had been there for at least a hundred years, so we made our way there. Horseshoe pits and washer boards claimed an area outside for entertainment. Rustic didn't come close to describing this place. It made rustic look industrial in design. The student body loved it because there were always students hanging out to drink beer, play the games, and meet new prospects for whatever reason.

When we walked in, I spotted the water boy squad sitting at a table at the front of the room. Naturally, they wouldn't go to the back like most guys did. The group needed to build some confidence before mixing it up with the upper classmen.

I tipped my head at the two facing us, and they sat up straighter alerting the three across from them of our arrival.

"Hey, guys," Noelle greeted them. They glanced in her direction but didn't take their eyes off me.

"Is that any way to speak to a beautiful woman who's spoken to you boys?"

Uh's and no's could be heard around the table as they jumped up and acknowledged her while pulling in two more chairs from the closest table.

"I'm Noelle Jefferies. I'm a junior transfer student and don't know many people yet. Please introduce yourselves so I can have five new friends." Her smooth introduction helped ease the stiff looks on their faces.

Each guy took a second to say their name and a word or two to help identify them. When we'd gone around the table, they all looked at me.

"I'm assuming you know Blue Myers already," Noelle added.

The eager nods and hellos indicated their answer. I stood and shook hands with each one. I wasn't a total asshole. They looked scared to death, and that was no way for Noelle to have to spend her time with these boys.

"I'm headed to the bar. What are y'all having?" I glanced around to see dark colored soft drinks and realized they were too young to drink. Hadn't thought about it before we came. Guess I don't have to worry they'll get drunk and hit on Noelle if she kept their meetings here.

"I'll bring back a pitcher," I told Noelle, and she nodded at me and smiled. Wow. Is that all it took to get a beautiful smile from her? I needed to remember she appreciated small things like being considerate.

I stood at the bar waiting for the pitcher of Coke watching her talk to the boys. They all seemed to calm down the longer she carried the conversation. As I made my way back, I heard laughter all around the table. Laughter was good, eased them into feeling more comfortable with a gorgeous woman sitting at their table.

"I was just telling them about how we met by falling into the pool. They thought it was funny."

"It's funny now." I looked around the table as they all watched me. "At the time, I thought she might come up and crack me over the head with her empty cup of beer I spilled. Or worse, she could have punched me in the nose. She's got a strong right hook so watch out."

The laughter erupted from them, and she laughed too. I loved hearing the soft sound and watching her smile. Her mildly pink, luscious lips turned up slightly at the ends when she grinned, but a big smile involved her perfect white teeth. Her eyes lit up, too. It signaled her happiness, and I knew that was a look I wanted to keep seeing.

We spent a few hours talking football and the upcoming game. I found the water boys to be entertaining and knowledgeable about the game, which surprised me. Most were in the program with intentions of being athletic trainers. I didn't know that was a degree until tonight. They took being on the team seriously, and I should be more considerate of their time.

She'd spent the evening creating an easy friendship among us all. I sat back and watched it unfold, enjoying watching the way she drew them into the conversation. This woman had a way about her that made people feel at ease. I wanted that feeling all the time, too.

Our dynamic struck me differently, though. I felt a current of electricity constantly running between us. Even as I watched her enjoying the camaraderie with this group of enamored guys, a pull kept calling to me to be near her. The desire to touch her smooth tanned skin held me. Noele was out of reach, though. I didn't want to interfere, but damn, it was difficult to be close and not touch her.

We stood to leave, and Noelle agreed to meet them again after practice tomorrow evening.

"Okay, guys, you have a job tomorrow with Noelle." They all looked seriously at me. "If I can't make it another day, I need to know you'll make sure she gets home safely after dark. I'm leaving it up to y'all to see to it."

There was never a question that this group would rise to the occasion and see her to the door. The request met positive responses all round, and I knew I didn't have to worry the rest of the week—at least not on this end. Whatever Aubry had planned might be a different story, and I didn't want to be a part of it.

We walked to Noelle's door as she dug out her keys.

"I guess it would be too much to ask for Quinn to be coming home tonight," she chuckled a little at her joke.

"Yeah, I wish they would move some of their loudness here. It gets old in a hurry. Jenko gives them hell about it."

"Like that bothers Quinn. It'll take a lot more than a few choice comments from Jenko to keep her quieted down."

"Don't we know it." I had to laugh. Some of the things that came out of Quinn's mouth when they were going at each other were comical. She could make a sailor blush, and when sex was included, it rose to a whole other level. I'm not even sure what some of her colorful phrases meant.

As Noelle opened her door, she stopped and turned to face me. Under the neighbor's porch light, I could see her gray eyes turn an iridescent silver. They captured my attention so I couldn't look away.

"Thank you, Blue. I know spending the evening with the boys probably wasn't what you were looking forward to after practice, but I appreciate you taking the time. I know they did, too."

"I enjoyed myself. You helped make it fun carrying the conversation until they got comfortable with talking. It's a gift you have, Noelle. Not everyone can do that." I reached out for her and slowly pulled her closer to me until we were toe to toe. The lightly sweet fragrance she wore wafted around her mixing easily with the faint vanilla from her hair. The two scents together created an erogenous memory to take home with me.

"I liked seeing you talk football with nerdy guys. It's pretty damn hot if you ask me."

She smiled and looked up at me, licking her bottom lip. I didn't know if it was intended to be an invitation to kiss her, but I took it as one. As I lowered my lips to hers, she sucked in a quick breath and joined me halfway. My lips skimmed over hers at first, kissing the edges and then full on before I ran my tongue across the slit seeking entrance to her warm mouth. She opened enough to allow me access before I deepened the kiss with tongues dueling for control in the heated space.

When she sucked my tongue in further, I gripped her perfect ass cheeks and pulled her to me tightly as I squeezed the globes against my growing erection. I knew she felt the force when she moaned into my mouth. The kiss broke, but I wasn't through. I nuzzled along her jaw and moved to her ear where I kissed and nipped down to the smooth curve of her neck.

She ran her hands through my long hair, and when she reached my scalp, her nails took over the assault by skimming up the back of my head. A slight shiver ran through me, and I bit down on her collarbone harder than I intended.

"Oh, Blue." Her husky voice made me want more. "We've gotta stop. I don't want to give the neighbors a show."

I reluctantly let her go and stepped back hating the moment her warm body was no longer against mine. "You're right. Not the time or the place." Our eyes locked in a magnetic pull.

She finally took a step backward to her doorway, kicking it open some with her foot.

"Will I see you tomorrow?"

"Probably. I don't know your schedule." She stepped inside.

"I'll text it to you." I leaned forward and gave her a little goodnight kiss. "G'night, babe."

She smiled. "Good night, Blue."

Dates in college never went as I expected. Most people had little time and even less money, so I never saw a real date coming in my near future. I couldn't be more wrong, though. When Blue finally asked me out, he meant what he said about a date.

We'd spent the week before the game hanging out or texting every night. I had my water boys, as I dubbed them, and he had to make an appearance or two with Aubry's group. What a disaster that must have been since they usually ended up doing whatever Madelyn scheduled with her group.

Funny how she had a group of one, Timms. This was okay with Blue, though, because he got to spend time with friends on the team. He wasn't close to Timms, but they hung out together some. After all this time together, they seemed like they had a better understanding of each other. At least Blue felt that way when he talked about it.

I planned burgers at my house—they planned bowling parties with a female for each guy. I baked cookies and handed them out after practice—they took their groups to dinner at all-you-could-eat locations. I learned to play washers at the Horn—they had a party at the frat house with paint balloons.

By game day, I knew all five of the water boys well. Blue confirmed the girls who came with Madelyn did whatever she said to do. More than once, he called me on his way home telling me when the twosomes and threesomes started for the night, he was out of there. Most of the girls were way too 'experienced' for his tastes which I found hilarious. The only two who were from the squad were Madelyn and Aubry, and the other women seemed to be older. It wouldn't surprise me if she'd hired prostitutes for those guys.

The cheerleaders made their way onto the sidelines after the team finished running through the tunnel, and we took our spots ready to cheer the team to victory over Dallas. The coaches preached all week how this game could turn the tide in their favor. A victory needed to happen, and the captains felt the responsibility on their shoulders as well.

After I jumped into hands and then shoulders on my base for the kickoff, I heard Madelyn's voice yelling her at base. The two moved over closer to us.

"I need to talk to you after kickoff, so don't go anywhere," Madelyn informed me.

Where was I going? We were on the sidelines for the duration of the game. Once we kicked off and my base let me down, she came running up beside me with pom poms in hand.

"Do you know why Blue left early every night from our group?" Her fake picture perfect smile she used for the fans was glued to her face and made me want to barf.

"No, do you? I had my group out every night, just like you said to do."

"Someone said he was with your group the first night instead of being with Aubry's."

"Yeah, he was. He wanted to get to know the water boys assigned to me. Didn't want to be afraid they'd poison him or something." I laughed as I said it. My guys were too sweet to do something of that nature.

"I think it was you who kept him there. Do you not remember me telling you he was off limits? Aubry wants him."

The squad started a new chant as the Rams got the ball after the first set of downs and Dallas had to punt.

"I think that's between Blue and Aubry, don't you?" She whirled around and locked eyes with me.

"How do you ever think that's going to happen if you fuck him seven ways to Sunday before she can even say hello."

I turned away. My first instinct was to grab that flowing bleach blonde hair and yank it out by the brown roots showing, but I didn't. Walking calmly over to the water, I picked up my bottle and took a long drink. I needed to calm down. Catfighting on the sidelines was strictly prohibited. Fighting of any kind was beneath me, and I wouldn't allow her to bait me. It's what she wanted, or she wouldn't say things like that where others couldn't hear it.

I moved off to the other end of the field. We usually rotated down the sidelines but not this quickly into a game. The last thing I needed to do was be close to her. This end offered a better view anyway.

Blue lined up even with the line on the opposite side of the field from me. When Timms snapped the ball, Blue took off down the field at an angle and then cut over leaving his defender behind with the quick cut. He caught the ball close to the sideline and ran it out of bounds straight at me.

I screamed trying to get out of his way, but he dropped the ball and grabbed me up to keep me from being plowed over.

He spat out the mouthpiece. "Babe, if you wanted me to pick you up, I'd have come over before the game." He grinned, stood me up, and trotted back onto the field where his team congratulated him on his catch.

One of my water boys came running up. "Are you all right, Noelle?"

I laughed, but he was genuinely concerned. "Yeah, I'm fine. Thanks for looking out for me."

"No problem. It's our job." He smiled and ran back to the others sporting a grin.

And just like that, the happy moment deteriorated in a flash. "That's what I mean. You've been hooking up with Blue all week, haven't you?" Half the squad and the football team heard her yell it and probably the entire front section of the fans. "He can't keep his hands off you even in a damn game," she shrieked.

I felt humiliated from her comments especially since we hadn't done anything yet. I walked directly up to her, tightly grabbed her arm, and pulled her as close to the front of the tall bleachers as I could so no one in the stands could hear what I said.

"First, like hell will this play out in front of the student body and the fans. I have more dignity than that. Second, if I choose to fuck Blue, you will never, *never* know about it, because neither of us will discuss it with you or anyone else. Third, if you ever pull this shit and try to humiliate me again, I will take you out so fast, you'll never see it coming. I'm not one of your minions, and I'm not going to dote on your every damn move. Get that through your small mind, Maddie. Understand?"

She looked at me and then behind her before she smirked in my face. "This is far from over, bitch. Remember that." She jerked out of my grasp and walked back to the middle of the sidelines. Her little minions ran to her rescue, and she examined the spot where I had my hand wrapped around her stick of an arm. Part of me hoped I left bruises while the other part prayed I didn't.

By the middle of the fourth quarter, we were behind by one field goal, but we had the ball and plenty of time to score once or possibly twice. The Rams gave it their all against this bigger university and had the marks to prove it. Many late hits received penalties for the Dallas team, but they didn't care. Their goal seemed to be to take out as many of our players as possible. They sacked Timms several times, but Blue moved some to defense and gave it to their quarterback, too. I'd be surprised if he didn't get an award for the sacks and assists after the dirty game Dallas played. I'd heard his team call him Half sac several times when he came off the field. I wondered how many assists he'd made in this one game.

The coach called a time out, and starters came to the sideline. As cheerleaders, we spent this time pumping up the crowd to keep the energy up for the team. I knew the coach would have something ready to score the needed touchdown for the win. In no time, the ref blew his whistle to restart the clock, and time started ticking away.

The team lined up, and Timms shouted the cadence to start the play. On the second hut, a defensive lineman charged across his opponent on our line, almost taking Timms in an unanswered tackle, but Jenko stepped in his way stopping him. This made the lineman angry, and he took a swing at Jenko who managed to step back fast enough to keep from getting hit.

A fight erupted and benches cleared before coaches and refs could stop the ensuing battle. Whistles blew, players and coaches scrambled, and eventually, it came to a halt. From my vantage point, it seemed like it took forever to clear the field, but the refs got everyone back to their positions. While the players waited, the refs conferred.

The refs ejected Jenko and the off-sides lineman from the game for fighting. It was a bad call on their part because Jenko kept the big guy from running over Timms. After our coach had an angered pow wow with the ref, he finally allowed Jenko to be benched, but the other player had to go to the dressing room.

This call fired up our team, and nothing could stop them from scoring the needed touchdown and one more before the clock ticked to 00:00. Timms fired off perfect passes without a hitch, and his intended receivers caught all he threw. Our fans screamed and yelled the praises of the team for thirty minutes after the game.

As I rounded up my things on the sidelines, I kept an eye on Madelyn. I might not make it to the end of the season on this squad. I'd never quit anything I started in my life, but she would not talk to me like that in front of or behind groups of people. I patted myself on the back for leaving the fighting to the players, but my emotions ran as deep as theirs.

She walked toward me as I stood with my bag over my shoulder. "You might be seeing the bench just like Jenko after the stunt you pulled threatening me on the sidelines."

"Gladly, if it means I get to tell my side to the sponsors of the squad. You had no right to say what you did. Don't think I won't take in witnesses. They've already told me they heard it all and are willing to speak up if needed."

Madelyn rolled her eyes and glanced back over her shoulder at the other squad members. "We'll see. That's all I'm saying." She flounced off in the other direction.

The ending of the game set events in motion that no one saw coming. Coach's anger rolled off his tongue with every word from his mouth. He threatened to suspend several players who directly participated in the fight caused by the bastards from the other team. Those actions didn't matter in his book. We came to play and win as a reputable team, and while we did win, our reputations as scrapers on the field now captured the attention of the media. A reputable team didn't fight. A reputable team didn't have players ejected. A reputable team won against the entire other team, not some in the locker room.

He laid down the law on how the rest of the season would go and ended his rant by saying more decisions would be made about current team members once they reviewed the films. Those words made us all nervous. Who knew what the coaching squad would see in the films? In the heat of the moment, all bets were off when it came to defending our teammates.

Coach went into his office calling the captains in behind him. Once the door closed, he started his rant again.

"I will not have my players acting like hooligans on the field. Do you all understand me? When I told y'all to keep the players ready to play all week, I meant keeping their heads in the game, not this bunch of bullshit that happened out there. Hell will be paid this week in practice, and that's what you better convey to the bunch of pussies that stand in that locker room right now. Do you get what I'm saying? Do you think the four of you are capable of getting my message across to that sorry group of good for nothings out there? Get out of my office, *now!*"

The office vacated as quickly as we could get out. No coach had ever talked to me like this, especially a TAU coach. I'd heard stories from other teams about their coach going off on them, but his name calling shocked all four of us. My anger built as I tore off my uniform. We'd won the game, hadn't we? What more did he expect? I prayed that film showed what we all knew happened out there.

After a lightning-fast shower, I shoved my gear I needed into my team bag and tore off out the door. Fans and parents stood around waiting for us as usual, but I didn't want to deal with it. The news teams shoved microphones in my face, but I didn't say a word to anyone. I climbed into my truck and headed directly home. The last thing I needed to do was take my mood out on the news media because shit would hit the fan over the things going through my mind.

I pulled into my spot at the apartment, threw open my door, and stomped all the way to my room. I had no interest in talking to anyone at that point. The adrenaline from the win ran high through my body, but the desire to work it off didn't.

I heard Jenko and Gerrod come through the door talking shit about the game behind me. I picked up my headphones and remote and turned the music up to drown their comments out as I fell across my bed. Something hit my foot, and I rolled over to see both standing there staring at me.

"What the fuck? Wasn't my door closed?"

"Yeah, but we could hear the damn music all the way in the other room. We knew you were here," Jenko informed me.

"We're thinking about going out and pounding back some beers and pussy and not necessarily in that order," Gerrod smirked at his comment.

"Not interested."

"Why not? You sure as hell can't lay here and sulk because the Coach scolded us like middle schoolers fighting in the fucking schoolyard. Bottom line, it went down in the books as a fucking 'W.' That's all that matters." Jenko slapped Gerrod on the back as he said it.

"Still not interested in celebrating. Y'all go and have all the damn fun. I'm not fucking feeling it right now." I rolled back over and put my headphones back on and turned down the music slightly. This conversation was over.

I sat up against my headboard and picked up the tennis ball I kept on my desk throwing it hard against my closet door, careful to not put it through the cheap veneer. This kind of win blew just like Coach said. A key team member missed from both sides and anger fueled our plays. Playing in control of the game calculated the best win—not the bullshit we allowed. We had to figure out how to prevent this from happening again. We needed to control the situation.

"I need control of this situation." I jumped off the bed throwing my headphones down intending to leave when my phone chimed. I looked down at the screen reading Noelle's name.

Nope, babe. You're not what I need now.

It chimed again before I could get to the front door. The screen displayed "HELP."

Dammit, I couldn't ignore it now.

Me: *What?*
Noelle: *Where are you?*
Me: *Headed out*
Noelle: *Call me*

I took a deep breath and hit her name to call. "What is it?"

"Hello to you, too. I wanted to see you, but not if you're in a bad mood."

"Well, yeah. I'm in a fucking bad mood. That win was shit, and you know it."

"No, all I know is we won, and I thought you could take my mind off the shit Madelyn caused today."

"Listen. Today is not the day. I'm going out to the XOX house to... to get rid of some aggression."

"Oh, so you're going to fuck some bimbo while I sit at home and sulk?"

"Probably..." I took in a deep breath to help calm me. "Hell, I don't know." Wow! She went straight for the jugular on that one.

"Why? Come over here, and we'll work it out together."

Yeah, like she'd ever be down for my kind of sex. She wasn't one who would want to be tied down and blindfolded. "Nope, that's not going to happen."

"What the fuck, Blue? We've hardly even gone out, and I agree to sex, and that's the answer I get?"

"Today it is. I'm in a bad mood. I need to work through this shit before I see you, Noelle." I fell back against the wall by the front door. “I’m sorry, truly sorry, babe, but I just gotta to do this today. It has nothing to do with how I feel about you or anything like that. I’m pissed at everyone including myself. I’ll get past this, and then I’ll see you. Please don’t take it personally because it’s not.”

“Fine, Blue. You do what you gotta do.” She hung up on me, but not before I heard her whisper, “And so will I.”

What kind of comment was that?

I ran and started my truck. Backing it out, I slammed it into gear and skidded out of my space. The sooner I did this, the better off I’d be.

I arrived soon after at the house to see a full-blown victory party taking place. The other teammates had arrived long before me and started the festivities. Fucking fine by me. I wasn’t in the partying mood anyway.

“Blue,” Jenko called as I stepped on the porch. “Glad you changed your mind.” He slapped me on the back. I glanced left to see Timms sitting in his favorite location. I tipped my head to him about the same time Madelyn came out with two long necks and two shots with amber liquid in them.

“Your girlfriend too freaked to show up? I figured my little talk would put a stop to her intruding where she didn’t belong.” She handed one of each drink to Timms and sat down in his lap.

"What the fuck you talking about, Maddie?" Timms asked before I could.

"Oh, baby, it's not important at all. Let's toast to the win." She clinked the glass with him and shot the whiskey down only to follow it by a gulp from the beer bottle, and he did the same.

With no intention of watching those two get drunk, I followed Jenko back to the beer and drew one from the keg.

"That was some fucked-up speech we got from Coach today," Jenko started.

"Don't want to talk about it." I downed the beer in three gulps before stepping up to fill my cup again.

"Well, Gerrod and I already did before you got here, so I'll let it slide."

"Where's Quinn?" Now I had Noelle on my mind from what Madelyn said.

"She's with Noelle. Said they were going to stay home tonight. Didn't much feel like partying, so I guess it's the guys tonight," he added and nudged me with his elbow tilting his head toward a girl I knew I'd hooked up with before. She knew my brand of kink. "Looks like Cassie's got her eye on you, Blue."

"Whatever, I'm not drunk enough for Cassie, yet." We both laughed knowing if I kept drinking one after another, I would be. I stepped up and grabbed a second cup, one for each hand. Double fisting worked even better.

I downed two more and poured two before I stepped out the back door. Being a big guy, it took a lot before I'd had enough. I didn't want a limp beer dick, though, so I decided these would be my last two until I walked into a shot-gunning contest. That shit was for the freshmen, but I was in the mood to show them up tonight. I needed to take control of some situation so I'd start here.

After five rounds, I'd beat all the players. I stumbled over to a lawn chair and fell in.

"I wondered how long it would take you to get out here," Cassie said before landing in my lap. "You up for a little play tonight? It's been a long time, Blue." She walked her fingers down the front of my shirt unbuttoning as she went. The fingernail of her index finger worked its way under the material and lightly scratched across over to my nipple. She scraped around the flat disk causing my dick to perk up in a hurry. When she lightly drug her nail across the nipple, I'd had enough. Being pissed off and horny always led to one thing—rough sex—and she knew the kind I liked.

I stood, taking her with me and carried her to the side door of the house that went directly to the bottom of the stairway. As I rounded the corner and started up, I glanced at the crowd, and Noelle stood in the same spot as the last time I did this.

"Well, fuck."

"That's what I'm hoping for," Cassie said in a breathy voice by my ear, and I turned and looked down at her before looking back at Noelle. It didn't matter because Noelle was gone. Cassie took this as a good sign and started biting on my ear and neck. I didn't want to feel anything, but my dick said otherwise. I needed to get laid, and I wanted it rough. Noelle wasn't the girl for that, but Cassie had proven she was always down for rough.

Cassie opened the door to the room we used last time, and I stood her up.

"Strip and get on the bed face down. This is going to be rough. Sorry but I'm frustrated, pissed off, and in a bad mood."

"Oh. Sounds like my kind of night." The stupid girl giggled at my comment.

"Good, because it's that or nothing tonight. Now do what I said." My voice held no nonsense in it. When she got down to her panties, I stepped up behind her and ripped them off from the sides.

"Bend over." She immediately put her hands on the bed. I opened the drawer behind me and pulled out two wide black ribbons. I leaned over her and tied one around her eyes first.

"Are you good?" I asked. I never wanted to hurt the girls I played with, but they would never see me naked either.

"Yes, Blue. I'm good." Her calm voice told me what I needed to know.

I ran my index finger slowly down her spine causing goosebumps to appear all over her legs. When I reached her ass, I parted it and continued until I reached the opening I sought.

"Wet for me already, I see." After dipping in, I moved some of her juices forward to circle her clit. I wanted her to have all the pleasure I would have, too. She moaned softly on my first pass around the swollen nub.

I moved back to the slick channel and pulled a little up to her other opening. I rarely did anal play, but I knew Cassie would go for it if I were in the mood. I rounded the little bud with her nectar before slipping my pinkie past the tight muscle to my second knuckle.

"Oh my God, Blue."

"How does that feel, Cas? You down for it?"

"I... I don't know. It's been a long time since I've done that."

"It's your choice tonight, and you should feel special since I'm not really in a giving mood." Her hands were clasped together as she leaned on her elbows, so I took that opportunity to wrap the wide black ribbon around them carefully while she fought with the decision.

"I suppose we could try. I mean, if you want to."

"Forget it. I asked, and you're not sure. We'll move on." With her hands tied and her eyes covered, I dropped my jeans and stepped out. I grabbed my dick and ran it up and down her slit that stood open in this position causing me to erect to full length. I rolled the condom on after a few pumps. Again, I ran my dick up and down her, stopping at the entrance we agreed on to cover myself in her precum.

"Are you going to tease me all night, Blue?"

"I can feel your body's ready. Are you?" She knew what I meant. We'd had rough sex the last time.

She backed into me to answer my question, and I pushed to the hilt in one move. God, so tight. I stayed there giving her time to adjust before I started pounding her pussy until we both got what we wanted.

When we were done, I took care of the condom and stepped into my jeans. Reaching forward, I pulled the tie on her blindfold and hands at the same time letting her loose from the side position she laid on. I'd taken her in all the positions I could come up with to make her come, and the noises she made told me she loved every one of the three she had before I shot my load filling the condom.

"You good?" I asked as I sat down on the side of the bed to look her in the eyes.

"I'm great." She nodded as she said it. "I'm sleepy, though."

"Stay here as long as you want. I'm leaving, and no one uses this room but me."

I wasn't a bastard to the women I fucked. I made sure they were satisfied and okay before I left them. Tonight, I felt like one, though. As I buried myself balls deep in Cassie, again and again, all I could think about was the look on Noelle's face.

Would she be waiting like the last time?

I prayed she'd be gone.

My descent this round was slower than the last so I could look around for her. I felt like a real dick for treating her like that, but she would never allow me to take her the way I needed tonight. I would lose her before we even started. Now I wondered if I already had.

As I wandered around the house and outside, I continued looking for her. In my mind, I knew she'd left, but I had to make sure. When I stepped back in the kitchen, I ran into Quinn and Gerrod.

"Well, here's the fuckwad now. Feeling like the king, asswipe?"

"What are talking about, Quinn?" I needed her to say what was on her mind. I knew she would anyway.

"You let my girl down is all I'm saying. She needed you today, and you chose to fuck her over."

"Yeah, I probably did. Why did she need me anyway? She sounded fine on the phone."

"What a walking douche you are. She had a fight with Madelyn and will probably lose her scholarship, and all she needed was a little TLC from the only person who fucking mattered to her, and you were too busy getting off on some skanky piece to even notice."

"A fight?" What about?"

"You are one stupid son of a bitch. I gotta give that award to you tonight. Who do you think, twat monkey?"

I assumed she meant me. "Why would they be fighting over me?"

"When you almost took Noelle out on the sideline, it opened up speculation about the two of you, and head bitch told her to leave your slut-ass alone. I think Noelle told you that."

"And I told Maddie to back off."

"Lot of damn good that did," Quinn added. "Look, I'm done with your stupidity. I hope she is, too. Leave her alone. She's got things to work out and doesn't need you fucking with her head anymore."

"Where'd she go?"

"Home, to her parents' house for the rest of the weekend to tell them about the scholarship. They won't care, but Noelle took paying her way seriously."

"Fuck."

"Yeah, that's what you did all right. And now you're fucked."

My parents didn't give a shit about the scholarship money. They'd started my college fund before I even came along. Plenty of money sat unused in an account to finish college and even get a master's degree. My dad had invested the money all my life. The money had grown exponentially. I hoped to use that money to keep me afloat after I graduated and before I got the job I wanted.

Tears began to flow again as I exited the freeway on the last leg of the journey. I didn't bother to call and tell them I needed to come home for a couple of days. I never did, so when I pulled up to the house, and it was shut up, I sat staring at the closed garage doors.

Me: *Where are y'all?*
Mom: *Houston visiting your grandparents. Yeah for the win*
Me: *Oh good. I know grandma's glad*
Mom: *Why?*
Me: *Just wondering. Y'all have fun*
Mom: *We will. Hope you celebrated in style! Love you*
Me: *Love you too*

"Well, shit. This didn't turn out like I wanted." Reaching up, I pushed the garage door opener and drove into my mom's spot closing it behind me. At least I had the house to myself for the rest of the weekend. I could hold my own pity party without causing a problem. Bring on the gelato.

After sliding out, I unloaded a few things from the car and walked into the quiet house. Grabbing the remote, I set the TV to music and went to my old room. They'd not changed a thing since I left. I flung myself across my bed. Even though I didn't want to cry anymore, slow tears ran down to the bedspread.

Rolling over, I moved up on my pillow, grabbing the other and wrapping it around my head for comfort.

Why was I crying? Madelyn embarrassed me in front of the crowd and the rest of the squad. I refused to let her affect me for another minute. On Monday, I'd take my uniforms into the sponsor and quit. There is no way I'm going to let this bitch run my life any longer. She could control her gang, but she never would control me.

Blue. The beautiful smile he hit me with when he held me off the sideline lit me up inside. He looked like perfection in his uniform, and the grip he had on me was tight and warm.

God. Why did he have to look that way all the damn time?

Tears slid down my cheeks this time. I thought I could count on him when I needed him, believing we had something growing between us over the past couple of weeks. Our start was rocky, but we'd smoothed things over. We'd laughed on the phone, spoke of dreams over coffee, and sent flirty texts all week. In my mind, feelings had developed between us. Apparently, it was one sided.

My phone pinged.

Quinn: *You make it home?*
Me: *Yeah*
Quinn: *Do I need to come down there?*
Me: *No, I'm fine*
Quinn: *I fucking hate "fine."*
Me: *I'm great then*

Quinn: *Good. Great is better than fine*
Me: *You're crazy*
Quinn: *That's fucking crazy to you bitch*
Me: *Haha right. I knew that*

I threw the phone back on my bed and laid over hugging my pillow. I needed to sleep. I'd feel better. The look on Blue's face when he saw me kept coming to mind. Twice the son of a bitch took another woman to bed.

What was wrong with me?

Drifting off into a light sleep, I woke up startled and sat straight up.

"Oh, hell no. You're not dragging me down, you bastard. There's not a damn thing wrong with me. This is all on you."

No one heard this, but it made me feel better. I laid back on my soft pillow and knew I was done with cheer and with him. Monday would be a new start. No more football and no more football players. Fuck them. I fell asleep listening to the new music by Ed Sheeran floating around my house.

Later, I opened my eyes to a dark room. I'd lived in this room all my life, so it didn't bother me. The music still played in the den, so I climbed out of bed and turned on lights heading back to the main section of the house thinking about ordering pizza. It would last me through lunch tomorrow when I needed to head back.

I looked at the screen intending to pull up my contacts where my favorite pizza store held a place of honor since my parents bought my first phone. I saw some messages waiting, but didn't want to talk to anyone yet.

After ordering and fixing a soft drink, I scrolled through them. Several of my water boys had left fun messages about winning—they were so cute. I needed to return a fun message to that group.

Quinn sent some stupid dirty gifs to make me laugh. What else would she send? Mom sent a pic of her and grandma in their team t-shirts I'd sent them before school started. My family was all about winning.

Several messages were mixed in from numbers I didn't know. I could see Madelyn having the minions send me shit.

The last one was from Blue. Because it was only a few words, it appeared on the screen. "Call me."

"Like hell, I'll call you. I don't owe you shit. Have all the slutty women you want. Do whatever you want. I don't have a single fuck to give you. All of my Blue fucks have been given out," I said this all to myself. I believed those words. Too bad I didn't say them to him. I refused to be told what to do again by him or anyone else that didn't matter in my life.

The doorbell rang, and I was glad for the distraction. I planned to catch up on my favorite TV shows, eat greasy pizza, and drink a liter of soda. I was never able to do this, so today I was going to do what I wanted, for me.

I opened the door with cash in hand for the pizza boy. Blue stood there instead, holding my pizza.

"Pizza, lady? It's hot and smells good." He smiled his panty dropping smile at me, and I wanted to throw up.

"Give me my food and leave. Here." I shoved the cash at him. "I don't want you paying a dime toward anything that concerns me." He let the bills fall to the concrete.

"I don't want your money, babe. I came to talk to you."

"I'm done talking to you. I'm done talking to anyone who has anything to do with football and that stupid university. Now hand it over and get in your truck and go home. I don't need you, and I don't want you here."

"That's harsh considering I drove two and a half hours for a few minutes of your time."

"Dumbass, you don't even know harsh. Give me the pizza and get the fuck off my porch. Is that better?" My hands reached, but he jerked the box out of my grasp.

"I'm not leaving until you talk to me."

"What? I have nothing to say to you."

"You're right. I'm not leaving until you let me talk."

"Don't care what you have to say. We tried... twice. Remember? It didn't work. You're busy doing what you do, and I've got a life of my own to lead. We don't mesh. Our paths don't cross or intersect from any direction. I'll be damned if I let you take me down that path ever again. Go back to your team, your skanks, your boys. I'm done."

I moved back and slammed the door before he saw the tears fall. After sliding down the door, I sat there silently crying over a relationship that never had a chance. Then I heard noises against the door.

"I'm not leaving, Noelle. I'm going to sit here and wait. You have to go back to campus sometime." The door groaned as he sat behind me.

"Go home, Blue. You can't stay there."

"I can, and I will. I'm more stubborn than you'll ever be."

"I don't want you here." The cruel words didn't make me feel better.

"I know you don't, but this is where I want to be."

"If you know this, why would you stay?"

"I let you down today and I'm sorry. You needed me, and I did something stupid instead."

"That's for damn sure," I said this more to myself, but he still heard me.

"I didn't know what was going on, Noelle, and I was too messed up to stop to think about it. I know I'm a selfish prick."

"Yep. You said it, not me."

"I'm so sorry. That's all I know to say."

"You can say it all day, Blue, but your word doesn't mean shit to me. Your actions tell me otherwise."

"I know. I'm not going to deny anything at this point."

"Go back to campus, Blue. I need to deal with this by myself."

"Deal with what, Noelle? With my stupidity? With Madelyn's stupidity? With my fucked-up problems?"

I had no idea what he was talking about now. I knew the stupidity, but what were his fucked-up problems? What the hell was he referring to?

"You don't have problems, Blue. You're selfish just like most guys, only caring about yourself when it comes right down to it. You pretend to make sure I'm okay, like sending the guys to see I get home. Then, when it comes down to you being there, you're only in it for you."

"That's because I have other problems to deal with, babe. Things you'll never know about."

"How can I deal with them if you'll never let me in? Forget it! I'm not sure I even want to deal with your shit."

"It's not something you need to worry about, trust me. We can only be friends. I realize that now. I thought we could maybe try, but I can't do it. It's me."

"Oh *please,* Blue," I say sarcastically. "The 'it's not you, it's me' speech. *Really?* Is that the best you can do?" I chuckled at the absurdity of it.

I heard him let out an exasperated sound. "This isn't something to laugh about. I'm messed up, Noelle. I'm not right. I haven't been right since I was fifteen."

I sat straight up. "What? What's wrong with you?" My mind went all over the place.

Was he sick?

Was he abused?

"Look, please let me in. This pizza smells so fucking good, and I'm starving. We can talk about it later." The tone of his voice held a note of sadness. Was he playing me to get inside the door?

"I don't know if I'm ready to see you. Why would you want to talk? We obviously can't seem to get things right."

"We can get things right, or at least we can give it a fair try."

"I thought we did that."

"No, dammit. You did. I didn't. I let my shit get in the way. I'll do better, I promise."

"How many times will I hear this from you, Blue?"

"Never again. If I screw it up again, I'll leave you alone. I'll lose your number. I'll forget you're on campus. I'll turn the other way if you walk by."

Hmm. That's pretty rough. I stood, wiped all the tears away, and unlocked the door. As I slowly opened it, he stood too, holding out the pizza box.

"Your pizza, ma'am." He smiled at me.

"I guess you're expecting a tip?"

"No, ma'am. Just seeing your beautiful face is enough for me."

"You're so full of shit."

He grinned at me. "Yeah, maybe that was a bit cheesy."

"You think?"

I stepped back to let him in and took the box. He followed me to the kitchen where I took out paper plates and napkins.

"Drink? I don't know if we have any beer."

"Water's fine with me. I need to back away from the alcohol for a while. The whole team does."

I looked at him like he'd lost his mind.

"Yeah, we got another lecture today after the game. Coach's going to kill us all week at practice from the fight on the field." He finished off his first slice as I took my first bite.

"How did you know I was here?"

"Quinn. She told me you went home. I thought she meant to your apartment, but she informed me of all of my mistakes including that one." He looked at me over the bar. "She also said you and Madelyn had it out on the sideline."

I rolled my eyes. "I'll be sure to thank Quinn when I see her for blabbing."

"She was pissed at me, and I think she's upset with you."

"I know. We talked." I dipped my pizza in the ranch dressing enjoying every single bite.

"Noelle. I don't know how to stop this nonsense with her. I'll do whatever you suggest, though. I asked Madelyn to fucking leave it alone. I told her I had no intention of seeing Aubry or anyone else but you on the cheer squad."

"It doesn't matter anymore. I'm quitting the squad. I don't need the problems that come along with it. Like I said before, I can pay for school." I looked down and picked a piece of pineapple off the top of my piece of pizza popping it in my mouth. "I just liked the idea of helping my parents out and using the college fund when I needed it after college. You know, like a car or down payment on a house or whatever to get me started in the real world?"

"Shit. That makes this even worse." I didn't tell him that to make it harder on him. This wasn't even his fault.

"It's not your fault. She's a total cunt." As soon as the horrible term left my mouth, I felt bad. I never used that term even with girls I hated. I felt the heat rise to my face. It crawled up my neck leaving a glow in its path. Blue laughed so hard I thought he would fall off the bar stool. The redder my face got, the louder he laughed.

"I can't believe you said that. You never go that far. Too funny, babe. Too funny... but so true."

BLUE

Noelle never ceased to surprise me. She was good at everything she did. She's a caring person, especially to the people she loved. A lot of college students didn't lift a finger to help pay for school, but she put up with all kinds of shit to pay for it all.

"You aren't going to quit, are you?"

"The cheer squad? Yeah, I am. I don't like my life in a constant state of drama. I feel like Madelyn wakes in the morning making a list of idiotic tasks for the cheer squad. After that, she devises plans to fuck with our heads, create havoc between us, and draw all favorable attention to herself by making us look bad."

"Yeah, you're probably right about that. She thrives on it, but I think it might have bitten her in the ass this time. I heard the sponsor made some noise about what went down on the sidelines."

"See right there. That's what I'm saying. Why would you hear this kind of thing? It's dumb-ass girl drama. I'm done with it."

"I can't believe you're going to let her win."

"I'm not running a race with her. I'm in college, for one thing, to get a degree and move on to the next phase of my life. She's obviously here for a different reason." She took a deep breath letting it out slowly. "I'm done talking about it and her."

"Okay, let's talk about something else." I hit her with my best smile.

"Yeah, that's not going to work anymore, Blue. You can drop other girls' panties with it from now on, remember. I'm done."

My smile dropped immediately. "I know, and you have every right to feel that way about me or us." I pushed the empty plate away. Suddenly eating greasy pizza turned my stomach. How far did I go with an explanation? How much did she need to understand? Less is better, right?

"I realize I've been a total douche bag to you more than once, Noelle, and for that I'm sincerely sorry. Some issues came up in my life when I was younger that were life changers for me. I don't talk about it because I'm over it and like to keep it in the past."

"Are you sick?" I knew where she was going.

"No, I'm not sick. My problems have nothing to do with an illness and never have." It would be so much easier if I just told her the truth, but I couldn't risk exposing myself. I knew she wouldn't use it against me, but she might tell someone who would.

"I don't like things normal people like." Whoa, where did that come from? Now she's going to think I'm a total perv.

"What do you mean 'things normal people like?' That's a strange thing to say, Blue."

"I know it is, but it's the truth. It's not what you think, though. I'm talking about in bed."

She lifted her eyebrows in question, but I wasn't ready to continue this line of conversation. "I don't like talking about it, but that's the reason we can't be together that way. I like you, babe... a lot. Hell, what's not to like. But we can't go that direction in a relationship. It doesn't mean I don't like sex because, believe me, in that respect, I'm a normal guy."

"Are you trying to tell me you're gay or bi? It's totally cool if you are. I'm not judging."

I leaned over laughing so hard. "No, babe, definitely not swinging for either of those teams. I like women... all kinds of women."

"Then what's wrong with you?" She looked point blank at me to ask the question.

I looked away trying to come up with something that would satisfy her curiosity and stop this line of questioning. “Let’s just say, I like things a little more controlled in the bedroom, and that’s all I’m saying about this. Can we drop it now?”

She stared at me for what seemed like forever. I’m sure her mind bounced around on my comment coming up with all kinds of kinky things. Shit, she probably thought I was some sadomasochist or something. Let her think what she wanted as long as we didn’t have to talk about it.

“So, okay. No more questions then.” Her words were very stilted. After a bit, she looked at me again. “I have one more, and then I’m done.”

I stared hard at her. I wanted this to be over. “One more. That’s it. No more questions.”

“Do these girls you choose to, to, uh… see. Do they like the same things you like?”

Oh, great. That’s a loaded question if I ever heard one.

How could I answer this without giving too much away?

“Yeah, they do.” Short and simple. I’m not giving any more.

“Okay, I said no more, and I meant it.” She picked up the half-eaten pizza and put it in the fridge. “You want more water?”

I shook my head. I didn’t know how long she would allow me to stay, but she surprised me.

"You want to watch some mindless TV? That's what I was going to do with my pizza. I also have some yummy Talenti gelato in my freezer."

"Never had it, but if it's frozen and sweet, I'm down." She got the quart container of gelato out and two spoons before we settled in front of some episodes of *The Walking Dead*. I'm not a big fan, but hey, killing zombies can't be all that bad.

Our evening together with no pressure left me feeling good. We talked and laughed about things happening around campus that didn't involve problems. I discovered we were both reading freaks, but she's all about romance. I like fantasy and am reading some Terry Brooks' books right now. Noelle had never heard of Terry Brooks, which shocked me. How did she get out of high school and not read anything by him? Of course, I'd never heard of any of the romance authors she claimed to love either. Maybe I should try one.

I reached out and picked up a strand of her soft hair hanging past her shoulder. I rolled it around my finger and slid it out leaving a slight curl.

"Your hair is a great color and super soft." What I wanted was to wrap the lock around my hand and pull her closer to me. The smooth skin on her neck stared at me all night. I had to look at it because if I looked at her lips, I didn't know if I could keep from kissing her.

It was all I could do all night keeping my hands to myself. Every time I got a whiff of the fragrance she wore, I wanted to pull her to me. There was no doubt I wanted this girl, but I knew I couldn't have her. Maybe it was all about the forbidden fruit thing she had going on.

"I guess I better head out. It's late and a long drive back to campus."

"Yeah, it's not too bad a drive, though." She walked with me to the front door. "It's been fun having you here." She looked around the den as she opened the door.

"It's been a great relaxing time. Chilling was what I needed for a change." I leaned against the doorjamb facing her. Before I could stop it, I yawned covering my mouth with my hand.

"I know you're tired after playing and then driving. Why don't you stay the night? You can sleep on the couch here or in the guest bedroom."

"No, I don't want to bother you. I know you came for some downtime and having me here might have made it harder for you."

"Blue, I wouldn't ask you if I didn't want you to stay. You're welcome to stay. Driving while you're tired is a bad idea. If something happened to you, I'd feel responsible." She looked at me with sleepy gray eyes that held my attention for all the wrong reasons. Damn, this girl stole my breath away when she leveled them on me.

I turned and leaned my back against the doorjamb to keep from looking at her. Her body wrapped around the end of the door with her face leaned against the edge. All I could think about was her wrapped around my body with her beautiful face resting peacefully on my chest. I stared down the road and then looked back at her.

"Well, cowboy, you riding away or staying. I'm sleepy." Her lips turned up in a quick smile.

"Yeah, I guess I'll head on home. I'm awake. I'll drive somewhere and get some caffeine to get me there." Damn, I wanted to stay but not with those sleepy bedroom eyes staring at me. I didn't know if I could stop myself from starting something with her.

"Okay, will you text me when you get there? I'll hear it and know you made it safely."

"Sure." I stepped outside the doorway and looked back at her. "Thanks for letting me come in, Noelle. I'm glad we spent the time together."

"Yeah, me too. You're a pretty fun guy when we aren't both angry." She smiled once again and shut the door, turning off the outside light.

I pulled my keys out and shook my head with a grin. Noelle was the kind of girl I could take home to Mom. I didn't think I'd ever meet one of those while I was in college. Now that I found one, though, what the fuck was I going to do about it? I had some shit to work through. I might need to head home next weekend to talk to my dad.

Maybe I'd start with Jenko. He knew all my crazy shit even better than my dad, but Dad would be more understanding. Jenko, not so much.

I drove home thinking about all the weird sex I'd had since my first encounter. I was sure most guys' first was a spur-of-the-moment kind of thing with the first girl they found willing. Mine couldn't be so simple. It had to be weirder than most guys. I had to plan it way in advance and get the perfect girl lined up, which is why I was a virgin when I checked into college at eighteen. High school girls couldn't be trusted. Hell, now I knew most college girls freely spoke about their experiences.

When I told the girl she had to let me tie her hands, her eyes became wide, but she agreed. I slid the blinders over her eyes covering the wild look in them. She asked me if I was going to hurt her, and I assured her the only hurt would come if she didn't enjoy it enough.

I knew I wouldn't last long as I rolled on the condom. A beautiful naked female body lying spread open on my bed almost caused me to nut before I even got inside her. I'd jerked off several times that day to make sure I could last longer, but when I got to this point, I felt the tingles already heading up my spine and my sac tightening up.

I said all the right things to relax her, kissed her like I meant what I said, and touched her in places I knew would drive her insane. I kept my mind on football plays while I worked her gorgeous body over. When I finally slid the second finger inside her and hooked them both upward, she detonated on the spot. Watching her come made me so hard I knew I was going to come, so I started saying the plays out loud—54, 22, hut hut, 4, 16, 72 hut hut—over and over I called plays we used on the field.

The sweet thing started breathing normally as I crawled over her. She finally asked me what all those numbers and words were, and I told her we'd talk about it later. I needed to concentrate on what I was doing. Sliding inside her warm wet channel felt like heaven on earth. Nirvana couldn't feel that good. I smiled when I lasted maybe ten minutes, but I'd yelled plays for the last two and decided to hell with this and filled the condom.

As I untied her hands and removed the mask, I explained to her what the numbers were, and she laughed, but I didn't care. Nothing she could say to me at the time would've ruined it. I checked her wrists making sure they wouldn't bruise from my soft rope, and she assured me she enjoyed it. Finally, I laid back on my pillow and slept like a dog after a hunt. She'd left by the time I woke up which thrilled me because I had no idea what I'd say to her.

After that experience, life became easier. I knew what to say to figure out where most girls' heads were at regarding being tied up. I guess I also should thank that *Fifty Shades of Gray* lady, too. If E.L. James only knew what she did for my sex life, maybe she'd have written that book sooner. Freaks like me thank her every time we have sex.

I laughed to myself as I pulled into my parking space and dragged out my phone to text Noelle. I figured she'd be asleep by now, but I promised, and I needed her to trust me to keep my promises. I shot her a brief '*home*' and put the phone in my pocket. Before I reached my door, she replied to me.

Noelle: *Glad you made it*
Me: *It wasn't too bad*
Noelle: *Good. Thanks for coming out*
Me: *I should be thanking you for letting me in*
Noelle: *You had my pizza. How could I turn you down?*
Me: *I still had to beg*
Noelle: *Begging never hurt anyone*
Me: *I don't do it often, so it kinda did*
Noelle: *Maybe humbling yourself more often would change you*
Me: *Maybe*
Noelle: *Anyway, nighty night, Blue*
Me: *G'night, babe*

I smiled at the 'nighty night' since it's something my mom would say. They were words of endearment and made me feel good reading them. Damn, this only being friends thing was going to be harder than I thought.

"Well, look who finally rolled her lazy ass back to campus," Quinn commented as I opened the door to the apartment.

"Yeah, I stayed until my parents got in from Houston so I could talk to them. It was late, so I slept over and went straight to class this morning. It's a brutal drive that early in the morning. I probably won't do it again." I threw my overnight bag and backpack on the floor at the door to my bedroom.

"I guess you told them all the stupid shit going on?"

"I did. They're cool about it all… happy, actually. They want me to concentrate on school. No more practices for this girl, which also means I don't have to go to games. Score one for me." I put both arms up like a ref.

"No fucking way. If I've got to watch Gerrod play, you're gonna sit your cute little ass down right beside me. The good news is you can bring your flask like everyone else and enjoy the stupid shit on the field."

"Does he know you feel like this?" Her comment surprised me because anything to do with Gerrod was high on her list.

"Hell, no. I suppose when I think about it, I don't mind watching him get all hot and sweaty in those tight pants, especially when they wear the white uniforms. Those are fucking hot because you get little glimpses of their hunky bare asses under that spandex."

I couldn't help but laugh. Most of the time the material was too thick to see anything but an outline, but that didn't stop most females from wishing for X-ray vision and using it every chance they could.

"You might convince me to watch a game. Maybe I could see one from the stadium since you sure as hell can't from the ground. We're lucky they have the big screens to watch."

"Just plan on it then. You, me, flasks... Saturday afternoon." Quinn waved the water bottle she had in her hand around like it was alcohol before putting her nose back in the textbook she had on her lap.

I unpacked my weekend things and came back into the den falling onto our couch. It wasn't super comfy, but it was good enough for studying.

"Want to tell me about your visit with Blue boy?"

"Not much to say. He came down. We talked and decided we could be friends. We ate pizza, watched some TV, and he drove back to campus."

"Chica, you have the perfect damn specimen of fine man meat sitting with you in an empty house, and that's the fucking best you can do? Need I remind you what to stick where?"

"We won't be having sex anytime. As in, ever. He's not interested in going there with me. Told me so himself. He only wants to be friends. Nothing more."

"What the fuck, Noelle? Is he gay?" She expected a direct answer.

"Uh, no, and I know for sure because I asked him the exact question." I gave her a hard look, so she knew I did.

"Tell me about this. How did that convo go?" She sat up placing the closed text on the coffee table.

"We agreed not to talk about it. All he said was that he had different tastes in the bedroom, and I wouldn't be interested in them."

"What the hell does that even mean, Noelle? Is he some perv or just into weird kink?"

"I don't know. Apparently, he had some problems when he was younger, and now he has control issues during sex. Issues he didn't want to experience with me."

"That's fucking strange. I think I'd have to tell him he was damn wrong, and I would be more than interested in playing kinky with him. Did you consider that?" I could tell she was overthinking this from the look on her face. Before I could say more, she pulled her phone out. "I'm going to ask Gerrod about it."

"*No,*" I yelled and grabbed her phone. "That's what he said girls would do if word got out about it. He doesn't want to share his private life with the world, Quinn. He'd like some things left alone, and this is one of them." I let go of her phone when she stopped tugging back.

"Okay, okay. I get it. He's private and secretive about who he is and what he does. I don't give a flying fuck what the dude does in the sack. It's his damn business, but aren't you even a little curious about it? What if we talked to one of the skanky hoes he's been with?"

"*No,*" I yelled again. "We can't do that either, or we're just like the girls he's talking about. It's his private life, and he'll share his secrets with me if, and when, he's ready. Until then, I'll be his friend. We can do stuff together and have fun, but we can date people, too. It'll be a platonic relationship."

"Oh, hell, please. You and I both know he'll be wanting in your pants in no time. Guys can't do platonic."

"This time, I think it might be true, though. If he's getting it from someone else, I won't be necessary."

"Girl, you are all kinds of fucked up. Gerrod doesn't go out with me just for the sex. I mean, don't get me wrong, our creaming the twinkie is fan-fucking-tastic, but we enjoy doing other stuff, too. Why would you even think that's all he might want you for?"

"I know he's banged a lot of girls on campus. I heard about it from Madelyn, remember? It's just that he's pickier about the girls he chooses to do it with. I'm simply not one of those girls."

"You might not be 'one of those girls,'" she used air quotes. "Maybe he is freaky in bed and only wants girls who are, too. You don't come off as a freak, Noelle, which is a good thing." She stopped and thought about it for a minute. "Hey, maybe he's like a Dom or something, and he needs a sub. You'd never be a candidate for a sub. You're too headstrong to let some guy paddle you're a... uh, aren't you? I mean, we've never talked about it, but I can't see you wearing a collar and being led around."

"Uh, no. I'm not exactly sure that's how it's looked as in a D/s relationship, but I'm not into that at all. He doesn't strike me as being a Dom either. He's too nice a guy."

"So you're saying badass Doms have to be mean?" She grinned.

"No, I'm not saying that at all, but I think they would at least be bossy, and he's not bossy. This is weird. I'm done talking about it. If he doesn't think we are sexually compatible, then I'm good with being friends. A guy friend I can count on will be great." I leaned back on the couch and opened my textbook. "I need to read."

I could feel her studying me from her chair, but I refused to look up. Knowing Quinn, she would have to mull this over a while before she made any more comments. The bad thing was, I knew she wasn't done with it, though.

When I didn't show for practice the next day, HB sent a text.

HB: *Where are you?*
Me: *Home*
HB: *You're late*
Me: *Nope, I'm done*
HB: *What does that mean?*
Me: *Not playing your games anymore*
HB: *I don't play games. Get over here*
Me: *Never again. Don't text me back*
HB: *I have every right to text you when you don't bother to show up*

I moved over to her profile in my address book and smiled as I blocked her number. There, that's done. With my travel bag cleaned out, the uniforms loaded, shoes and poms inside it, I headed out.

All of it sat in my back seat while I drove over to the sponsor's office. Unfortunately, so did Madelyn. We met in the parking lot.

"What are you doing?" She pranced down the sidewalk behind me.

"Turning in my stuff," I called over my shoulder.

"I never took you for a quitter."

"Not talking to you about this, Maddie." I opened the building's door, and let it go behind me.

"Thanks." I heard her call.

I knocked on Ms. South's door before I opened it. She sat behind her desk reading student papers. "Hey, Noelle. What's going on?"

"I'm turning in all my stuff." Before I could unzip the bag, Madelyn walked in without even bothering to knock. The look on her face said it all.

"Ladies, is there a problem here I need to know about?" Ms. South stood and walked around her desk.

"No problem here. My schedule is too busy to devote the kind of time needed to do a good job. I don't like doing anything halfway, and honestly, the aggravation of it all is too much."

"You realize you are going to be forfeiting your scholarship by doing this, right?"

"Yes, I do, and I've got it covered so no problems with that at all."

She eyed me carefully and then looked around at Madelyn. "Did you know about this?"

"No, ma'am. I found out when I walked in behind her."

"She knew on Saturday when I told her I was done, but in all the excitement at the end of the game, she failed to hear or understand what I was saying. Then, when she texted me today during practice, I told her again. Obviously, she has a difficult time accepting information she doesn't want to hear." I looked over at Madelyn when I said it and waited for a response.

"I understand perfectly. You see, Ms. South, Noelle has a hard time following directions and didn't like being called out on it. I feel like it's my job to direct them to do the right thing in all actions involving the cheer squad."

"I'm sure you do, Madelyn. Anything else you'd like to say, Noelle?"

"No, not really, except I'm sorry. I've never quit anything before in my life so this is bittersweet for me, but I feel like it's best for all involved if I do so."

"Okay. Well, it's been a pleasure working with you, Noelle, and I wish you good luck with the rest of your days here at TAU."

"Thank you, Ms. South. I appreciate it." I turned to leave but couldn't resist getting in one more jab. "And Madelyn, now that I'm not on the cheer squad, you can expect me to see whoever I want, whenever I want, especially Blue. Oh, and you can kiss my ass." I walked out the door feeling like I'd had the last laugh because Ms. South would want an explanation about that comment. My days of cheering might be over, but I cheered all the way to my car and drove home.

"I'm in love with the shape of you." I sang the words to Ed Sheeran's song while I put my car in park in front of my apartment. The song made me happy every time I heard it, and once I did, there was no getting it out of my head. I sang the last few lines as I got out.

"I'm in love with the—" I stopped when Blue stood up on the front steps.

"Someone's in a great mood."

He unfolded his long body for me to peruse behind my sunglasses. The tight jeans from all those highly toned muscles trying to hide behind the denim captured my attention first. I followed the line up to the navy t-shirt fitting snugly across his pecs and stretched the arms just enough for perfection. Damn, he had a drool-worthy body.

"He's my friend, he's my friend," I mumbled to myself so he couldn't hear.

"Hell, yeah, I'm in a great mood. Not only did I turn in my cheer gear, but I also got the last word in with Madelyn. Do you know how happy I am right now?" I jumped up and clicked my heels in the air. "Yep, that happy."

"Well, damn, don't let me stop your little celebration. Should we go find a karaoke night so you can show off your singing?" He pulled me in for a brief hug. We fell into a mutual understanding that a friendly hug was acceptable for coming and going but nothing more.

"Uh, no, that will never happen." I turned, grabbed both his biceps, and looked him right in the eyes. "As my friend, if you ever see me attempt to sing in public, you will immediately know that I am highly intoxicated and need to go home. Understand?"

A hearty laugh greeted me. "Yeah, BFF, I think I got that loud and clear."

I unlocked the door to let us in. "What are you doing here this time of day anyway?"

"I got a text saying someone might need a friend today and since that person couldn't be here, I was more than happy to provide you a shoulder to cry on. Obviously, said texter didn't truly understand the situation because if anything, you're happier than I've ever seen you." He followed me into the house and sat down.

"Well, it's not that I don't appreciate the effort, but you're right. I don't need cheering up. A huge burden flew off my shoulders today, and I feel like dancing or doing something fun." I turned on Pandora and danced around my kitchen. "You hungry?"

"I'm always hungry."

Glancing into the near-empty fridge. "There's not much in here. Let's go get wings or something. Hey, I know. Call your boys and tell Quinn to come, too, and we'll celebrate at Chewz. They have a dance floor, too.

I can get my jam on." I spun around dancing some more.

"Works for me. Let's do it."

"I think we should Uber over. I plan to celebrate." I nodded my head showing him exactly how this would go down.

"Let's take my car. I promise to get you home safely. I'll even be the DD tonight for you. Can't let my girl here get a DWI or worse."

We pulled into Chewz about the same time as the others. Quinn bounded out first coming straight to me. "You okay?"

"Hell, yeah, I'm okay, bitch. I'm better than okay. I'm perfect and to prove it, I'm going to break a cardinal rule and drink on a school night."

"Ohhh. The girl is breaking one of her damn rules, boys. Can we help her out with that?"

Laughs and fist bumps came from all over for me, not that this bunch needed a reason to party.

"Can't overdo it, guys," Blue told them all. "Remember what Coach said?"

"Drink blocker."

"Haterader."

"Buzzkill. Dude, really?" This came from Timms. Seeing him here surprised me since he's Maddie's main man.

"Timms, you're a team captain, too. You're supposed to be enforcing Coach's rules." Blue slapped him on the back as he spoke.

"That old bastard can kiss my ass. My passes have never been more accurate, and he knows it." He cocked back his passing arm and let an imaginary ball fly. "See what I mean? Right on the numbers." In an imaginary announcer voice, he added, "It's a miracle. Blue Myers catches the perfectly-thrown ball and steps in the end zone, and the TAU Rams win the championship."

We all laughed at his animated play-by-play action as we make it inside. We gathered around a huge round table and ordered and received several pitchers of beer and water for Blue.

"So what exactly are we celebrating? Not that we need a reason or anything," Jenko asked as he poured and passed the full mugs around.

"I quit cheer today," I told them all. This was easier doing it all at once.

"And she told Madelyn off in the process," Blue added.

This caused me to look up immediately to see how Timms took that little tidbit I didn't divulge. "Sorry, Timms, but it had to happen. We couldn't get along for shit."

"Girl, you don't owe me nothing. She means very little to me."

"But she's your girlfriend, right?"

"Awe, hell no, she's not my girlfriend. She's more like a fuck buddy if anything. We both like it, so we do it when the mood strikes. That's it. We don't date. We don't hang out except at parties at the house, and then that's only until we go to my room. When we're done, I'm done."

"Dude, that's an asshole move. Are you sure she knows this?" Quinn asked him.

"Yeah, she knows. I didn't try to hook up with her. She's the one who initiated this friends with benefits. I told her from the get-go, I'm not getting tangled with any one girl while I'm here at TAU. Even after she knew the rules, she was down for threading the needle whenever. Worse than that, the girl's got a thing for it in public."

I remembered it from the first party. Everyone at the table seems to know it too, which surprised me.

"Hey, it's her kink. Don't down it till you try it," Quinn added.

But Gerrod spoke up quickly. "We will never have sex in public, Quinn. I'm not into sharing, and you're too damn loud."

Jenko put his hands to his ears. "Don't we know it." He pointed to Quinn. "You need to learn to keep it down in the morning. I hate waking up to your screaming and the headboard bumping against that fucking wall."

"Yeah, fucking's what's happening on that wall all right." She stood up and did some pelvic thrusts in his direction. "You're just jealous 'cause it's us and not you." Everyone at the table started laughing except Gerrod, who hid his face. Quinn could give as good as she got, and none of these guys could hold a candle to her in a verbal contest of wit.

As the laughter died down, I couldn't help but wonder about Madelyn and Timms. He could be funny or moody. I never knew exactly how to take him. His confidence never wavered, though. Maybe that's what she saw in him, strength and confidence.

The evening wore on, and I danced with everyone except Timms who never got up from the table other than to hit the bathroom. Quinn and I twirled, and line danced and stomped to Copperhead Road and drank too much beer to be good at any of them, but we had a blast.

We danced back to the table just as the guys were ordering another pitcher at last call.

"Damn, I need to go home. I've got a nine o'clock class in the morning," I told the table before I tripped on the chair leg and fell back in Blue's lap. "Oh, my savior. I knew you'd be there for me."

"Always, babe. You know that. It's what friends are for."

"What if I don't want to be friends anymore?" I wrapped my arms around his neck. "What if I want the same thing that Timms has?"

This comment got the attention of the table since my drunk voice was louder than necessary.

"Yeah, that's not happening, babe."

This struck me the wrong way, and my lower lip came sliding out in a pout. "Am I not pretty enough for you to fool around with, Blue?" I felt the tears welling up in my burning eyes. Damn beer.

"I think someone's had too much to drink," Quinn spoke up quickly. "Beer does it to her every time."

Blue spun me around and looked me right in the eyes, at least the one I could focus. "Babe, you're gorgeous even when you're not trying. Don't ever let any guy try to tell you otherwise."

"Any guy except you. You take all those skanky girls at the XOX house, but I'm not good enough for you. Do they have magic pussies or something? I can have a magic pussy, too. You just won't give—" Before I could finish the sentence, Blue put his hand over my mouth, and that caused the tears to flow freely down my face.

"Babe, we need to get you home. You're saying things you are so going to regret in the morning. I hope you don't even remember that statement." I could hear the others laughing around the table, and it made me mad.

I pulled his hand away from my mouth. "What? Do y'all know he only takes girls to bed with some sort of magic." I rounded back on Blue. "I know. They have forked tongues and no gag reflexes. I might not have one either, but you're never gonna find out."

"Okay, we're done." Blue stood taking me with him. He held me close against his warm body.

"Does done mean we are done being just friends?"

Everyone behind me laughed even harder. "Take her home and show her your little friend," Jenko called after us."

Timms piped up. "Yeah, you know that one that comes with blinders and a rope."

This caused Blue to whirl us around which was a bad idea. He leveled a look at Timms that could have killed him. "Shut the fuck up, Timms." Then he added, "We're out. See y'all tomorrow."

"No problem, Blue. Sleep in my bed. I'm not gonna need it," Quinn called after him and laughed.

"Babe, you are so gonna regret this in the morning." I stood her up beside my truck.

She leaned against the bed as I opened the door. "Nope, I refuse to regret anything tonight. I'm giving myself a pass on tonight. I can drink what I want, say what I want, and do what I want, and I think I've done a pretty good job of it. What do you think?" Her speech wasn't slurring yet but not far from it. I picked her up and slid her into the seat.

"Yeah, I think you hit all three of those pretty well." After buckling her seatbelt, I slammed the door. Damn this girl. She tested my ability to keep away from her at every turn. The fragrance of her hair when she wrapped around my neck attacked my senses upping my need for her. I focused on what she said.

"That's not what I want to be hitting, though," I said aloud to myself. "Wait, is that a backward statement?" I opened my door to her laughter.

"What happened on my way to the back of my truck that's so funny?"

"I was thinking about the term 'hitting that.' I mean guys say it all the time." She did her best male impersonation. "I'd like to hit that. And dude, I'm gonna hit that tonight. You know what I'm talking about?"

I looked at her and smiled. "You're pretty funny when you've been drinking."

"I'm telling the truth, and you know it."

I started the truck. I needed for her to be out of my truck as her scent was invading the cab. Before we made the first corner, she started again.

"No, not tonight but other times. I've heard guys say it a lot of times." She dropped back into her male voice. "Yeah, you see that hot chick over there? I'd hit that so fast she wouldn't know what happened until I had her screaming my name."

This earned another laugh. "Babe, I would never say something like that, and you sound like one of those douche bags off Jersey Shore. I never knew you had a Jersey accent like that."

"I do not sound like a meathead." She took in a deep breath. "Maybe just a little, but it's funny, right?"

"Oh yeah, babe, very funny Paulie D coming out of those beautiful lips."

"You think my lips are beautiful?" She looked at him and stuck them out in extreme kissy lips.

"Of course. Everything about you is beautiful, Noelle." I glanced over and saw her lips still holding that form. Before she could pull back, I leaned over and stole a fast kiss.

"See, they just begged to be kissed."

"I did not beg you to kiss me." The indignance at the idea of begging apparent with her tone.

"I didn't say you begged me to kiss you. Why are you turning all my words around?"

"Because you don't ever try to kiss me. You don't ever try to hold my hand, and if you hug me, you make sure you don't get close enough to let me wrap around you." Oh God, and the tears came again. "What's wrong with me, Blue?"

"Babe, absolutely nothing. I like everything about you."

"No, you don't. I must not do anything for you then, and I thought what I was feeling had chemistry behind it. You told me you're not gay, and I believed you." I pulled to a stop at her apartment and came around opening the passenger door.

"Let's get you inside. You need some water, ibuprofen, and sleep."

"Yeah, alone again. I always sleep alone. Guys just don't like me. Are you sure I'm not ugly?" All this came out through tears and shuddering hiccups as her head laid over on my shoulder. She pulled out keys from her pocket as I carried her to the door and took them to open it. I bypassed the couch and walked straight to her bedroom and sat her down on the side of the bed.

Squatting down in front of her, I ran my fingers across her cheeks, my hair and palms resting over the warmth of her jawline. My thumbs wiped away her tears. "Listen to me, Noelle. You are a gorgeous woman. You're smart and thoughtful, a good friend, and a great daughter. You do kind things for people you don't even know, like the water boys. Any guy would be lucky to have you as a girlfriend."

She sucked in a stuttered breath. "Any guy, but the one I want." Her eyes never wavered from mine. "I want you, Blue. I need you to want me back. The last thing I need is another guy friend."

"Noelle, babe, we've already agreed this wouldn't happen." I wiped away more tears.

"Now you're mad. Just go home. I'm not going to beg you, Blue. If you don't want me, then fine." She jerked open her nightstand drawer and pulled out a vibrator. "Bob likes the action. He gets me. He never says no unless I forget batteries." When she took the lube out and poured it all over it, the excess dripped down on her jeans. "Leave, Blue. We got this. Bob's hot for me, and I like it hot. Again." She pushed down on the button, and it began a slow vibration and a slower rotation.

Damn it.

"See, he's hot and ready for me, so go home to one of your slutty girls."

Before she could move back on the bed, I jerked hot Bob out of her hand and threw it over my shoulder. I pushed her back as I slowly covered her body. Our faces were barely inches apart as I peered into her eyes and shook my head. I knew this was a bad idea, but fuck it, I could only take so much.

My lips descended down on hers with a scorching kiss that burned me from the inside. I tilted her head using the hand I wrapped through her hair so I could deepen the mauling I determined this luscious mouth needed. My tongue slid in and explored every angle and spot before beginning a tango with hers.

My lips left her and inched slowly across her jawline to the shell of her ear where I left a line of warmth down the outside with my tongue. I scraped across her earlobe and gave it a tug.

"Blue," she said like a plea. My brain lost its ability to think with the feelings building inside me. Shit, I wanted her. I wanted to take her in the frenzy she had worked in me, but I pulled back some.

"Babe, you are the most perfect woman on campus. I've wanted to do this to you since I had you in my arms in the pool." I knew my breath fanned across her neck from the little shiver she made before I bit and lavished the spot with my teeth and tongue down to her collarbone. "Having to be your friend is the hardest job I've ever had."

"God, I've wanted you so bad, Blue, since that same day. When we watched those two go at it under that beach towel, I thought I would combust in my chair. My feelings haven't changed." She wrapped her legs around my waist in a tight hold. She had me, and I wasn't getting away, not that I wanted to at this point. If anything, I wanted the clothes that separated us to be gone. My hard dick stood between us, and she had to know how badly I needed her, too.

My hands worked their way under her shirt as my mouth slid down her chest. The two met in the center of cleavage covered by her bra. I felt a front clasp. In a snap, I released her sensitive breasts that demanded attention as she arched into my hands. Pulling her shirt over her head, I released them both to pleasure with my hands and mouth.

"These are even more perfect than I dreamed they were." I ran my tongue around the nipple and blew a breath across the wet skin causing the pert nipple to strain into a hardened peak begging for my attention. With an assault happening on one with my fingers, I bit and lavished the pink tip of the other.

She rubbed her flaming lips up and down the length of my dick, digging her heels into my ass causing the friction to be hard and rough.

"Blue, please. I need this. I need you."

I kissed down her taut stomach. The strenuous work with cheerleading had her muscles tight. While my tongue circled her belly button, and I bit my way to her hip bone and unbuttoned her jeans tugging them down to her hips. The hot pink lace covering a little trail of cropped hair looked so fucking sexy.

"Hot pink. I like it." I bit down on her lips on the outside of the lace. Noele began wiggling and writhing under me telling me she wanted more. I pulled back more and pulled her legs from around my waist so I could dispose of the offending denim and hot underwear.

With both her calves captured in my grip over one of my shoulders, I had a perfect view of her when I bent her knees forward. "Shit, Noelle, you are so beautiful. I slid a couple of fingers between her legs just above her thighs and worked my way down slowly. Holding her this way, she had no choice but to lay there and take it. I moved down to her center, and when I reached it, she bowed up off the bed trying to get me closer to where she wanted them. I breached her lips feeling the warm liquid waiting on me to use for our pleasure. Sliding my finger down to her opening, I took more with me as I trailed back up to her clit—its impatience evident as the nub was swollen and ready for attention.

I bent her knees more, opening her to me as I leaned in and licked the same path my fingers had taken. Working her clit over while my fingers pushed inside her, once again she bowed off the bed using my shoulder as leverage.

"Lay back, babe. Let me love you like you need to be. I want you to feel everything you need." I pushed inside her as I flicked her clit at various speeds with my tongue. "Put your hands on your tits and squeeze those peaks." She followed my directions without question. I knew her mind hinged on the edge of perfect pleasure.

"Blue, please, please." The raw sound of her voice made me realize how close she was already. She squeezed her nipples, probably harder than I ever would, and I plunged two fingers in her curling them around in search of that spot she needed me to find.

Tremors inside her started to seize around my fingers, and I took that moment to bite down lightly on her throbbing clit. She captured my fingers in a tight embrace as she jerked wildly in the orgasm ripping through her. My eyes landed on her face capturing the bliss. Damn, she made me want to come in my jeans from the ecstasy spreading across her exquisite features.

I knew then I was in deep shit. This could be bad for both of us, but right then, I didn't want to do or say anything to spoil this moment.

I slowly let her legs down to the bed. At the moment, she seemed lost in another dimension as she came down from the high.

"You okay in there?" One arm was slung over her eyes before a slight grin graced her lips.

"I couldn't be more perfect if I tried."

"Good." I leaned up and kissed her lightly.

I needed to get out of there.

God, I wanted to stay.

I wanted to be with her.

If I ever hated being so fucked up, now was the worst time of all.

I inched off the bed, taking care not to rock it any more than my weight would allow. Reaching over to the other side, I pulled her comforter over her bare skin. She hardly moved. I was torn between wanting her to forget the encounter and needing her to remember the pleasure we shared.

I let myself out locking the door behind me. Starting my truck, I drove back to my apartment. Every turn caused my anger to grow. My need to be with her filled my mind with all the problems I caused for myself. Why couldn't I just be honest with women? Maybe I was too fucked up to have a normal sexual relationship. Maybe I needed to get professional help.

I screeched to a stop in my parking place, rammed the truck into park, and stomped in the house only to be greeted with Quinn, Garrett, and Jenko all sitting there watching TV.

"Didn't think we'd see you tonight, dude," Jenko called to me as I headed to my room. I didn't bother answering him, but before I reached my door, Quinn stood right behind me.

"Is Noelle okay?"

Without turning, I spoke, "She's fine. She's resting in her bed under her covers with meds and water right beside her. Don't worry."

"Thanks, Blue," she said it softly like she knew it was okay but not right which surprised me.

"No problem." I closed the door behind me. "No problem at all."

My class alarm buzzed beside me on my nightstand, so I rolled over to stop the obnoxious noise.

"Holy shit." Opening my eyes caused pain. Moving my body caused extreme pain, and rolling over turned my stomach. I leaped from the bed, at least it felt like a leap, and ran to my bathroom barely making it in time to throw up something foul.

"What the hell?" I leaned over the toilet buck naked. I never slept naked. I moved to the sink and splashed my face with cold water. I finally looked in the mirror and staring back at me was a green-colored human. At least I thought I was human. My hair was wild, my face was a strange color, and upon further inspection, I had some bite marks on my breasts.

I let my mind drift back to last night, and it all came rushing back.

“Holy shit isn’t strong enough. What the fuck, Noelle?” The memories of my legs over Blue’s arm, while he ate me, caused red blotches to start at my neck and work their way up until I glowed. Green and red didn’t mix well, but then neither did the raw little places on my breast, stomach, and abdomen where his scruff scraped my skin. That led me to think about what my thighs probably looked like, and I covered my face with my hands.

What did I do? Did I goad him into going down on me? Did I lower my standards to the point of begging him?

“Fuck, you are so pathetic, Noelle. Pathetic.” I glanced at the big clock I’d hung up in my bathroom the day I moved in. “And late for class.” I turned and started the shower. Like it or not, I had classes I couldn’t miss.

All the way across campus, I berated my stupidity. He’ll never want to be my friend again. I pushed him into something he swore he didn’t want to do. How would I even be able to look at him knowing I was the only one drinking. Some celebration it turned out to be if I ended up sick and sick of myself.

It took everything in me to listen to the lectures and offer a word or two of participation. Showing up late was frowned upon but not attending at all was worse. I slunk in and took a seat in the back where I never sat and started taking notes immediately. At least doing this mundane chore kept my mind off the fiasco I'd caused.

When I trudged back across campus through the quad, I passed the Coffee Bean, and there he sat almost as if he waited for me as usual. I kept walking, and he caught up to me.

"Good morning, sunshine. It's a little cloudy to wear your sunglasses, don't you think?" He provoked me to get an answer as I continued moving forward.

"No." That's all I could muster up.

"Headache this morning?" He grabbed my arm and stopped me so I could witness his brightest smile, the one that dropped panties on sight. Damn him.

"Uh, no. Not really. I had some pain relievers on my nightstand, and they came in handy." Total lie as I walked on.

He moved alongside me. "Oh really? That's good. Wonder who put them there?"

I never expected I'd be able to have a normal conversation with him at this point, but he seemed hell bent on having one.

"Hmm... I wonder. Certainly, nice of whoever got me home and put them there, though. If you see that person, be sure to say thanks for me." I stopped at the crosswalk to wait my turn.

"Going home so soon today?" I looked up at him and then glanced down at my watch. Shit, I had another class. I guess he was the only one who remembered.

"Uh. No." I turned and started back to where I came from.

"It's our morning to meet up, remember?" Again, with the smile.

"Oh, right." I veered off the path toward our spot. "That's great because I need coffee."

"I thought you might." He held out a cup.

"I don't want to take yours. I'll buy one."

"No, this is yours. I bought it waiting for you." I took it and drank a sip. "Hope it's still warm enough to drink. I know you like it hot." He winked at me when I looked up at him since he'd emphasized 'hot.'

"Shit." I shook my head.

"Oh, babe. We're good. I didn't want it to be a thing between us, so humor is the best way to look at it. You were a little drunk, and we had some fun. Let's laugh about it and move on."

I glared at him, but with that smile, I couldn't stay angry at either of us, so I started laughing, too. This beat crying by a long shot.

"So, how hot do you like that coffee?"

I punched him in his thick bicep. "Shut up."

He'd made it all okay for both of us. I knew he had more to him than looks and a great body.

A routine developed between us making our worlds meet in something much more comfortable. We met for coffee on campus two days a week. We studied in the library two nights a week. He went to practice, and I hung out with Quinn. Football Saturdays turned out to be one of the highlights of the week. Our little part of university world fell into place better than I ever dreamed it could.

On the Saturdays the Rams played out of town too far for us to go, we tailgated and watched the games on big screen TVs. I never knew this went on while I cheered.

I dragged some of the water boys' friends into our little circle. These guys' sense of humor kept us laughing all the time. Who knew geeks could be so funny? Quinn and I did our best to fix them up with girls we met on campus we thought would be perfect matches for them, but nothing good had happened yet. We didn't give up trying, though. These guys were perfectly happy drinking beer under our tent with just Quinn and me. I guess no pressure suited them just fine.

During homecoming week, the school's festivities ramped up on Saturday. My parents came down, and so did Blue's. I invited them all to come to our tailgate party since not everyone could get a ticket in the stadium. Dad cooked all kinds of great things on the pit while we watched the pregame activities and visited.

I spotted two people walking through the area looking around. I knew it was Mr. and Mrs. Myers from the pictures Blue showed me. I walked out into the lane and waved at them to come our way.

I stuck out my hand. "Hello, I'm Noelle Jeffries, I'm so glad y'all came."

His mom looked down at my hand, and I thought she was going to turn me down.

"Noelle, I don't do handshakes with people I feel like I know, honey." She wrapped me in a big hug.

"Oh, okay." I hugged her back knowing I would like her right away.

"Blue has told us so much about you, Noelle. I feel like we should already be friends."

"That's great because he talks about y'all all the time."

"He does? I hope he tells the nice stories." Greg winked when he said it. Oh God, this guy's charm reminded me so much of Blue. They made a perfect couple, both beautiful in their own way.

"This is my husband, Greg Myers, but please call us Gina and Greg." His dad hugged me as my parents made their way over for introductions, too.

After Quinn and the boys were introduced, we sat down to talk about the game. They had only made it up for a couple of games this season since Greg's job forced him to be gone so much, but they never missed one on TV.

"I'm glad we were able to get tickets for today's game. I'd hate to drive all the way here and not get to see my son play," Greg told us all.

"Yeah. Blue stood in line to make sure you both would be in the stadium. He's really happy you made it."

"Oh, honey, we wouldn't miss a game if Greg didn't have to work. We made all the games the first two years when Blue didn't even play all the time. I wish we could come more often. I know Blue likes us to be here for him but at least he has you and his friends to watch."

"Yeah, I didn't think I'd like going to games all that much after cheerleading, but I like it much better."

"Blue told us of the unfortunate incident with that horrid girl you had to deal with. I'm so sorry she caused you to quit and lose your scholarship." Wow, I didn't know Blue shared so much with them.

"Honestly, I'm not sorry at all. The first two years were paid for, and my parents were more than happy to let me concentrate on school for the last two."

My dad came up with appetizers teasing about how we were going to miss the best part inside the stadium. I knew there would be more than enough for later. He never cooked small amounts of anything on the grill.

Eventually, we made our way over and found our seats. Quinn and I had student tickets and couldn't sit with Blue's parents. I liked them. They seemed fun and energetic, sort of like mine.

Once we settled in, Quinn looked at me with a strange look. "What?"

"What? Did you notice his mom and dad eating up every little piece of shit that came out of your mouth? It's like they fucking worshiped your every comment. I believe they had their mind made up about you before they rolled in here." Quinn looked out over the field to spot Gerrod.

"What are you talking about? They are nice people, and they know Blue's my friend."

"When are you and your 'friend' going to wake up and realize you are more than friends?"

"Never. We decided back in the beginning that it's all we'd ever be."

"Yeah, and what about the night you celebrated quitting cheer *in your bed?"*

"Shhh." I looked around. "You don't have to announce it to the world."

"As if any of these people know us."

"Quinn, I told you we discussed it and decided to let it go. It was a mistake made when I was intoxicated. We don't date. We don't hold hands. We certainly don't kiss. What makes you think it's anything more than a friendship?"

"Uh, let me see. Neither of you dates anyone else. You go everywhere together. He makes sure you are always safe. You eat most meals together. The only damn difference between us and y'all is the fucking."

I glanced around to see if people looked at us. "We don't sleep together."

"You damn sure have. Maybe not all night, but I've found y'all in your bed several times."

"Yes, asleep. Sometimes we fall asleep when we are talking or studying. We don't touch each other, though."

"Says the girl who sleeps all over the bed. And how the hell do you know you don't touch if you're asleep? No touchy feeling in your sleep, little girl." She wiggled her fingers at me, and I laughed.

"If we touch in our sleep, it's all innocent. We don't plan it or consciously do it."

"Maybe you should, though. Shit, how do y'all go so long without sex?"

"Please Quinn. I don't want to talk about this with fifty thousand of my closest friends around." The man in front of me had the nerve to turn around and nod his head. When he turned back, Quinn and I both made ugly faces at him before we cracked up laughing.

"Down set, red, 29, 26, hut hut," Timms called off the play, and Blue took off through the hole in the line that Gerrod opened for him. The game turned into a runaway for us unlike the sportscasters predicted. When Blue caught the ball in the end zone, the score had us winning by thirty-five points, and it was closing in on the end of the fourth quarter. After the kickoff, the first string stood on the sidelines cheering on the second string.

Quinn and I headed back to the tailgating section to visit with my parents before they headed back home.

"Oh, sweetie, we're glad you're back. We wanted to talk to you about some plans we have." Mom cornered me with this.

"Yeah, what's that?" I sat down as she handed me a cold beer.

"We've decided to take an extended vacation. Your dad's going to join me in the ranks of the retired, and we want to travel to celebrate."

"That's awesome, Mom. I'm glad you're finally going to go to some fun places." I pulled her in for a tight hug.

"We'll be gone for the rest of the year so we wanted to make sure you'd be okay with it all."

I never thought about them being somewhere besides a couple of hours away from me, but there was no reason for them to stick around here.

"Sure. I've got plenty of friends around if I need help with anything."

"Yes, and Blue to take care of you, too." She smiled a strange smile at me like she knew something I didn't know.

"Yeah, I guess?"

My dad walked over and sat down with us. "Did you tell her?"

"Yes, she did," I answered for her. "I'm thrilled for you two and jealous. You'll have so much fun traveling together. You've wanted to for so long now."

"Right, and we feel it's a good time for us to go knowing you'll be in good hands."

"What are you talking about?" I looked around at all three of them. What was going on?

"Didn't Blue and Quinn talk to you about this already?"

I looked at Quinn who looked like her dog had died or something equally catastrophic. "Quinn, what's going on?"

She looked at Mom and Dad and shook her head. "Well, we hadn't talked about it yet, but I knew you'd be fine with it all, especially after our talk in the stadium."

"What? What did we talk about in the stadium?" I thought back, and we'd had a lot of short conversations while the game went on.

"Gerrod and I have decided to move in together."

"Okay?" Where did that leave me? No roommate, that's where.

"Blue volunteered to move in my room and be your roommate. Since you said yourself again today, you're nothing but friends and that's all you'll ever be, we thought it worked out perfectly."

"You did, huh? Without even asking me how I felt about it? Don't you think I should have had some say so about living with him?" This pissed me off to no end. How dare they make a decision that directly affected me without even talking to me about it.

"I tried to talk to you about it, and you told me all y'all were ever going to be was friends. I called and told your parents about it because I didn't want them to think I was leaving you high and dry."

"Did you call and tell his parents, too?"

"Uh, no. Gerrod and I figured he could take care of that shit."

"So just like that, y'all made a huge choice about life-changing events and didn't think I needed to know anything about it?" I jumped out of my chair and took off. Being pissed at them all, I had no place to go even to sulk. Quinn ran up behind me.

"Blue said he would talk to you about it this evening. He was going to tell you and his parents on the same day. Besides, I would hardly call getting a new roommate life changing."

"Well, if it was no big deal, why didn't y'all tell me when you made the decision? Oh, yeah, because it is a big deal. His parents will flip out. Then what? I'll be left alone with no roommate, that's where. I can't ask my parents to pay all the rent."

"Listen, if it sucks, then I'll move back in until the year's over. It'll only be for seven months, Noelle."

"Yeah, seven months living in a two bedroom alone to pay all the rent, and you wait to do this until after I forfeit my scholarship."

"Your parents assured me the damn money didn't mean shit to them."

"I'm saving that money to live on when I graduate until I can get a good job, Quinn. You knew that. You know what, never mind. I'll deal with this on my own." I took off home since it was *my* home.

I decided to let this go until I had a chance to talk to Blue in person. I prayed he took the time to tell his parents before we talked.

BLUE

I checked the phone when we ran off the field and saw a text from Noelle asking me to come over when my parents left. They had decided to stay the night, though.

> **Me:** *Parents aren't leaving til Sun. Go to dinner with us?*
> **Noelle:** *OK. Picking me up?*
> **Me:** *Yeah at 7*
> **Noelle:** *Great*

Usually, she sent a little more than the necessary words, but I guess she was busy. The parents were waiting, so we left immediately.

"We're picking up Noelle on the way," I told them when we climbed in the car.

"Oh, honey. I thought we might get you to ourselves, but it's fine." My mom rarely ever disagreed with plans like this.

"I have some things I need to tell y'all and her, so it's better if she's with us."

My dad spoke up, "That's great. We both liked her, and she's certainly beautiful. Her parents seemed like fun people, too." He turned and shot my mom a look that I couldn't quite understand.

"Yes, Blue, it'll be great," Mom added.

"Good, because I've already invited her and that'd be awkward to have to tell her she couldn't come."

"No, son. We wouldn't want to do that." Dad ended the strange conversation as I pulled up to her apartment.

I walked to Noele's door finding her ready to go, which was good since I was starving and a little nervous about what I had to tell them.

"You have fun today at the tailgating?" I put my hand on her lower back as we walked out. I tried to keep my hands to myself, but sometimes, I needed the contact with her. This was one of those times. I prayed she liked the idea Gerrod, Quinn, and I had come up with but wasn't sure about myself.

"Yeah, I guess." Her gray eyes had an unusual look to them. "Yes, it was fun."

Something was off. I didn't know if telling her now was a good plan.

The door opened, and my dad stepped out to move to the back seat with my mom.

"Greg, you didn't need to do that. I'm fine with sitting in the back seat."

"And deprive me of sitting with my beautiful wife? No way." His smile said it all.

"It does my heart good to see parents still in love. It gives me hope that maybe I can find love like that someday."

"You're looking at true love right here. Been that way since we started dating, too."

Dad was pouring it on thick. "Please, Dad. You're gonna make me look bad," Blue spoke up.

"Why? We're only friends. They are in love still after all these years. I think it's sweet."

I knew she loved romance. How could she not with all the romance books she had piled up on her Kindle.

Gina leaned over and gave her husband a kiss on the cheek. "He's always been the charmer."

Noelle looked at me and grinned. All I could do was shake my head as I pulled out of the lot and drove to the restaurant.

The dinner conversation centered around the game and then moved to talk about our classes. I decided now was as good a time as any. Everyone had finished dinner, so there wasn't too much time left.

"So, I wanted to talk to y'all about something while we were all together."

"Oh," Mom looked at me with a smile. "This sounds interesting." She leaned in.

"What's going on, son?" Dad asked.

"You know that Gerrod and Quinn are together now, and it's Gerrod's senior year. He's hoping to go pro if everything works out." I glanced at Noelle. The look she wore told me she wondered where this was all going.

"Jenko and me, well, we've been together for a long time, and he's good with whatever we want him to do. Y'all know he's a go-with-the-flow type person." Everyone nodded their heads. He rarely got mad about much, which made him great as a player and even better as a friend.

"What are you trying to say here, Blue? It seems like you're not getting to the point." Dad preferred a straight line.

"So, Quinn and Gerrod are going to move in together for the rest of the year." I glanced at Noelle expecting her to be surprised, but the look on her face was anything but surprised. "Anyway, everyone wants it to be an easy move all the way around, so I'm going to change places with Quinn. It would be too crowded with four of us living in our apartment. Jenko doesn't know Noelle as I do, so we all thought it would only make sense for me to live with Noelle. I'm great with it if she is."

No one said a word. Mom and Dad looked at each other, but when I looked over at Noelle, she was staring down at her empty plate. I had a bad feeling about the decision now. What if she didn't want me to live there? When Gerrod, Quinn, and I talked about it, we thought it was the best plan.

"It's only until the end of the year," I added after the fact.

Mom finally spoke up. "So you didn't know about this, Noelle?"

"Yes and no. Quinn told me today after the game. She'd already told my parents, and they were fine with it because they know we're friends. Blue and I aren't going out and have no intentions of doing so. We'd be roommates until May."

Noelle's argument was convincing, but something was off. I'd spent enough time with her to know when she was covering, and she was definitely covering.

I smiled at them all. "So, that's settled. Y'all want dessert?"

After dinner, we left, and a lively conversation happened all the way to drop my parents off at their hotel with a promise of brunch before they headed home. They extended an invitation to Noelle to join, but she declined with homework excuses.

When I shut the door to the car, I looked over at her. I knew she had things to say, but waited until it was only the two of us, which was probably the same thing my parents would do in the morning. I needed to hear her out before I said anything to them about it.

I drove out of the hotel parking lot and pulled into the convenience store next door. Putting the car in park, I turned and looked at her. "What's going on, Noelle? I know you too well. You're dying to say something."

"How could you even make a decision about my life without talking to me? The three of you made a hugely important change in our lives and didn't wonder if I'd have something to say about it?"

"Yes, we did wonder, but we thought you might not go for it." I glanced in her direction as she crossed her arms in front of her chest. Yeah, she's angry. I needed to make this right.

"The decision's not etched in stone yet, Noelle."

"Sure as hell sounds like it to me. You didn't tell your parents it wasn't a done deal? You said I'm moving in with Noelle. You made it sound like something was going on until I spoke up telling them it would only be a roommate situation."

"That's all it's going to be, Noelle."

"I know that, but did your parents? No. They thought we were more than friends. Did you see the look on your mom's face? She's not happy about this."

"I realize it's a surprise for y'all, but would you deprive Quinn and Gerrod of living the life they want? I wouldn't do that to my friend, and I thought you wouldn't either." I knew this would get her. She never wanted to come between them. Neither of them had had much luck with relationships until they found each other. Hell, I was happy for him. He said he would have a girl this year, and he made it happen.

"It's going to be weird, Blue. Like when you bring girls home. How's that going to work?"

"How does it work when Gerrod stays over?"

"It's... it was weird the first time, but we got used to it."

"So you'll get used to it when I bring girls home?"

"And you'll be okay when I bring guys home, and we're all there the next morning?"

Yeah, I didn't see that coming.

"Well..." I sat back and scratched my head. "Honestly, I didn't give that part too much thought when we were talking about it."

"Think about it now, Blue. You and a strange guy wandering around in your underwear in the apartment. That's gonna be weird."

"Does Gerrod wander around in his underwear in your apartment?"

I wanted to laugh but decided this might be the wrong time. "Yeah, and the first time, I screamed. He's a big guy and him wandering around in boxers was crazy, and we won't even talk about how it is with Quinn being a screamer. Or the time that Gerrod broke the bed banging her so hard."

"Stop. Enough. I know this already. Don't need any more info. I get the same thing on my end." Damn, this could be bad. What would she think if she happened in while I had a chick tied up and blindfolded? It might scare the shit out of her, or she'd decide I was a perv and never want to speak to me again.

"So, yeah. How's it going to be if you bring home a screamer, or I bring home a loud banger?"

"Stop, Noelle. I get it. We'll have to come up with some system or clue."

"Please, Blue, don't tell me you want me to come home to my apartment and look to see if there's a sock on my door. I'm not doing it. So you better learn to fuck your women at their house or the XOX house."

"And what will you do? Go to some guy's apartment with a bunch of other sweaty dudes hearing you, knowing you're getting laid in the other room?"

This pissed me off. Thinking about her going to bed with another guy bothered me enough, but with others in the same house listening to her. Nope, I didn't want this to happen. She was better than that.

Noelle looked at me with a sad look in her eyes, and I wondered what thoughts ran through her mind.

"What?"

"Nothing."

"It's something. Just tell me, Noelle. We can talk about anything, remember?" I wanted her to trust me.

"You'll laugh at me."

"No, I won't." I reached over taking her hand running my thumb over the soft skin. "Tell me."

The look she leveled on me brought forth all kinds of wrong feelings. I couldn't let this happen, especially not now. We needed to keep it in the friend range and had been doing such a great job of it so far.

"I don't sleep around, Blue."

"What? I never said that." Is that how she took what I said?

"You assumed I brought guys home, and I don't do that."

"But you're the one who brought it up."

"I know, but I needed it to sound real because I know you do, but I don't."

"Like you've never done that?"

She got the strangest look on her face, and I didn't know how to read her. Then something dawned on me.

"Are you saying you've never had sex? That's what you're trying to say?" I knew I had a shocked look on my face.

"No, I'm not a virgin. I've had sex." She lowered her eyes to our hands clasped together. "Just not in a long time. Like since I've been here at TAU."

"You haven't even been here all that long, Noelle." Thank God. Her being a virgin made things even harder as far as I was concerned. I wanted this girl, but I didn't know how I was going to get past my kink with her.

"So you're saying you probably won't be bringing guys home?"

"I'm saying I don't know if I will, but if I do, I don't want it to be awkward for either of us."

"It won't be. I promise you. We'll have to take it one day at a time. We'll cross those bridges together."

She finally smiled a little. "Okay, I can do that."

"If you ever find something uncomfortable happening, tell me. We can talk about it. That's what friends do, talk shit out."

She nodded. "Only if you promise to do the same thing."

I squeezed her hand. "We good now?"

"Yeah, we're good." The bright look on her face told me we'd weathered this storm easily, and it gave me hope about a possible future.

"So when's this move taking place?" She seemed more eager now to move forward.

"Truth? If you ask Gerrod, tonight." I laughed, but I felt sure that's what the two lovers wanted. "But I'm going to push for tomorrow."

"Guess you need to start packing then."

I looked at her for a second. Were we doing this? My life was about to get very interesting.

"Right, my favorite thing, moving." I let go of her hand and started the car for her house.

BLUE

My parents took the news better than I guessed. After we talked it over and they understood the situation, they decided to head home. I knew they were only okay with the plan, but they'd get over it. I waved goodbye to them and went to my room to start packing up my stuff. Fortunately for me, I didn't have that much to worry about. My closet had a few items I wanted to keep to myself, so I packed those first. The last thing I wanted to be revealed right off the bat to Noelle was going into one box that I would handle on my own. I closed the box and set it under my jacket to carry separately.

"Hey," I called to Quinn from my doorway. "Go home and get your clothes packed. I need this move to happen today. Moving and practicing on the same day blows."

"Yeah, yeah, lover boy. You're trying to get your shit done so you can spend quality time with the new roomie."

"Whatever. It's not going to be like that, and you know it already." She loved giving me hell because I gave it right back.

Quinn stuck her head in the doorway. "Honestly, I'm kinda afraid what kind of shit I'm going to find when I get to the apartment. I know Noelle's going to be pissed at me."

"I think she's cool with it all now. At first, she wanted to kill you, but after we talked, it's going to be fine."

"That's how it looked to you, I'm sure. She's going to have a lot of different comments for me."

"So turn on that rarely seen Quinn charm and kill her with it. She'll come around."

"Right." She pulled back from the doorway but departed with her middle finger hanging on the frame causing me to laugh a little.

I loaded all the boxes in the back of my truck and clothes in the back seat. The special box I put in the front under my jacket. I'd take it in first and store it away for later. I walked back into the apartment I'd shared with Jenko and Gerrod for the last year and few months and looked around. We'd had some sick times in this place together.

Jenko and I had been roommates since I left home. I hoped having Quinn live here with him would work out okay. I knew it had to open his eyes to women. He didn't have sisters so the arrangement should be interesting.

I left the key on the dresser in my old room, and I made a pass over it for anything I'd missed. "This is the right move." The four walls heard me, and I shut the door.

Moving Quinn was a different ordeal. This crazy chick had a shit ton of stuff. Did females need that many scarves or shoes? When I got to my new place, Quinn, Gerrod, and Noelle walked from the doorway with hanging clothes. No way that would all fit in my old closet. I opened the back door to Gerrod's truck for him to stack in his part.

"The fuck, dude? Are these all hers?" He looked at me like I'd spoken Greek and stepped back scratching his head.

"Uh, yeah, just wait and see." He moved out of the way.

"Move, dipshit. These are heavy." Quinn piled her load on top of Gerrod's. "Make yourself useful and go bring some shit out." Then she added in a sweet tone, "Please."

Gerrod and I walked together to their rooms. "Gerrod, what is all this mess?"

"Shhh. She'll hear you. Dude, do all women come with this much rando stuff?"

"Hell if I know. The question is why?"

"Who knows but wait till you see the damn boxes from her bathroom. We have to share one remember? I might see if I can pay Jenko extra and share his instead."

I laughed so hard. "Yeah, might be a plan."

"Laugh less, work more. Two jocks should knock out a load twice as fast as regular people, and there is no double entendre meant by that."

"Quinn, don't say that for everyone to hear," Noelle tried to correct her.

"Little momma, I'm sure living with a guy you'll hear a whole lot more you don't want to hear."

Noelle shook her head. "She's never going to learn."

Gerrod came out with a stack of boxes. "God, I hope not. I love her just like she is."

The unloading went a lot faster, but by the time I got back over to my new place, we were tired. Damn, one girl couldn't possibly own so much stupid shit. I carried several boxes of picture frames and for what? She informed me they were so she wouldn't miss home, but I doubted her sincerity from her tone.

I told everyone I'd take care of unloading my stuff by myself. I needed to do my unpacking, so I knew where items ended up. I liked things organized and from the looks of what we unloaded for Quinn, she didn't. I hadn't gotten a look inside Noelle's room yet.

I wondered if she owned the same amount of things Quinn did.

Noelle walked in the door behind me with a box from the back of my truck. "Don't worry about unloading on my part. I'll get it all. You've been working with Quinn all day. I know you're tired."

"Thanks, I'm sick of carrying boxes and clothes." She plopped down on the couch while I took the box and my jacket into my room and put it in the bottom of my new closet. When I came back out, she sat there with her eyes closed. She looked beautiful. Her perfect face with long eyelashes fanned out across her cheeks was relaxed and unconcerned about a change.

I walked out the door without a sound. If she needed a little break, it was fine by me. On my way to the car, Timms drove by in the parking lot.

"Hey, bro. 'Sup?" His use of language made me smile.

"Not much. Finishing up moving in here." I poked my thumb over my shoulder indicating the new place.

"Yeah, I heard at the house you're moving in with the hot new cheerleader."

"I bet you did. Get an earful from Madelyn?"

"No, someone on the team told me. They'd been talking to Gerrod, and he told them about the switch. Good plan on your part." He smirked when he said it.

"It's not like that. We're only going to be roommates. Nothing more, and she quit cheer, so she's sitting in the student section now."

"Now that I did hear from Maddie, a huge earful that lost my attention on 'bitch quit.' You know I hardly listen to anything she says. We just like to fuck, that's it."

I shook my head at his bluntness. He had no feelings for Madelyn, and she seemed okay with it, but I wondered sometimes. We continued to talk about this week's game for a while, and I was happy for the distraction from moving. Besides, Noelle could sleep longer.

He finally took off, and I grabbed another armful of clothes so I could start in the closet and work my way to the door. When I walked in, she wasn't there, but I heard her.

"Oh my God. What the hell is this?"

I knew before I turned the corner what she'd found and immediately went on the defensive. I walked in my room, in my closet, and there she sat with my toys in both her hands—soft rope in one and the leather cuffs in the other.

"Noelle? I told you I'd take care of my stuff, didn't I?" My tone told her how pissed I was. "Why didn't you listen to me?"

"I, uh… I, well… I was just trying to help," she stuttered through her words. "I… I… I don't know what to say."

I took the stuff from her hands and shoved it back in the box. After closing it up, I returned it back to its spot in the bottom of my closet. She never moved from her spot, but the look on her face said it all.

"I'm sorry. I didn't mean to pry into your private... stuff." She had a difficult time coming up with terms for what she'd found. "I didn't know. I never knew."

"Look, Noelle. It's no big deal. Just some toys to make things... interesting. You know, like to experiment with. It's not like I planned on using them on you or anything, and I sure didn't plan on you finding them."

"Right." She quickly stood up and edged toward the door. "I'll leave you to unpack. Do you want me to help you carry anything from the truck? I can carry in hang-up clothes. That should be safe." She stepped into the hallway to speak from there like she was afraid of being in my room now.

"No, thanks. I'm good. I'll take care of it. I like to organize as I go. Makes things easier to find later." I never took my eyes off her face. I wanted to say a lot more but decided less was better.

"Okay, then. I think I'll do some reading in my room then. Yell if you need anything." She took off down the hall and shut the door to her room behind her.

"Well, shit." I headed back to my truck to get another load. I knew better. I should have kept those locked in my truck for now or threw the box in the dumpster. I only needed two things, rope and a blinder. I gave myself a pep talk on every trip I made.

As I folded up the last of my t-shirts, I heard Noelle's door open. I figured she'd head out and bypass having to talk to me, but I was wrong.

Her head peeked in my door. "Hey."

"Hey." The tension hung between us, but I wanted it to end. "You heading out?"

"No. I thought we might get something for supper. Are you hungry?"

I looked at her and smiled. "What have I told you a million times, babe?"

We said the words together. "I'm always hungry." We both laughed.

Snap, the tension ended.

"We need to talk about food. It'd be cheaper if we shared meals, at least in the evenings."

I followed her into the kitchen and opened the fridge. Not much in there. Do these girls not eat food? We'd have to make a grocery run tonight.

I pulled a bottle of water out and downed it while she stood there.

"Wow. Do you drink water like that every time?"

I looked down at the bottle, crunched it up and shot at the garbage. "Yeah. I've been busy and forgot to drink. Got to stay hydrated. So, don't you and Quinn eat food?"

"Yeah, why?"

"Unless Quinn took it all, this fridge is bare. Where's all the food? I mean, I'm not going to eat your food or anything. I'll get my own, but what do you eat?"

"I eat. I have some yogurt in there, and I eat oatmeal." The indignant look on her face told me she knew what I meant.

"Noelle. There's no food. We can't live like this. I need protein, fruits, and veggies. Do you cook?"

"Yes, I can cook, but we never take that much time. I've always been too busy."

"What about Quinn?"

"Please. Quinn can't boil water. I hope Gerrod knows what he's getting into if he thinks she's turning into Suzie Homemaker. Never gonna happen," she laughed while she spoke.

"Okay. Make a list, and I'll buy groceries. I don't expect you to split the bill since I'll probably eat twice as much as you."

"No, but say I'll pay a third. Will that work?"

"How about we let me buy this time, and we'll see how much you eat and revisit this? I think you'll eat less than that." She had a smoking body, and I felt sure she ate only good things for it.

We decided to go together so it would take less time. Walking in and getting a basket, she picked up an over-the-arm basket and turned back to me.

"What's that for?" I pushed toward her.

She looked down at it. "It's what I always use, but I guess it won't work anymore."

I couldn't help it. The incredulous look on her face was too funny. "Nope. Not gonna work for us." A smile ghosted across her lips.

Strolling up and down the aisles, she added a few things, but I loaded the basket down. With our list made up of mostly things I planned to eat, we covered ground quickly. As we rounded the last corner, we ran into Madelyn and the minions.

"Well, if it isn't the quitter. I guess we all know why you quit. You'll be too busy entertaining."

"Fuck off, Maddie. I have nothing to say to you," Noelle came right back at her.

"Wait, this looks like stuff for two. Are y'all living together already? I must say I didn't see this coming. You must have a voodoo snatch to get him hooked this fast."

I stepped up. "Back off, Madelyn. That's uncalled for. We are only roommates, nothing more. Don't talk about Noelle that way."

"Oh poor, Noelle. She doesn't like being called out on her shit and has to have her big, strong, hunky, football player care for her." The bitch looked directly at Noelle. "I guess you got your way, though. Stole him from the girls who truly cared for him."

"I don't need to steal roommates. He came willingly, Maddie."

"Most guys do with your kind." The other girls laughed at Madelyn's quick return.

This turned into a cat fight waiting to happen. We needed to get out of her line of fire. I turned to Noelle and jerked my head to the side letting her know I wanted to get the hell out of there. She nodded in return.

"Oh girls, isn't that cute? They already have their own language." This had to be the most immature woman I'd ever encountered. "I'll be sure to inform the right people of this new arrangement for you."

I guessed she couldn't help herself. Noelle said over her shoulder. "You be sure and do that, bitch. I know everyone is dying to hear your news. Better yet, post it on the internet unless I beat you to it."

"That was a bad idea goading her." I picked up a case of bottled water. "She'll do anything to use it against you."

"You're right. I should've let it go, but she makes me so damn furious. Over stupid shit, too. Why do I let her do it every time?"

"She'll be over it as soon as someone else does something that pisses her off."

I fumed all the way back to the apartment. Why did I allow that bitch to get to me? I needed to stop because it made me look as childish as she was.

He stopped the car and looked at me. “Don’t let her get to you, Noelle. She’s got control if you do, and that’s the last thing you need is for her to continue to control you. Forget about her. Live your life however you want. What she thinks no longer matters. Agree?”

“You’re right. I agree.”

We carried in more groceries than I’d ever seen in that kitchen. I hoped he planned to eat all this. I began putting items away as he brought in the last of the bags.

"What do you want to cook first?" It occurred to me that we rarely ever cooked. It looked like that was all about to change.

"I'll cook whatever you like." He stood at the end of the bar taking items out of the bag. This looked so domestic on both our parts. Quinn and I never had this conversation in our entire time together.

"Whatever you're hungry for is fine with me."

"K, let's have spaghetti. It's easy, and I picked up wheat pasta. Good carbs, you know."

No, I had no clue. "Yeah, now that I'm not working out so much, I'll probably start paying more attention to my diet."

"Working out is good for you anytime."

"I don't want to gain any weight, but I like to eat."

"Obviously, whatever you've been eating is fine just add in the gym a few times a week, and you'll stay the same."

"I've never had to watch what I've eaten. I'm lucky that way but working out with the squad was always part of my routine."

"Then do the same thing you were doing by yourself. I could go with you a few times to help set up a plan if you want."

"That'd be great. Let's do it one day this week when you're feeling up to it. I don't want to interfere with what you already do, though. Now that I don't have cheer, my schedule is pretty much free when you are."

"We'll work around our classes then."

"Great, roomie. I'm kinda likin' this new situation already." I smiled at him.

Blue put our plates on the table filled with more spaghetti than I'd eat in a week. The serving size plainly fit Jenko or Gerrod. I had to smile when I sat down.

"That's a lot of food, Blue."

He looked at his plate and then at mine. "Oh, yeah, I suppose it is. Just eat what you want, and I'll finish the rest. Food never goes to waste." He picked up his fork and dug in.

Silence filled the air as we ate. I wanted to ask questions about the box of items I'd found but couldn't decide how to bring it up. Several times, I started to say something but thought better of it.

"What's going on in that head of yours because clearly eating isn't it? You've hardly touched your plate, and you said you were hungry."

"I'm eating. It's really good, too. Are all the things you make this good?"

"I guess. No one's ever complained before, but then I could feed them leftover shit and that bunch would probably eat it."

This caused me to laugh out loud. "That's a little bit of an exaggeration."

"Yeah, you're right. How about week old food? They'd eat it if I poured gravy over it." He grinned at me after taking another bite. "You're avoiding my question, though."

He put his fork down and looked directly at me. "What's going on, Noelle?"

I did the same and folded my hands together under my chin staring back at him. "It's none of my business, and you can say that to me, and it'll be fine." Before I could finish, he held up a finger to stop me.

"You want to know about the box?"

I nodded my head. I couldn't tell if he was pissed from his tone. "It's okay. Don't feel like you have to tell me."

"It's not that I don't want to tell you. What I don't want to do is scare you or disgust you."

"No, never. What you do is your business."

"Look. I like things a little different than a lot of guys. It's nothing too extreme so don't worry."

"I'm not worried. It's not my place to judge you, and I won't." He seemed to like this comment because his face relaxed.

"Good. I promise nothing happens that's not consensual and never will. I'm a little OCD about stuff, and I like control. It's not about sex, it's about control for me."

"So you like to control the girls you have sex with, but it's not about the sex?" This confused me.

"Right. I want control in the bedroom to a certain extent, but if she's not into it, then it's fine."

"Is this like a Christian Grey thing? You have issues?"

"Who's Christian Grey?"

I looked at him like he'd stepped off another planet. "*Fifty Shades of Grey*? Surely you've heard of it."

"Oh, right. Never watched the movies and sure didn't read the books, but I've heard enough about it. He's a lot more fucked up than me. So, no, not like Christian Grey... nothing that intense or dealing with inflicting pain. The only pain I ever inflict is on the football field, not in the bedroom. I promise you."

He picked up his fork and started eating again finishing off his plate. My mind filled with at least a dozen more questions, but I decided to hold off.

"Anything else you want to know?"

"No, but can I get a raincheck on that question? I might think of something I want to know later."

He nodded his head. "Anytime. I'm not going to hide any of this from you. I don't want it to be a thing for us to tiptoe around. I mean, at first I thought I would keep it all from you, but I wouldn't want you to hear something around campus and wonder about it. Just ask me first, okay? I'll never lie to you."

He looked hard at me. The emerald of his eyes captivated me. If I didn't know better, I'd say they smoldered with lust. I knew better, though. He didn't have those feelings toward me. We'd already been down this road. He'd made it very clear.

"Great. Yeah, I'm good with that. Just one question, though."

"What's that?" he said as he pushed his plate to the side and looked at mine. I handed it over to him, and he dug in.

"How do you find girls who you know are into it? I mean, it's not like every girl you're with is going to be happy with being tied up, right?"

Again, he put his fork down. "No, they don't all like it. If things between us progress to the point that she's in my bed, I ask her or pull out the bindings and ask. If she's down for it, then that's all I need to know. If she's not, then I'm cool with it. I'm sure as hell not forcing anyone to do something they don't like."

"That's good to know, and thank you for trusting me enough to share your private life with me. You're right about hearing it around campus. I've heard some comments but didn't know what they were referring to."

He looked up from the plate again. "You've heard things? From who?"

"Madelyn made some comments that I didn't understand, but they make more sense to me now."

"Should have known. Dammit, I've never had sex with Madelyn." I knew he was angry. "Uh, just saying." Then he smiled. "Never wanted to have sex with her either."

"Just saying, huh?"

"Right." We both laughed now, and the intensity of the topic ended which made me happy. He'd given me more than enough to consider.

Our first week together lined out pretty quickly. He went to practice, and I spent more time studying than ever before. We still met on campus for coffee because some days we never saw each other, which I found strange since we lived together. We'd managed to eat dinner three times, and that seemed like a miracle.

I volunteered to cook on Friday night and made twice the amount I usually would so he had enough to eat. His appetite amazed me. This meal would be my first try to impress him with my abilities, so I cooked one of the few things I knew how to do, chicken fettuccini. It probably wasn't on his list of approved eats, but oh well. It was only one meal.

My body rejected a pizza-free week for grilled chicken, broccoli, brown rice, roasted chicken, baked chicken, grilled steak, broiled steak, and green things of all sorts. Where was the variety or fun in that?

The door opened, and his backpack hit the floor. "Wow. That smells fucking amazing. What'd you cook?"

"Tonight it's chicken fettuccine. I splurged and used whole grain pasta since that's what you bought. I've never had it before now. I also made a salad with all kinds of interesting things in it." I prayed he found it all edible.

"Good job. I'm sure it'll all be excellent. Of course, since I'm starving and didn't have to cook it, I can't wait to dive in." He sat down at our small table.

I'd set the table to look nice and stuck a candle in the middle. I wasn't going for romantic, but when I put his plate down in front of him, I noticed he was staring at it. Maybe I overdid it.

"Uh, I didn't have flowers, so I decided a candle made it more like an Italian restaurant."

"No, it's nice. I never think about any of that kind of shit. Guess I'm more interested in the food." We both laughed because we knew it was true. "Hey, thanks for doing this. I appreciate it."

"It's the least I could do. You've cooked all week, and I figured after the game tomorrow, you'd be going out with the team to do something."

"Yeah, probably." He stuck the first bite in his mouth and didn't spit it out. Whew, I had my doubts if he'd like it. "This is great, Noelle. You did an awesome job. Maybe you should've been doing the damn cooking all along."

"Uh, that would be a hell, no. I'm good with yogurt, remember?"

"Right, you mean something I'd stand at the fridge and suck down? Yeah, not a meal."

I took a bite and surprised myself. I'd made it a couple of times for my parents, so I was glad it came out tasting good.

"How was practice? Y'all ready for the game tomorrow?"

"Yeah, it's a conference game, so it's important, but the team we're playing isn't that great, so we're feeling good. I hope we're not overconfident, though. That shit happens all the time, and these smaller teams sneak up and win. Coach's been giving us hell about it all week. Can't let our guard down."

"He's right. Gotta rise for each occasion. Not let the little guys worm their way in and ruin y'all's record."

"Okay, Coach Jeffries. I'll keep that in mind." He smirked when he stood to refill his plate. "We'll get the job done. You're coming, right?"

"Oh yeah, got my student ticket. Quinn makes sure to pull both of ours each week."

"Good. I like knowing y'all are cheering for us from the stands."

We stuffed ourselves with too many carbs and did the dishes together before we moved to the den to watch TV. I watched him sitting back in the overstuffed chair with his feet propped up on the coffee table scrolling through the listing. Talk about a homey scene. Dinner, dishes, and Netflix. The feeling unsettled me. Did either of us think we would end up this way? I knew I didn't.

I believed he spent more time at the XOX house, but if he'd been there this week, he failed to mention it to me. Not that he had to, but he came home each evening usually studying or watching TV.

"It's Friday night. Don't you have plans with your boys out at the house?"

"Nope. We gotta be at the field house early tomorrow, and I need to rest tonight. I know they're partying, and I sure as hell don't need that."

"Right. So what are you going to choose?"

"I don't care. What do you want to see?" He scrolled through the pictures of the titles and passed over *Fifty Shades of Grey*. "Hey, we should watch this since I've never seen it. Did you read the books?"

"Yeah, but I'm not sure it's your type of movie. It's low keyed until the very end." Were the two of us ready to see this movie together? I'd seen it, more than once at the theater. Both times there were no men in the audience.

"Low keyed, huh? Am I going to fall asleep? Is it mushy and girlie?"

"Mushy and girlie? Uh, no, it's more intense, and there's nothing girlie about it." With his preference in bed, I wasn't sure about this. "Are you sure you want to watch this? I mean, I know it's nothing like what you enjoy."

"How do you know what I like? I might learn some new skills from the infamous Christian Grey."

"No doubt." I wanted to laugh but thought better of it.

"Let's do it."

He pushed start, and I pushed panic.

At the beginning of the movie, I silently fought with myself over whether we could get through the show... it's not going to be so bad or would it? "You know it's been a while since I've seen it. I only remember the main points."

"Yeah, I bet I know which parts you remember." The smirk he followed his comment up with caused my cheeks to get warm.

The movie's final scene belted out the ending, my feelings the same as before—rage and anger. The only saving grace at each viewing being I'd read the trilogy and knew the outcome. Blue's initial reaction surprised me. He stood, his posture ramrod straight. The body language he exhibited told me he was angry, too.

"That was bullshit. How could she lay there and take it? She had a safe word. Why wouldn't she use it? That was abuse, plain and simple." The show affected him far more than I anticipated. Exploring his feelings would be far easier if I knew more about his particular kink.

"Yes, but it was consensual, just like you said you always ask for." I knew I pushed some buttons and should've left it alone.

"No, nothing I do is even close. Nothing. I wouldn't hurt a woman that way. Never would I take my anger out on a woman over my issues."

So he could admit he had issues. This had to be a good first step.

"The thing you don't understand is, he has baggage from his past." I'd hoped with mentioning this, Blue might open up, but he didn't take the bait.

"I don't have baggage, Noelle. My childhood was normal with great parents in a nice home."

"So what you're saying is you needing control during sex has nothing to do with anything that happened to you as a kid?" He didn't say anything for a long time. His facial expressions told me his mind churned. Pain or sadness haunted his beautiful features. I didn't realize until now the expressiveness in his eyes. Watching the green change to a dark emerald, I knew a heavy tale tumbled around begging to be told.

Would he want to share these thoughts with me? Maybe we weren't there yet which was fine. I prayed we'd get there someday.

After a few silent minutes had passed, I decided to help him move on. "Look, Blue, you don't have to share your personal life with me. I get it, I do. We all have secrets we choose to keep to ourselves."

He sat back down and leveled sea green eyes on me. "I know I don't have to reveal anything to you, and I appreciate you not pushing me, but I also feel like I should tell you some things. I don't want you hearing random shit around campus about me, and God knows some of the girls I've been with can't keep their mouths shut. People say guys are the one to kiss and tell, but I've found the opposite to be true."

"Yeah, sometimes, especially when alcohol's involved, bedroom gymnastics tend to be shared." I smiled thinking of the bragging I'd heard from Quinn. If anything, she overshared until I claimed TMI.

He took a deep breath. "I told you I like control, but the truth is, I demand it but only with two things. I like to make sure my partners' hands are kept out of the mix. Tying wrists are the only thing I use the rope for."

Before I could stop myself, I blurted out, "You have a problem being touched or something?" I couldn't understand this. He held my hand and hugged me often. I'd seen him hug other people, too. It seemed extreme to tie his lovers' hands away from him.

"No, I don't have a problem being touched. Hell, if that were the case, how would I ever play football. Think about being tackled or on the bottom of a pile."

"True. I'd feel claustrophobic finding myself under all that weight."

"All that weight would kill little you." We both laughed lightening the moment which helped us both.

"Riiiggghhhttt. There's more to this body than you think." I ran my pointed finger up and down me. What female didn't worry about an extra five pounds weighing her down? "Okay, so you don't have a problem being touched, but you like the girls to be tied up while you... have sex."

"Yes, I want their hands tied to something, so I don't have to think about where they are."

I know my face said what the fuck. I couldn't help myself. I tried hard to see it from his point of view, but this moved to the weird side.

"Don't look at me like that." I'd hurt his feelings now. Damn.

"Sorry. I'm trying to keep an open mind, but you can't expect me not to question it all."

"You're right, and you're the first person I've tried to explain myself to."

Wow. Now I felt bad when I should be honored with his trust enough to talk about it with me. "Okay, go on. I'm not here to judge you, and I appreciate you opening up to me. You said you used ropes, but I saw black furry handcuffs in the box. You use those, too?"

"Hell, no. I know you're going to think this is strange, but they were a gag gift for graduation from Jenko. Said he wanted to help me branch out a little. I threw them in the box to keep my mom from finding them when I moved to college. She'd freak. The truth is, I've never used them."

"What? Jenko's known about your kinkiness since high school? Are y'all attached at the hip or something?"

"No, but he's been my friend forever. We went through school together. He knows everything about me."

I made myself drop the face I was making. He struggled with talking about everything, and I wanted to know it all. "Sorry. I promise I won't question you again. No handcuffs, ropes only. What else?"

"Blindfolds. I either tie something around her eyes, or I have sleeping blinders or blackout masks."

I nodded my head up and down digesting the new item. No touching and no looking. I couldn't wrap my brain around it. I'd seen him in a bathing suit. Michelangelo couldn't paint someone who looked like Blue. There's no way he had body image issues.

His pecs were perfection, and his arms kept a t-shirt taut. The abs he sported called to any red-blooded female to run her hands, or better yet, her tongue over to feel the valleys defining them. The Adonis V on his abdomen pointed a perfect line to heaven, didn't it? Why would he want to keep this from a lover? Top that off with his beautiful dark blond hair that I'd love to run my fingers through. I'd die if I ever found myself in the situation where I could be with him and couldn't do so.

"Are you anorexic or something like it?" It was the only explanation I could come up with.

"What, no. Why would you think that?"

"Come on, Blue. You're beautiful… your face, your body, your hair… everything about you is beautiful. Why wouldn't you want women seeing and touching you unless you had some strange body issues? Do you want me to be honest with you?"

"Absolutely."

"If you and I were not simply friends and we were going to uh... you know, have sex, and you told me I couldn't see or touch you, I think I'd cry from the loss. I'm not sure I could go through with it. And it's not about being tied up because I think I could handle that and covering my eyes, too. I could so do that, even though I never have." I wanted him to understand it had nothing to do with the things he liked doing for the sake of enhancing our pleasure during sex. Isn't that what a lot of people who played like to do?

I saw now his need to control the situation had completely different ramifications in his life. It wasn't his need to control his lovers, his kink had underlying causes. That's what we needed to talk about, but I knew he'd had enough sharing for now. I'd pushed further than he wanted to go from the look on his face.

BLUE

I wanted to go all caveman and drag her by the hair to my room, slam the door, tie her down, cover her eyes, and fuck her until she couldn't walk. She admitted she could see being tied up and blindfolded. I wanted to high-five the sex gods. Now we were getting somewhere, but I couldn't let on how happy this made me.

I needed to keep my happiness with her admission to myself. She still had some valid questions, but I wasn't ready to get into anymore tonight. Guess I'd save my celebrating for the shower later.

"Can we change the subject for now? I think I've overshared enough tonight."

"Sure. Hey, and thank you. I know you probably didn't plan to hand over that info to me so soon. I appreciate the trust you've placed in me." It was a sincere thank you, and I appreciated it.

"You're right. I don't share often, so please keep it between us."

"Right. No problem. Roommate secrets. I get it. If you only knew the things about Quinn that are on the Do Not Share list." We bumped fists to make it official.

"Movies?" I picked up the remote. "I don't think you have to worry about me watching the next Grey."

"Yeah, but you need to. It'll change how you feel."

"Doubtful. Nothing about that show sparked my interest." I finally relaxed back in the chair.

"It's early still. You want to watch something else to get your mind off that one?"

"Yeah. Let's do something scary this time. That'll take my mind off it for sure." I flipped through the listing.

"Scary shows give me nightmares, but I'll give it a try. I can always hide my eyes at the bad parts."

"I can move over next to you and keep you safe." What a lame excuse to sit next to her. After our talk, I wondered if she would say no.

"Good plan. I can hide behind you." I slid in next to her, and she wrapped her arm through mine."

"See, this way I can tuck my face behind your shoulder." She dipped her face behind me. She slid down enough that her head was even with my shoulders which didn't take much, but it was enough to have her leaning on my arm. All I could feel were her amazing tits hugging my bicep, one on each side.

This innocent situation would have my mind on anything but a scary movie. I'd better pick a good one.

The sun rose with me glued to her backside on the couch. My arm held her against my hard morning wood nestled between her firm ass cheeks. Damn, this had the potential for embarrassment.

Her head rested on my arm which was curled around her neck and down between her tits. Talk about firm. I wanted to roll her over and see for myself or gently palm the closest one. This line of thinking made my dick harder.

A line of drool dripped down my arm tickling the sensitive skin. I wanted to laugh at the feel and the situation. Who knew a week ago my 'friend' would be close enough to my wood to feel it on her ass, while I had her tits wrapped around my arm? Yeah, not this guy.

"What time is it?" Her raspy morning voice surprised me.

"Uh, I think it's around nine."

"Nine. I need to get up. I need to do some homework before the game." She moved against my hard length, and I wanted to groan but kept it in. Her entire body froze stiff. Yep, she felt me. She turned her head a little to see my arm located in a great location.

"Uh, Blue?"

"Yeah?"

"I… I… I think you need to… unfold from around me."

This stuttering she did when she was nervous was cute.

"Sure, babe. Hey, and don't worry about the drooling. We'll add that to the DNS list, too."

"Sorry about that. I must've been sleeping hard."

"Yeah, me too." I started laughing. My fourteen-year-old self popped out. I tried to hide it, but it was too easy. She sat up immediately.

"Blue! That's… that's just wrong."

"Babe. It's a natural phenomenon." My laughter got louder.

"Well, keep your phenomenon to yourself, please."

"Hey, you were the one backed up to me." I was all but crying looking at the indignant face she made.

"Ugh. Men."

"That's right, babe. Me man, you woman." I stood and beat my fists against my chest. "Me Tarzan..."

Before I could finish the statement, she stomped off down the hall yelling, "I'll never be a Jane, you overgrown manchild. *Never!*" No stuttering involved.

"Manchild. I'll show you, manchild." She took off running to her room as I chased after her. I laughed all the way to my shower. This female for a roommate might be a pretty sweet deal.

I stared at the scoreboard shaking my head, tied with only two minutes left. The B-Bombers freshmen from my old high school played better than we did today. Dropped passes, Timms sacked three times, two fumbles in the red zone.

What else could go wrong in one damn game? Oh yeah, we could lose.

We got the ball back with a minute-six on the clock. We huddled, and Timms called two plays. First, a screenplay with a pass to the secondary. Coaches designed the play to advance the ball downfield picking up over twenty yards or more. The second play would end across the goal line for the win.

I hated playing this way. The risk of losing was great if these two plays didn't come off exactly as planned.

We lined up, and Timms started the cadence. "28-15-Blue-Blue-hut." We executed the play perfectly and gained thirty-eight yards. With Timms calling two plays in a row, we kept the defense a little off kilter. The chains barely had time to move and the defense set on the line when Timms started the second play sequence.

"32-12-Red-Blue-hut-hut." He dropped back and three receivers, me included, took off for our spots. All of us were designated to catch the winning pass. It all came down to who Timms found open.

He fired the missile. Since I was the usual receiver, the defenders double-teamed me leaving Powell standing wide open in front of the goal post. He caught the pass like we were playing a game of Sunday afternoon family football in the yard. The team swarmed Powell before Timms could get to him to jump mid-air and spin.

The PAT floated through the uprights putting us ahead by seven points. Only two seconds left on the clock made it all the sweeter. Greely kicked the ball to their receiver who barely took three steps before our kick-off team nailed him. The clock ran out, and we'd managed to put another 'W' in the books.

The stadium erupted, and the few who didn't attend the game heard it across town. We managed to pull it out when we should've won by fifty or more points. We deserved the ass chewing we were going to get in the locker room and all week long on the practice field. Our coveted spot in the top twenty could take a hit from this.

We ran to the locker room knowing what awaited us. Winning in the last minute always made us excited and this time was no different. Coach walked in behind us and nodded at the offensive coordinator.

His coaching fostered this win—that, and Timms' leadership on the field.

"Men, gather around." He waited until we stood close in to him. "Since I have nothing good to say, I'm going to save my comments for Monday's practice. Be ready." He turned and walked into the office leaving the room to drop-dead silence. We all knew we deserved it, but damn, it took away the euphoric feelings in a heartbeat.

This didn't stop the celebrating to move out to the XOX house as usual. This would be our last celebration there for three weeks since our next three games were on the road, making the winning harder. Standing on the sidelines to a stadium roaring for the other team made it more difficult to muster enthusiasm when desperately needed.

I parked my truck so I could leave when I was ready. Part of me wanted to celebrate, but part of me stood in front of Coach in that locker room thinking of all we did wrong on the field today. This caused me to be pissed off as I walked to the house. The usual shit went on around me. Drinking, dancing, playing games like normal. I couldn't be the only one angry over our fucked-up win.

"Blue," Timms he launched a can of beer at me. "He catches, he scores."

"Thanks, man. Hey, and good job on the pass to Powell today."

"Yeah, even you could have completed that fucking pass to him. No one was even around him. That was the shit you pulling his defender off."

"True. Glad I could make your damn easy job even easier." We fist-bumped when he moved to stand beside me to watch the crazy shit going on around us.

"Gotta teach these children how to play ball every chance we get. Powell will be taking your place soon enough."

"Yeah, not looking forward to that shit by any means."

"The fuck? You're not planning to make the transition to pro ball?" Timms' reaction made it sound like I spoke blasphemy.

"No, probably not. I love this damn game, don't get me wrong. Playing for the rest of my walking days, I just don't see it." This conversation seemed strange for us to be having. His graduation in May changed the game for all of us. "Besides, I gotta break a new quarterback in this summer and then leave next year. Yeah, not feeling that shit to go play with a different set of fucking rules the following fall."

"Not me. I'm all in for this. I've been having wet dreams all season about how playing pro next fall's gonna be."

"Good deal, dude. You'll go quickly in the draft. Your damn record proves you deserve the opportunity."

A few new people walked through the front door with Noelle and Quinn being the last two. Quinn looked around immediately for Gerrod. Nothing new there. What was new, though, was the way Noelle was dressed. Short skirt and a sheer looking shirt with long sleeves that started down at her biceps. Damn, she looked good.

Timms elbowed me when he spotted her. "Dude, if you don't make a move on that one, someone's going to. I wouldn't mind being that person. She's fucking hot."

"Yeah, not going to happen. We're friends and roommates. That's the way it needs to stay."

"So you're telling me she's fair game, then?"

Dammit, I hated even talking about this with him. I knew from some of his comments before he had eyes on her. "I don't know how fair it is, but yeah, I guess she is."

"Shit man, just waiting for your permission." He laughed out loud knowing I didn't need to give him permission. If Timms wanted it, he took it. I guess she was in the safety zone living with me. "Talk to ya later." He moved off to where she stood talking to Quinn and Gerrod.

I didn't know if I could watch this fucked-up scene. Already being in a bad mood and seeing him make his play, put me on edge. I moved out back to talk to the other team members. I needed to keep my mind on anything else. I found Powell surrounded by well-wishers.

"Good job today, Powell," I called to him as I walked in his direction.

"Thanks, Blue. I couldn't have caught it if you weren't out there. That guy would've been all up in my shit if you hadn't drawn him the opposite direction. Guess I didn't pose a threat in their minds."

"Yeah, they spent too much time watching fucking game films to think I was the only one who could catch Timms' damn pass."

"Sure as hell took that defender by surprise. I looked over at him when I threw the ball down and smiled. He was pissed." Being a freshman, Powell deserved a little time to brag. He'd need to outgrow it before he ruined his credibility with the team.

Powell waved over my head. "Crew, my man."

A tall kid walked over and gave a man hug to Powell. They both seemed a little cocky. Must be a freshman, too. They'd have it knocked out of them before they became starters on this team.

"Blue, this is Crew Devillier." I turned to look eye to eye with him.

"Hey, nice to meet you. I've been watching your career with the Rams since you walked on the field." I liked this kid already. We shook hands.

"Thanks, man. Appreciate it."

"Tuck's and my dad are big Rams fans. They make all the games they can."

"That's great. We need all the fans we can get. What position they got you playing?" I should know this, but I couldn't keep up with every team member.

"Right now, tight end, but I've played several positions since I started playing when I was a kid. My size helped when I was younger. Now I'm about the same as most on this team."

"Yeah, college ball has a way of bringing the cream of the crop together. Size in high school levels out on this field." I'd learned that the hard way.

"That's for damn sure. Crew and I thought we were big until we came down last spring to check out the school. We spent the summer trying to bulk up. Our dads laughed at us about it." Tucker and Crew laughed at their stupidity.

"Yeah, but we did add some size and muscle since then. We'll continue lifting through the season and the spring. Gotta get the size, Tuck, if we want to start with these guys next fall."

"Hell, yeah, we do." The two knocked fists. Damn, was I like that as a freshman? I laughed at the two of them.

We turned at a noise.

"Looks like Timms found his next bedpost notch," Tucker spouted off.

I looked around until I spotted the noise and Timms. He pulled Noelle in tight against him. Charging over there to lay him out with one hit crossed my mind before I remembered giving him the go ahead. Fuck.

"Shut the fuck up, that's my roommate. Don't ever talk shit about her like that again." I said it without looking at the kid, but he damn sure knew I was talking to him. No one else said a word.

The situation inside the kitchen looked heated between Timms and Madelyn. Why did Noelle want to get into that shit? She knew Timms and Madelyn were together at these things.

As we watched the scene unfold, Noelle pulled away from Timms and walked out of the kitchen. Thank God she decided to move away. I hoped she lost the desire to see what Timms was about. She knew already.

Finding my way into the house, I knew it wasn't my place, but I had to know she was okay. I looked around a little before I spotted her standing beside Quinn at the beer pong table.

"Hey. Problems in the kitchen?" I asked pretending to watch the ping pong ball fall into the cup.

"Uh, no. I'm not wasting my time getting involved with that again. I didn't realize they were attached to each other."

Before I could respond, an arm wrapped around her from behind. "Sweet cheeks, I'm not attached to any one woman. You should know that by now." He kissed her neck below her ear.

She pulled out of his arms. "Really? It looked like it to me. Honestly, Timms, I won't be a part of that. If she wants you, she's got you. No interference from me."

"Like I said before, she's nothing to me. That ship sailed a long time ago. She can't seem to get the message." His harsh comment bothered me since I knew they still slept together whenever he wanted to scratch that itch.

"Obviously, she hasn't, and I refuse to be the one to help her understand." Noelle stood her ground against his arguments.

"You want her gone from here, just say the word. I'll ban her ass. We don't need her shit here anyway. She's nothing but drama." Now, this was new. He'd refuse to allow Madelyn to come to the house? I'd believe it when I saw it.

"Do not put this off on me," Noelle stood straight and faced him. "It's not my house. Doesn't it belong to the frat?"

"Sure as hell does and as this year's president, I say who comes and goes." Timms stepped up, so their bodies barely touched.

I could see the fire between them. I'd never seen him put this much effort into impressing a female. He'd never cared enough to want to. If they didn't fall at his feet, he found one that would. Noelle would never be that girl. She wasn't built that way.

Watching this play out, made me want her even more, but I wasn't the one she bowed up to, though, a dick that wanted nothing more than a one and done was. Dammit, how did I let this happen?

My first instinct said to get between them before he put her over his shoulder and took her upstairs with her kicking and screaming. That would evolve to heated sex in his bed. The undercurrent burned in the slight space separating them. The more they argued, the faster the space filled with two hot bodies.

Mine and Quinn's eyes met up, but I couldn't read her thoughts. I wondered if she expected me to stop this before it went too far. How would it look if I did? Me taking Noelle upstairs would never happen even with her admission she might be into it. She still didn't know the reasons behind the ropes and masks.

I turned back to the two in time to see him grab her up like I predicted and carry her in a fireman's hold. He swatted her ass hard with his free hand and took off upstairs. Her protests weren't as loud as I thought they would be. She beat on his back but not as hard as she should've. If anyone thought she was going against her will, no one said a word.

I looked down at the floor for a second, picked up my beer can, and threw it at the wall sending a spray of beer all over the room. When I turned and saw Quinn glaring at me with an eyebrow cocked, it made me madder. Madder at who was the question I asked myself as I walked out the door.

NOELLE

Timms threw me on the bed and kicked the door closed. He fell on top of me and started kissing me. At first, it was nice. Nice, is this what I expected? Nice? Hmm. Where was the fire we had going on downstairs? He turned his head to gain more access to my mouth, but I wasn't feeling it.

When his tongue tried to play around with mine, it tickled. I couldn't help it when I started laughing. He immediately rolled off me.

"I'm sorry, Timms. Do it again. I promise not to laugh."

"Hell, no. I'm not kissing someone who laughed at me."

"I wasn't laughing at you. It tickled."

"I didn't kiss you to play tickle time, Noelle." I'd hurt his feelings.

"I'm sorry. I don't know what else to say."

"Yeah, I know. I'm not feeling it either. What was that downstairs, though? I wanted to grab you up and kiss the hell out of you."

"I wanted that, too, but now we're alone... it was just... eww."

"Eww? It was that bad?"

"No, it wasn't bad. I'm sorry."

"Stop saying that. Obviously, we had something else going on down there that's not happening here." We both rolled over and looked at each other. "What do you think?"

"I don't know. I mean our friends were all there watching which was weird."

"Yeah, and then there was Blue. Waiting, watching."

I looked hard at Timms. He's right. Blue stood by and watched the whole scene without comment.

"Did he say something to you about him and me?" Would he admit to Timms there was something going on between us that neither of us wanted to admit?

"No, he didn't. What he did say was there was nothing going on between you two, and I was welcome to take my chances."

"Oh he did, did he?" I rolled to my back and blew out my breath. "What's this all about, Timms? I tried, in the beginning, to see if there was any interest, and he told me it would never happen. I guess I just don't do it for him.

"So the two of you've never..." he seemed almost embarrassed to ask it.

"One night we almost did, but I was drunk, and we only fooled around a little. He assured me that nothing else would ever happen. Like I said, I guess I don't have what he's looking for."

"No, I don't think that's the problem at all." He laid back, too.

"You don't? He had me questioning myself. Was I not pretty enough, or smart enough, or thin enough. Were my boobs too small? Was I too bitchy? What the fuck is going on, Timms?"

"That's all just shit, and you know it. You're all those good things and none of the bad. He has his own problems going on. Y'all need to talk about that, though. Not you and me."

"You mean his need for tying women up and blindfolding them? We talked about it. He explained to me that he liked to be in control. I even told him I'd be willing to try that, and he laughed and said no."

"Is that all he said to you?"

"Basically, yes." Did he share more with Timms?

"Look, Noelle." He rolled back onto his side and propped his head up on his arm. "There's more to his story than being in control, but this is his to tell. No one else's. Not too many know or question him, so you'll have to hear it from him when he's ready."

"Well, hell. What more do I have to do to get him there, strip naked and beg? If that's the case, never gonna happen." I blew a stray hair off my forehead. "I'll never beg a guy for sex. I'm not that girl. I'll never be that girl." My frustration with the situation grew with this conversation.

"Noelle. I'm not the guy to ask. I believe Blue has real feelings for you, but he needs to see that you're the one he can be himself with." I began to see there was more to Timms than being a jock.

"Blue is complicated in a lot of ways. Some athletes can only dream about the drive and determination he has on the field. He has a 4.0 GPA, but almost no one knows it. His parents are good people who raised him right. The guy has a lot going for him so if he's got a problem in the bedroom, then maybe you need to figure out how to get past it."

I stared at the ceiling a long time while Timms stared at me. "You're a beautiful woman, Noelle, and I'm disappointed this won't work between us, but I get it. You need to decide if Blue's worth the trouble to pursue. Hell, make a plan and do it."

"After today, that might be under the headline of impossible. I don't think he was too happy when we were facing off downstairs."

"Yeah, I thought he was gonna call me out on it before we got up the stairs, but he stood and watched it happen."

"Right. Do you have any idea how that makes me feel? Like shit, that's how. And that's what he did before. He chose a skank over me."

"No, don't think that. It wasn't over you. It's over his ways in bed. He wouldn't be able to do those things to you. Don't take it personally."

"Oh, I get it, 'it's him, not me.'"

Timms laughed a little. "That's a good one. I've used it a couple of times myself."

I hit him on the arm. "You're a mean bastard when you want to be."

"Hell, yeah, I am. It's a rep I gotta keep up, too. Not looking to carry any gold diggers off to the pros with me."

I sat up and pulled my knees up to my chin. "You *are* a mean bastard. Surely none of these fine girls here would be a gold digger."

"Woman, you need to look around. They're all potentially dying to fill that role."

"You're so full of shit, Timms."

"Maybe, but I'll be rich and full of shit." He laughed at his own joke as he sat up, too. We climbed off the bed and continued our humorous banter back down the stairs.

A few of Madelyn's minions gave me go-to-hell looks, but I no longer cared about any of them. Fuck 'em. I didn't care what they thought.

I walked back to the pong table where the same group stood around playing.

Quinn looked at me. "Are you fucking insane, bitch?"

"No, why?"

"Were you just horny and couldn't help yourself from becoming his latest conquest or is there some shit I don't know about you?"

"The truth is nothing happened."

"The hell you say." The look she gave me made me want to laugh in her face.

"No, the truth, I say. We laid in bed and talked. After he kissed me and I started laughing, it killed the moment."

"You fucking laughed at the overgrown manwhore? That's classic, Noelle."

"Yeah, it was. We did have a great talk opening my eyes to a lot of stuff."

"Really? I hope it was about Blue because some shit went down after Timms He-manned you up the stairs for all to see."

"Like what?"

"See that cup on the floor and the wet wall? Blue slammed that bitch against the wall sending beer everywhere. People scattered trying to miss a full cup of that piss they drink."

"He was mad?" Blue confused me at every turn.

"No, it was a hell of a lot more than that."

"Where is he?"

"Left right after the shit-fit he threw, and no one tried to stop him."

Gerrod walked over to us and wrapped around Quinn. "Hey, babe. I think we need to head home. I prefer a more private celebration."

She turned at me and grinned. "Think my hot boyfriend is hot for this body." She pointed up and down herself.

"Hell, yeah, I am," Gerrod said loud enough for all to hear.

"We'll see ya later. You good here with all these dicks swinging for a position with the women?"

"God, Quinn when you put it that way, I think I'll head home, too."

She leaned in and kissed my cheek causing Gerrod to pipe up. "Now if y'all are down for a threesome, I'm good with it anytime."

"Hell, no. You got all the woman you can handle, big boy."

"You're right, baby, so right." He picked her up, and she wrapped her legs around him. "Let's go home."

"Fucking right." Their lips were still attached as they walked out the front door.

I made my way to the porch where Timms sat in his lawn chair drinking a beer. A black-haired hottie with tattoos sat in his lap.

"Heading out?" he asked while she continued to kiss on his neck.

"Yeah, had all the celebrating I can stand for one day." I waved and walked to my car, but before I could open the door, Madelyn appeared.

"I guess you think you can have the whole team."

"Not doing this, Madelyn." She pushed the door closed before I could get in. "Go back inside. I don't want any of them. Go for it."

She gave me a strange look. Maybe she finally decided. "Damn right I will."

"Good for you. I hope you're successful." She gave up too easily moving away from my door. I stepped in and drove away. I had more important things to deal with at home. I didn't need to stir this pot, too.

Blue's truck took up his spot next to mine. Our house was empty. I wonder where he went that he didn't drive. I went to my room to change into yoga pants for the evening. Another Saturday night at home alone. My social life sucked a big one.

I heard the door open as I made my way down the hall. As I rounded the corner to the den, I almost ran into Blue kissing a woman I'd never seen.

"Oh, uh. Sorry." I stammered out as I began backing up.

"Thought you'd be busy with Timms till tomorrow."

His words burned and what was worse, I felt like he wanted them to.

"No. I'm home for the night."

He looked at me and then at the girl he'd yet to introduce. "We're here for the night, too. This is our cross-the-walk neighbor, Heidi." She raised her hand in a little wave. He grabbed it and pulled her to his bedroom door. I couldn't help myself watching them walk through the opening. He stopped, and we stared at each other for longer than necessary before he closed it behind him.

No way I could stay there knowing what was going on. I grabbed my books and keys and left. The only problem was where would I go for the night? There was an empty bed at Quinn and Gerrod's. I could stay there for the night, but for now, I needed another spot to study while they were busy.

The library echoed from the lack of people taking up space. "Great, got the whole place to myself." Comfy couches to sit back and study on waited for me.

Three hours later, I shut my books. I'd read everything assigned for the coming week, done all the assignments for Monday's classes. My stomach growled from lack of supper. I'd planned to cook at home tonight, but now that was out. Damn him. We'd talked about having a plan. Why didn't we settle on one? Deciding to head over to Quinn and Gerrod's apartment, I gathered my things and walked out into the nighttime and headed over to their place.

I knocked on Quinn's door, and she jerked it open. "Where've you been?"

"Hello to you, too. I've been at the library studying? Why?" She had no reason to be mad at me. I'd left them alone to have some afternoon delight.

"We've been calling your damn phone, and no one answered."

"Oh, I turned the ringer off while I was there. Forgot to turn it back on." I pulled it out of my bag and fixed it. "Why were you calling anyway? I wanted to give y'all time to do whatever."

"That would've been great except Blue started texting and calling both our phones before we could get our groove on. He's like a little bitch when he doesn't get what he wants."

"What'd he want? He seemed occupied when I left. I planned to spend the night here so he could have the house with his new friend."

"Apparently said friend didn't stay for the dirty deed when she found out his idea of fun."

"Oh. Well, not my problem. What'd he want me for anyway? He didn't need my help."

"Hell if I know, but could you call him so we can go back to enjoying our Saturday night?" She wiggled her eyebrows.

"I'll go home."

"You're welcome to stay, but we won't be around to entertain you. Sorry."

"No problem. I'll go home now." Quinn and Gerrod didn't need a cockblocker for the night. Not that me being around ever stopped her.

I took a deep breath before I opened the front door and walked in. I didn't know what I'd find, but as long as he wasn't holed up in his room with company, I was good with it. He wasn't in the den, so I tiptoed down the hallway. When I got to his door, I put my ear up to it and didn't hear anything.

Deciding to open it to see if he was there, I found him sound asleep. I pulled the door back closed trying not to wake him. I took a deep breath when I sat down on the couch. He looked so peaceful sleeping. I wished I could see it up close sometime, but it looked like that day would never happen.

I turned on the TV, but before I could decide on something, his door opened, and he came down the hallway sprawling in his chair.

"Hey, I'm sorry about that. I didn't plan to bring her home, but she has a roommate, too. I figured you'd stay the night at the house so it'd be okay to bring her here."

"Where is she?"

"It didn't work out." Instead of looking at me, he stared at the TV as he spoke. "We didn't have the same ideas of being in bed together."

"She didn't want to experience the real Blue in bed?" I had to grin when I said it.

"Yeah, something like that." He still wouldn't look at me.

"So, we need to make a plan, Blue, to make sure that doesn't happen again."

"Even if we had a plan, today would've happened. You weren't here, remember? It should've been fine."

"Right, but if it's going to happen, text me or leave something on the door so I'll know."

"Fine, we'll do it your way."

My stomach chose that exact moment to growl louder than ever before. "I'd planned to come home and make dinner."

"You and Timms work up an appetite?" I knew this whole evening was spurred on by Timms' little scene at the house. Let him think what he wanted. He didn't want me, and I grew tired of waiting around for him to come around. Wasn't I allowed to have sex, too? I didn't question his choices.

"Maybe. Either way, I'm starving, and I know you are, so I'm going to make dinner." I went into the kitchen and opened the fridge. "Chicken?"

He moved to the doorway looking at me bent over digging in the fridge. "Yeah, sounds good to me." The look in his eyes made me wonder if he was in the mood for something else. That smoldering green caused my girlie bits to tighten up. Down girls. That won't happen.

I pulled the chicken and fresh green beans from the drawer. He took the beans from me and started washing and snapping them. He loved them both cooked and uncooked, so they were a safe bet every time.

We talked about the game while we cooked the meal together. He placed some rosemary carrots in the oven last. The meal smelled awesome when we sat down at the table.

"Thanks for cooking, Noelle. I appreciate it."

"You helped, too. Team effort, remember?"

"Also, nothing happened with Heidi."

"None of my business. You're a grown man. Do what you want."

"Right. I don't owe you an explanation, but I wanted you to know nothing happened. When we got in the bedroom, I wasn't feeling it. Just wasn't in it with her." He reached over and laid his hand on mine throwing me off completely. "I just wanted you to know." He looked down where he held my hand captive and moved it to pick up his fork. "Looks great. I'm starving."

I stared at him for a full minute before I picked up my fork and started in on my plate. My confused brain barely told my hand to put the food in my mouth.

We ate the rest of the meal talking about nothing and everything. He'd met two freshmen players at XOX that he found comical but worthy of the spots they'd earned on the team. He didn't know much about them but felt like they would be assets to the team next year.

After we finished cleaning the dishes, he brought us both a beer, and we sat in the den. This time he sat on the couch beside me. Every move he made this evening threw me off.

I flipped on the TV to add some background noise to the room. Too much silence led to thinking. I wasn't sure thinking was a great idea for either of us.

"So, nothing went on with Heidi, huh? What happened?"

"Like I said, I wasn't feeling it. I told her so, and she agreed. She went home."

"Were you good with that?"

"Yeah. I was." He turned and looked at me. "Look, Noelle. When I watched Timms carry you up those steps, it squeezed my heart like something I hadn't ever felt before. I couldn't decide if I was pissed off, hurt, disappointed, or what. I knew I didn't like it."

I nodded in response. I didn't know what else to do. We were breaking into some new territory here. What was he expecting from me?

"I don't know what's happened since we moved in here, but I keep getting this possessive feeling when it comes to you. I tried to deny there could be something more in the beginning. When you'd had too much to drink, and we fooled around with a little oral sex, I knew then I had to back away. I thought I could do it. I've had female friends in high school. I never wanted to be with them. I can't do this with you."

Nothing was stopping me this time. If he rejected me this time with his admission, then I'd know it was me. I refused to believe it was, though. I think we both scared each other. I leaned over and grabbed the front of his t-shirt pulling him toward me. I kissed him harder than I'd ever kissed a guy.

In less than a minute, he took over. He hauled me into his lap. When that wasn't enough, he pulled one leg over until I was straddling him. He held me so tight and so close, I couldn't think. His kiss stole my breath, but I didn't care. His tongue sought entrance, and we started a dancing duel for control—it set me on fire.

His hands slid down my back to my ass cheeks and pulled me to his rock-hard cock. Through my yoga pants and his warmups, nothing was left to the imagination. I could feel the crown against my swollen clit, and it scorched my senses. I knew I was going to come from the friction. It was the heaven I'd been seeking and yet to find with him.

He continued to work me against him until he finally broke the kiss. His eyes were dark emerald green, and I knew we were both in too deep to not see this through. He grabbed the bottom of my t-shirt and pulled it over my head with my sports bra following. His hands found both breasts at the same time.

Starting under my ear, he left kisses and nips as he worked his way down to his hands and fingers that assaulted the hot skin of my nipples, which stood at attention begging for his attention. He rolled my hardened nipples between his fingers until his lips closed over one peak and then the other. While his teeth and tongue lavished easy bites and licks, his thumb and index finger tweaked and pulled unmercifully at the other.

My body responded with voluntary grinding in a dance it knew without being taught. I couldn't get close enough to him to reach the ending I desired the most. He let me go long enough to lose his shirt. I ran my hands down the hot skin of his pecs and lower to the cut abs I ached to run my tongue down. When my hands reached the tied drawstring below his waist, he let go and grabbed my hands and moved them behind me, holding them with one hand. The other went back to knead the aching he'd left.

"No." He bit down on my nipple sending sparks straight to my core.

"No? Blue, it's okay."

"No." He ran his tongue around the nipple and blew cool air causing it to harden more than I thought it could. "You said you might be willing to try my way. Did you mean it?"

"Does it mean we can continue what we've started?"

He looked up at me. "Only if you're okay with it."

I nodded my head. He let go of my hands and wrapped his arms tight around me pulling our chests together. The slight bit of coarse hair on his tanned body continued to tease my tender nipples as he walked down the hallway taking us both to his room.

Thinking about what we were about to do excited me even more, but the fact he'd come to the conclusion that we could give this a try... this had me squirming in his arms and rubbing up and down him.

"Be still." He swatted my ass. "The last thing I want to do is drop you right now." He kissed me hard again. He pushed the door closed with his foot but never broke the kiss. We fell together on the bed. He pressed against my clit and rubbed the length of himself up and down me.

"Oh, God, it feels so good, Blue." I kissed his neck and chest and even ran my tongue over the flat disc on his chest causing him to push down harder on me before he started sliding down my body. He dropped open mouth kisses across my breasts, then across my stomach as he worked his way down.

When he reached the tops of my pants, he pulled the tight material and stood off the end of the bed taking them and my thong all at once. "Your body is perfection, Noelle. If I had my way, we could stay here all weekend and never cover you up so I could admire every angle of you."

The hooded green eyes wandering over my nakedness left me feeling exposed. I pulled up one leg bending it at the knee in a wasted attempt to cover myself from him. His lips curved slightly upward. "No, babe. There's no reason to be shy. Every inch of you waiting to feel my touch makes me want you even more." His palm wrapped around my ankle and dragged it inch by inch down the sheet, allowing him to look at me. He moved to stand over me and started at my ankle. The kisses he planted in a line down the inner side of my calf were warm from his open mouth. Then he reached my knee, and then my thigh, pushing my legs further apart as he worked his way where I wanted him.

"Please, Blue. Please."

"Please what, babe?"

"I need you inside me. As great as this is, I've waited so long, and I want to feel you touching me in all the perfect places. I just need it, please."

"How can I deny you with that kind of request?" He reached over the side of the bed and pulled a wide piece of black satin ribbon. Taking both of my hands in his one, he moved them above my head. Straddling me, making sure to keep his weight on his knees, he tied my hands together and to the headboard.

"Are you sure you're okay with this, Noelle? If you ever feel afraid or worried or it hurts, just say stop, and I'll let you go. I won't have you scared in any way."

"Blue, it's okay. I get it. It makes you feel safe so you can give yourself to me the way I'm giving myself to you. I'm not afraid."

He kissed me, heating my senses all over again. His tongue slowly made its way to wrap around mine, his rough side connecting with my smooth. When he pulled back, he looked down at me. "Pull your arms and see how it feels."

I did, and it was loose enough for some movement away from the wooden slats, but my hands wouldn't come loose. "It's good."

"You're sure?"

"Blue, I'm fine. Now quit asking. You're ruining the moment." I popped up as much as I could and kissed him. He broke the kiss and pulled the elastic strapped night mask from beside the bed, slipping it over my head.

"Still good, babe?"

"Still good."

"Is it freaking you out?"

"No, but it's different." I turned my head left and right trying to follow his voice. I felt him move off the bed and heard the soft whoosh of his clothes hitting the floor. A feeling of vulnerability hit me, and my breathing became more labored.

"Noelle?" I felt him over me. "Babe, what's going on?"

"Nothing. I'm good."

"No, you're breathing funny."

"I'm a little nervous, Blue. Promise you won't leave me here like this?"

He rolled beside me. "Maybe we should stop. You're not comfortable with it."

"No. I am comfortable, but I'm unsure."

"Noelle. Do you trust me?" I felt his hand on my stomach softly running a finger around my navel. "Think about my finger. Nothing else." After he'd done that a few times, my breathing calmed some. "Babe, you didn't answer me. Do you trust me?"

"Ye... yeah... yes, Blue, I trust you."

"But you're nervous. You're stuttering which you do when you get nervous."

"Yes, I am nervous. I can't see and can't feel, Blue. Promise you won't leave me here."

He pulled one eye of my blinder up. "I'm right here, babe, not going anywhere. Right here, all the time."

"Okay. I'm good." He put it back in place.

His hand was still on my stomach. "Now where were we? Oh, yeah." He circled my navel again, but this time he leaned over and licked my nipple. "Your tits are awesome, Noelle. Beautiful, plump, soft, perfect." His words accompanied his finger as it traced down toward the small line of hair I kept trimmed short but not shaved. "And this." He touched the line of hair. "I like it. You look like a woman."

"Good?" I supposed that was a compliment.

"Hell, yeah, it's good. Who wants to go to bed with a girl? Not me. Puberty was a long time ago." He slid his finger between my folds and touched the swollen bundle of nerves that had been ignited but cooled off. It only took one brief flick to come to life again.

He sucked on my nipple hard this time and circled my clit before giving it a little pinch. I arched off the bed. "Oh my God, Blue."

"Yeah, babe. Just making sure you're ready. I want this first time to be the best ever, and having you ready for me makes it better for both of us." Two fingers traced down to my opening before circling both sides while his thumb worked my clit, and he kissed, sucked, and licked my nipple. When he slipped one and then two fingers in me, I felt the orgasm building.

I started bucking off the bed trying to get him to speed up his movements. My head jerked from side to side seeking what my body craved. The sensitive walls convulsed and clamped down on the two fingers he moved in and out pushing me further and further until I cried out with the ecstasy we both chased.

"Breathe, babe. Just breathe." His kisses started slowly at my jaw and worked up to my temple while he uttered soft words calming me from the frenzy of his creation.

"Damn, babe. I've never seen your face look more beautiful than at this moment. So worth the wait."

"No more waiting, please, Blue. No more."

I felt him move between my legs before I heard the sound of the package opening. He positioned the crown at my entrance. He lowered himself over me but kept the weight on his forearms. He pulled one leg up around his waist, and I automatically wrapped the other around his hips, so my heels pulled in on his ass cheeks. He pushed in far enough for his warmth to breach my slick passage. I bucked up again pulling him down, and he sank in all the way.

"Damn, Noelle. I was trying to take it easy."

"Fuck easy, Blue. I need you now." I knew my voice sounded desperate and maybe I was.

"Not a problem." He pulled out and slammed back into me, and the feeling was so damn good I thought I might faint from it, but instead, I cried out his name over and over.

"Holy shit. You're so damn tight, babe. Is this hurting you because it feels fucking perfect to me?"

"No, you're right. It's perfect." I pulled back moving him out some hoping for another hard thrust, but he sat back between my legs picking up my hips and pulling me to him over and over. Push. Pull. Push. Pull.

With each push, the hard motion went deep hitting that elusive spot most guys failed to find. Who knew elevating my ass this way would make him rub across it almost every time?

"God, it's so good, babe, so fucking good. I love being able to watch you this way with tits bouncing with each hard push. The way your body almost curls up when I pull you further on my cock. It's the best view ever." Looking for another way to please both of us, he leaned back over me and pulled my legs across his arms at the elbows causing his hard cock to plunge further than I thought it could reach. "Babe, you gotta get there. I am not gonna last much longer. It feels so good. I can feel it building up. I'm about to blow."

After moving to wrap my legs back around him, he put one hand between us finding my sensitive clit. When he rubbed across it with his calloused finger, he bit down on my nipple, and that was it for me. My eyes darkened, and I saw stars, my body seized up in a stiff pose that caused my toes to curl up as I screamed out, "Fuck, fuck, fuck."

I felt him frantically plunging inside me leaving no space between, as though the tip reached a stopping point. He made several short jerks inside me as he called out his pleasure. "Yes, babe. Oh yes, yes, yes."

A few minutes passed as we floated back to the reality of the living. "Fuck, Noelle. Breathing hurts. You killed me." He spoke between wheezes after rolling beside me. "Are you okay?"

"I'm killing you? You failed to mention gymnastics might be involved. And yeah, I'm good. I'd be better if I could see, though."

"Right." The bed moved. I heard clothing rustling around before the ribbon came loose from my wrists. The mask slid off my eyes causing me to blink with the dimness of the room helping to orient myself faster. Now I watched him lie back down beside me before snuggling me up to his warm side.

He took my hand in his and brought my wrist in front of his eyes. "No marks. Good. I'd never want to do anything to mar this beautiful skin. Make sure I see the other one when we get up, please." He kissed the wrists where the ribbon held me, pulled my arm across his body, and kissed my forehead.

The care offered surprised me. I didn't expect him to be as attentive to how his needs might affect me.

"Gymnastics, huh? Don't think I've ever been accused of using a floor routine in bed."

I raised up on my elbow to see his face. "What was up with suspending me between your legs and all the pushing and pulling?"

"I love it. I can get to your best parts easier. I can control the pace. You gotta admit the angle hit all the right places you want me to be. How is it wrong?"

"Wrong isn't the word I would use, more like awesome, and it's different than I've ever had."

"Let's call it an adventure instead of gymnastics, then." He pulled me back into him.

Lying there beside him felt right. I tried hard not to think, though. Thinking got me in trouble and overthinking was worse.

BLUE

I woke up huffing and puffing. I ran hard down the field, but I couldn't catch up with the ball. It managed to stay about ten yards ahead of me. Not a dream I liked to have but did sometimes. I realized no one was in bed with me, which is not how my night started. Where'd she go?

I grabbed my phone and saw 8:30 glowing at me. Shit, I had to get to class. She'd probably already left for hers. I stumbled into my bathroom and turned on the shower. I stuck my toothbrush in my mouth as I waited for the water to warm. I climbed in and leaned against the tile, thinking of our first night together. Damn, it was a sweet time.

As I woke up more, I decided maybe her being gone this morning was a good thing for us both. I mean, I didn't want it to ever be weird between us, but the morning after time can be tricky. Living together might get that way if we continued with the bedroom rodeo. This required me to do some thinking, and it was too damn early and not enough sleep.

Noelle and I normally met up at the Coffee Bean on Mondays—got to face her sometime. I wrapped the towel around myself and stepped out about the time the bathroom door opened. "What the fuck?" I reared back ready to hit whoever was coming through it.

"Blue?" Noelle's voice stopped me.

"Oh. It's you." She stood there with a cup of coffee in her hand.

She looked like I'd hurt her. "Sorry, I thought someone broke into the apartment. I thought you went to class."

"Class? Blue, it's only Sunday."

"What?"

"Yeah, you didn't sleep through an entire day. It's Sunday morning. I got up and made coffee. What'd you think?"

"I was getting ready to go to class. I thought you'd already gone to yours when you weren't in bed with me." The coffee cup she held out was warm in my hand. "Thanks for this. Smells great."

She edged her ass up on the counter with her steaming mug. "So, uh, ab... about last night."

"You're nervous again." I reached over and pressed a soft kiss on her edible looking lips. "Stop."

"Yes, sir."

"Sir? I like it." I grinned at her.

"Don't get used to it. You told me that like it was an order. I'm not good with taking orders, you know."

"Oh, yeah, and I'm not the head of anything."

"No, but you do have a nice head." She reached down almost slid her hand inside my towel before I grabbed her arm and brought it up and around my neck.

I pulled her off the counter and took the coffee out of her hand. "No hot coffee, please." I kissed under her ear and started down her neck, but apparently, she had other ideas. She wiggled out of my arms and started to drop to her knees, but I grabbed her by the shoulders and brought her back in front of me.

"Blue?" She gave me a strange look. "Don't you want me to?" She stopped and looked down at the tented towel. Damn a girl offering to give me head first thing in the morning and wood was bound to happen. "You know... don't you like that?"

"Yeah, I would like it, but not with you touching me."

"How am I supposed to do it if I don't touch you?" The look she gave me was almost comical if the situation had been different. As it was, there was nothing funny about it.

I rarely ever let girls do it. Not that I didn't like getting a blowjob because damn, what guy didn't? But damn, there had to be rules about it. Most girls weren't into rules as much as spontaneity for dropping to their knees.

"It's done all the time. You've gotta let me tie your hands behind your back and put your blindfold on."

"You want me to give you head with my hands tied behind my back?"

"Yeah, if you want to." We stared at each other for what seemed like forever. Neither of us backing down. There was no way in hell she would be touching my dick and possibly coming in contact with my half sac. Hell no, wasn't happening.

"Blue. We've had the best sex of my life. I've felt every important part of you inside me. I think it's safe to say I will be okay with whatever it is you've got hanging between your legs."

"You're right. I know you're right. It was the best sex ever, but you touched nothing, and that's the way it has to be, Noelle. No touching my junk."

She gave me a hard look for a few seconds, picked up her mug, and stomped out of my bedroom. Yeah, I knew this wasn't going to work.

We avoided each other most of the day. Out at the XOX house, I watched some football with my boys for the afternoon. Timms came home when the first game started. I wanted to hurt him for whatever went on with him and Noelle, but I knew I didn't have the right to bust his balls over it since I'd taken home someone else.

He wandered into the kitchen and came back out unscrewing a beer bottle. "Sup?"

"Not much. You?" My mind rolled over all kinds of words I wanted to say, but I played it cool.

"Nothing. Been over at Madelyn's."

"What?"

"Madelyn. You know the little cheer pussy who hangs out here waiting on whatever scraps I'll give her."

"Dude, I know you don't like her all that much, but that's just fucked up you to talk about her like that."

"Why? She's cool with it. Never says shit about what I say as long as I make sure she's the one getting a piece of this." He grabbed his junk and laughed. "She knows what I like, too. We're both a little freaky sometimes." He looked over the top of his bottle. "But hey, nothing like you are. We like to watch and be watched. You know what I'm talking about."

Yeah, I knew what he meant but him talking about her that way bothered me. Why did women allow themselves to be debased that way?

He must have known the topic pissed me off because he changed the subject. "So where's your little piece today?"

"I know you're not referring to Noelle that way, dude."

He threw up his hands offering no resistance. "Sorry man. Didn't know it was like that. Thought you two were only friends."

"Doesn't matter what the fuck we are. Don't refer to her as a piece." I kept my voice calm. I didn't want to get into it with Timms. He was my teammate. We needed to work together. "Let's not bring her up, okay? I think it'd be better for both of us."

"That's cool." He took a long swig of his beer. "But you do know she was here last night with me right? I mean, we did get in bed together."

He tested me with every word out of his mouth.

"Yeah, and I know how it ended, too. Must have been laughable." He laughed out loud when I said that, since he knew I was telling the truth. "And all you need to know is that she came home last night."

"Came home to your—" I knew I'd surprised him by the tone of his voice.

"Sure did." I never took my eyes off the TV.

"So you two try out your famous knots?"

"Dude, you know I'm not one for sharing." I took a drink from my bottle.

"You talked her into your kink-ass bed. Dude, I'm impressed with your abilities with the women." He laughed so loud the other guys looked over in our direction.

"Never said that, Timms."

"Didn't have to, shithead. It's what you're not saying that gave it away. She down for your fun and games then?"

"Not talking about it."

"Ohhh. Maybe you didn't hit it then."

"Not talking about it."

"She any good?" He couldn't help himself.

"Stop fucking talking about it," I said each word with a bite to them.

"Okay. Don't get all pissed off. If you'd just admit to it, then I wouldn't have to keep guessing."

"Stop guessing, asshat. It's none of your damn business."

"Oh, yeah. She's got your ball in a twist. Better straighten that shit out, dude. You know what happened last time you did that." He started laughing so hard he couldn't catch his breath.

I knocked back the last of my beer and walked to the door.

"Don't leave mad, Half sac. Getting angry won't change shit. You're still gonna love me tomorrow," he called after me while the rest of the guys watched.

I didn't want to go back to the apartment and face Noelle. I needed to get this shit nailed down in my brain before I could talk to her again. Where could we go with this? Was I ready to try having a relationship? I'd never actually had a long lasting one. In high school, I dated a girl once or twice, and that was it.

Mostly I hung out with my friends and left them alone, hence being a virgin going off to college. Noelle was a great girl—smart, fun, pretty. I'd thought of all this before when we first met. Could I try to explain myself to her? Was I willing to divulge my private life that way? Hell, I didn't know. I needed to talk to Jenko. He'd help me wrap my head around it. He'd been there all along. He knew the real situation.

I picked up my phone and shot him a text before I left the house.

Me: *Sup*
Jenko: *watching the game. You saw me here, dumbass*
Me: *Go with me to drink a beer*
Jenko: *You buying*
Me: *Sure*

It wasn't long before he walked out the door. He turned up the bottle and downed the beer before throwing it in the garbage can that sat on the XOX front porch all the time. He opened the door to my truck and climbed in.

"What's up, dude? You sounded needy."

"Don't talk to me like that. You know I'm not needy or a little bitch." I laughed as I drove off. We landed at the sports bar across from campus. Not too many people came in here on Sunday afternoon, which was good because I didn't need others hanging around.

"Wings and two beers, please," I told the waitress and watched Jenko admiring her ass as she walked away.

"Whoa. Now that's a fine ass right there."

"Right. Like you'd know a fine from a flat one."

"Dude. Where'd you sleep last night because I know what thighs I spent the night between."

"Nevermind. I'm not here to listen to your half-ass truths."

"Nothing half-assed about Cora's sweet spot. It's all perfect." He wiped a hand down his face. "Wore this bad boy out. I've been chilling all day after one night with her so I could drag my sorry ass to class and practice tomorrow."

"Are you admitting what others have known all along? You're a one and done guy? Not talking about a notch on your bedpost and you know it. No stamina, dude."

"Shut the fuck up. I'm good for three to four a night, and you know it."

"Uh, no, I don't know it. Don't want to know it either."

We laughed. He always knew how to make me laugh, but what I wanted to talk about wasn't a laughing matter to me. Everyone who knew the real deal, knew it could get to me sometimes. I look deformed like I'd been born with a birth defect or something. What guy wants a woman looking at his junk and laughing at the abnormality of it.

My dad assured me when I recovered from the surgery that everything would be fine. When the right woman came along, she would understand. Was Noelle the right woman? I'd never even considered telling a female about being one ball short of normal. I mean, I didn't stand and look at myself in the mirror or anything, but sometimes I caught a view, and it freaked me out. It made me feel like a loser.

"So, honestly, Blue. What's going on, dude?" He knew this was serious or I'd never opt to talk about it.

I looked down at the beer label and scraped on it. "I like Noelle... a lot."

"That's a start. How much a lot are we talking?"

My eyes finally raised up to his. I couldn't answer this. I didn't know how.

"You talking enough to be honest with her, or just enough to do a little sheet dancing?"

"Jenk, man, I don't have to like them to do 'sheet dancing' with them." I air quoted him.

"So, how much then? Gonna take her home to meet momma?"

"She's already met my mom and dad."

"What's going on then, Blue? I can't help you if you don't talk to me, bro."

The cute waitress came out with the wings and handed us napkins. She couldn't take her eyes off Jenko. Shit, I wanted to talk about Noelle, and he wanted to hit on the waitress.

"Forget I mentioned it. Just watch the game." I shoved the basket over his way.

"No, dude. No. You know I'm here to help you. I've always been here for you, dude. Now talk to me." He tore into the wings while I continued to peel on the label. "Are you afraid to use your toys on her?"

"No, we did that."

He looked up at me with his eyebrows raised up. "Really? Well, that's a step in the right direction. I'm taking it she ran screaming?"

"No, she didn't run. It was some good shit, too."

"Okay. Kinda weird, dude, but glad you liked it." He continued looking at his wings. I think he didn't want to look me in the eyes, which was fine by me.

"But the next day when we might have gone at each other again, she wanted to touch me and well... she got down on her knees—"

"You're killing me, Blue. Please don't tell me she was on her knees to give you head and you turned her down." Now he's staring at me.

"Yeah, something like that. I think I hurt her feelings or made her mad or something."

"Well, I can see why. She lets you do all your dumb-ass shit, and she's still willing to blow you, and you turn her down? You probably pissed her off. I mean, how often does a guy turn down a blowjob? Uh, *never!*" He throws the eaten wing in the basket and downs half the beer.

"Yeah, that's pretty much how it was. She got all pissed off and left. Now I gotta go home and face her."

"That damn sure doesn't sound like a place I'd want to be going tonight."

"I know. I should just strip down and show her. Hell, if she goes running, then I'll know we haven't got a chance. But if she laughs, just shoot me. So I'm telling you, I need to borrow that pistol your dad gave you."

"Uh, no, I don't even have the damn thing at school. It's locked up in Dad's gun safe at home. Besides, if she doesn't go running, then you'll know it's okay with her."

"But what if she's not the one? What if we decide we aren't each other's one and end it? She'll know. Others will want to know, and she'll tell them."

"Dude. She's not fucking like that, and you know it. Look, I don't know her all that well, but she doesn't strike me as someone who does a lot of gossiping.

"Right. She's not."

"Then why do you think she'll go spreading private shit anyway?" He picked up his last wing and finished it off. "Look, Blue. You're friends, you're roommates, and you've had sex once. I'm not thinking you're ready for this heart-to-heart shit yet. Why don't you give it some fucking time? If she's down for your kinky ropes and masks, why not let that ride for now?"

I finished my beer and waved our empties at the waitress for another. "Yeah, you're probably right. It's too soon. If she's willing to continue as we are for now, maybe I can work up to letting her in on why I'm Half sac."

"Great. Now eat your wings, and I'll order me some more. The hot little thing's headed back over here."

NOELLE

As I moped around all day, the incident in the bathroom this morning controlled my thoughts. Everything about Blue was something I liked, but I fought with myself over his idea of enjoyable sex. Blue was a great guy, fun, ambitious, and according to Timms, smart but liked keeping it to himself. And then there was the matter of him being drop-dead gorgeous with a smile that lit up the room. And that damn hair and hot body drove me insane just thinking about it.

So what if he had a problem with me seeing and apparently touching him intimately. The touching thing only dealt with that one, yummy area. Could I live with that? Hey, if he didn't want me to reciprocate on oral, who was I to argue? Everyone had their quirks, right? The argument in my head played over and over all day.

When it came down to it, what bothered me the most was he didn't trust me enough to let me judge for myself. Shouldn't I get to decide that whatever he kept to himself would be a problem for me? Trust. I knew I needed to earn his complete trust. Could I bide my time and let him see, no matter what, he could trust me?

I was determined to talk to him the minute he walked through the door, so I studied and watched mindless TV. As the doorknob turned, I put my thick biology book down. When he stepped inside, immediately our eyes met. He walked in and sat down beside me, so our thighs touched.

"Hey," I softly spoke.

"Hey, yourself." The awkwardness drifted away the longer we sat.

"Listen," we both said it at the same time and started laughing.

I turned sideways and faced him. "You go first."

"Thanks because I want to say something important to you."

"Good, I have something important to say, too."

He took my hand and laid it in his lap, our fingers intertwined. "I'm sorry about this morning. I want you to know that I wasn't trying to be a dick about what you wanted to do. It scared me is all. I panicked and didn't handle it well. I should've considered if what I said would hurt you, and all I thought about was it hurting me."

"Yeah, it did kinda hurt my feelings, Blue. I won't lie. I felt like a ho begging to blow you down on my knees like that."

"I'd never think of you that way, Noelle." The honesty of his face told me it was true. "You have to know that. It's just... I have some problems, and it's something only a few people know the real story. I don't talk about it, and those who know don't talk about it. Some of the team know that I have this situation, but they don't know the story. Believe me, they don't even ask."

"Right. I get it. I wanted to say I'm sorry, too. I see now that it's extremely private, and we've only been together once, and I mean, we're not really together-together, and we've only had sex and fooled around a little, and you've been inside..." Before I could finish this long rant I was on, he grabbed behind my neck and pulled me into a fierce kiss. Maybe it was to shut me up. Maybe he thought I needed it. Hell, maybe he needed it.

When we finally came up for air, he pulled me across his lap. "Noelle, I want us to be together-together. Like exclusive. I want to build this trust thing with you. I need time. If you're willing to work through this with me, I believe we can get there. Together."

"Together." My smile stretched across my face. "I can work with that, Blue."

"Can you handle the idea of the ropes and blinders for a while?" He looked so sincere, I wouldn't turn him down even if I couldn't stand being tied and blinded.

"Yes, Blue. I'm willing to do whatever it takes to get us through this."

"Together."

"Together."

He kissed me again, and I moved over to straddle his lap. My hands slid up his hard biceps loving the feel of smooth skin and flexed muscles. As I reached his shoulders, the ends of his soft hair shifted across my hands. My hands slid up under it at the back of his sinewy neck. Damn, the guy had muscles everywhere I touched. My nails raked up through the dark blond hair, and I felt a shiver run down his back. Funny how it shot straight to my core, and I couldn't help myself from grinding against his growing length nestled between us.

He kissed down my neck and leaned me back so he could continue a path to my breast. Between nips of the delicate skin, he whispered. "Let's take this to the bedroom and test your theory, babe."

"Good plan. You got a ribbon, right?" I held him to me so he would continue the licking and biting assaulting my hardened nipple over my tank.

"Yeah, always." A growl left his mouth as I raked down his head and over his neck.

"Great idea, Blue."

He stood, and I wrapped my legs around his waist. "Together starts now, Noelle."

"Yes, right now."

Blue slammed his door shut with this foot.

Finding the words to describe the next three weeks of our togetherness were impossible when Quinn and I sat down to watch the last away game. The team traveling every single weekend left us lonely and needy. Two good things that came from the away games were, that Blue and I were ravenous for each other when he returned and spent the following week making up for the days we were apart, and the team won all their games.

"I'm so fucking glad they play at home next week." Quinn opened the door to Chewz.

"Yeah, I'm getting tired of sleeping alone two nights a week."

She leaned in. "Right, but damn it's been the best sex ever when Gerrod returns from the winning game. He's all horny and excited for me that he can fuck forever."

"Forever?" I looked at her.

"Yeah, do you know how many big O's he can give me in that amount of time. Dammit, that makes me wet thinking about it."

She has no filters which always makes me laugh. "No more talk about sex, please."

"Okay, Debbie Downer. Order me another glass of wine while I pee, and let's watch our hunky guys in their tight-ass football pants." She slid off the tall stool grabbing her purse.

She returned as the ball sailed above the field to the other team's receiver. As we watched each down, it became apparent how evenly matched the two teams were. By halftime, the score was tied at twenty-one.

"Ugh. They better come back ready to play harder this next half," I told Quinn. "Losing is not an option this late in the season."

"Right. They'll be bummed sons of bitches if they lose. That..." she looked me in the eye, "... does not make for good welcome-home sex."

I nodded my head in agreement as the Rams gained possession of the ball. Timms ran on the field ready to start the first set of downs. We prayed it was the beginning of several before they scored. They ran several running plays eating up yardage each time and making several first downs in a row.

When Blue and that freshman kid, Powell, came in together, I knew Timms would be throwing a long pass down the field. The experienced quarterback dropped back to pass with plenty of time for Blue and Powell to make their way into the red zone of the opposing team, the Stallions. He found his man, and we watched as a beautifully thrown arc landed directly in Blue's hands at the eighteen-yard line. He zigged and zagged around the player sent to defend him before making it to the six. The stadium's volume rose to record pitch with Stallions' fans' happiness that we'd been prevented from scoring.

The excitement died down quickly when everyone realized a player was hurt. I jumped off my barstool and got closer to the screen. I knew it wasn't Blue, but it could be Gerrod, but anyone injured worried us all. The usual crazy crowd at Chewz stood still watching the scene unfold.

As the name of the player came across the audio, everyone stood with their mouths hanging open. Timms' injury had to be bad. They brought in a stretcher and a cart to put it him on. Quinn and I held our breath waiting for any morsel of information. Timms being sidelined would devastate the team. Not only was he a great quarterback, but he kept the team in line. His leadership both on and off the field helped make the players into the winners they all were.

The announcer finally said that it appeared to be a knee injury, and he would be taken off for X-rays and examination in the locker room. He would probably be out for the remainder of the game.

I'd met the new backup quarterback, Crew Devillier, when I met Powell. With Timms in his senior year, the coach had him working with Crew after practice to get the kid up to speed for college ball. The coaching staff seemed pleased to have the two working together, and I'd heard Timms talking more than once about how natural the kid was at the position. Guess we'd all be finding out now since Crew put his helmet on and sprinted to the huddle formed behind the line.

We all knew how important winning was, but Timms' injury weighed heavily on my mind. This guy lived to play pro ball. It was his plan after graduation. I had no idea what his major was. Would a knee injury take that out of the realm of possibilities? These guys lived and breathed football. How would he take not getting to play? My mind thought of all the worst cases, and I knew I needed to be more positive.

I returned to my stool and climbed on downing the rest of my wine. "What do you think, Quinn?"

"I think this is shit. Why do they put so damn much importance on playing a game that could leave them crippled or brain dead?" She shook her head. I knew she only watched football to support her guy, but I'd never heard her be so down on the sport.

"This is their life, Quinn."

"Yeah, and what's Timms' life going to be if he never plays another game? His entire future is based on a stupid fucking game. And now what, huh? I'm not sure I can watch more of this shit today." She got up and pulled her stool around the table putting her back to the big screen we were watching.

"Okay, let's think positive thoughts. It might not be as bad as they say. It could just be for precautions."

She nodded her head. "Yeah, say some prayers."

It turned out that prayers for his knee went unanswered. With a torn ACL, surgery was imminent. He never came back from the locker room. Instead, a freshman took over leading the team to victory and received the much-deserved game ball in the locker room. The team flew back to Texas after the game with Timms on crutches and painkillers.

Sitting on pins and needles, I tried to write a paper at our kitchen table while I jumped at every noise that sounded like a car in front of our apartment. With a pretty good idea of the kind of mood Blue would be in when he walked through the door, I wanted to be there to greet him. We needed to share the good times and the bad.

He poked his head through the doorway looking around. Once he spotted me, he barged through the door and walked straight to me. I stood so he could pull me into a tight hug we both needed. I didn't let go until he backed away and pulled me with him to the couch.

"It's bad, huh?" I pulled his hair out the bun at the back of his head so I could run my fingers through it.

"Yeah, it's really bad. He'll be having surgery any time now or maybe tomorrow. The team doctors wanted to get him back here before they made a damn decision. I don't know why they waited on us. Hell, they could have brought him home earlier and got started." He pulled my hand to his mouth and kissed my palm before leaning his cheek into it.

"Did you get to talk to him?"

He shook his head. "Too out of it on the painkillers they gave him."

"I'm sorry, Blue. Truly sorry it happened to him. How bad will the team struggle without him?"

"Hell, if I know at this point. The kid's good. He proved that today against a tough team. Didn't seem phased at all by the stadium noise or the stress of coming in last minute like that. He settled down and did his job. Made me wonder if he's used to it all, but he's a freshman, so I know he's not played in the college arena before."

"Who knows. Guess y'all be getting to know him a lot better now."

"Looks that way." His stomach decided to growl like he hadn't eaten in days.

"You haven't eaten, have you?" I smiled at him because I knew better than to ask if he was hungry.

"Yeah, I could eat."

"Good because I cooked lasagna while I waited for you. I know it's one of your favorite things and decided today might be a good time for it."

"Thanks, babe." He pulled me over for a slow kiss. "I had a lot of time to think on the plane today about what my life would be like if I didn't have you in it. I'm glad I had you to come home to today. I wouldn't want to be alone right now or maybe ever."

I wrapped my arms around him. I knew it was too soon for the big 'L' word. I think we both knew it. We wouldn't be living together except for the roommate situation either. I knew my feelings for him were heading in that direction, though. I could only pray his were, too, and with this admission, I was fairly certain it was.

BLUE

"Damn, Noelle, that was excellent lasagna. You've been holding out on me." I leaned down and kissed her forehead when I picked up her empty plate and went to the sink.

"No, I've been saving it for the right time. It's a little extra work, so it's gotta be a weekend meal. The best part is it makes a boatload of food at once so we can eat on it for a couple of days." She finished off her water and turned to the sink and started laughing. The guilty look on my face had to be comical. Busted. I stood over the stove and lasagna pan, shoveling in more of the cheesy pasta.

"Blue, fix another plate if you're still hungry."

"No, I'm not hungry, but it smells so fucking good and tastes outstanding." I took one more big bite. "I can't tell you how long it's been since I had it."

"Thank you. I'm glad you're enjoying it. I'll try to make it more often now that I know how much you love my cooking."

"Oh, hell, yeah. Make it whenever the mood strikes you." I put the fork down and covered the dish before placing it in the fridge. "Outta sight, outta mind."

"You're so crazy." She stepped beside me at the sink, and we filled the dishwasher before returning to the couch.

I laid down and pulled her on top of me. "Can we just lay here a while, babe?"

"Sure. I love sprawling on your big warm body."

I wrapped my arms around her and closed my eyes. "Damn this feels great."

Her warm body and long legs entangled in mine caused my dick to get other ideas. Her leg brushed across it making it grow even harder.

She raised up and looked at me. "Looks like someone has something else on his mind."

"That's the little head talking. Dammit. His thoughts are always on one thing." I pulled her thigh down on my rock-hard cock pumping up and down it.

"One day, you're going to let me touch you for real." She sighed, and her warm breath drifted across my ear and neck. Fuck, it felt good. I moved her all the way on top of me, and she lowered her lips to mine.

Her full pink lips ghosted across mine before she sucked in my lower lip and nibbled on it.

My mind couldn't get off the idea of her wrapping those lips around my dick and looking up at me through those gray eyes of hers. I ground her down on my length, and she moaned into my mouth as her tongue wrestled with mine. Shit, I'd never wanted a girl to give me head so badly that I ever remember before this.

She sat up and pulled her top off leaving her in a thin, pink, lacy bra. Her pert nipples stretched at the material.

"You know that makes your tits look good enough to eat, but why do you even bother with something like that?"

"It's called a bralette."

"Waste of money, except damn, makes me need to taste them through it." I sat up and took one in my mouth as I palmed the other while I twisted the nipple. The lace created a little more friction for her, and she ground down on my aching dick leaving us both breathing harder and moaning for more.

I kissed across the tops of the smooth flesh and then lowered the straps, so the pink bunched around her waist before finding the wet skin of uncovered pebbles. "I like them all rosy from my teeth nipping at them." She must have liked it, too, because her grinding grew more forceful.

"Blue?"

I popped the tip out of my mouth. "Yeah, babe?" I ran my tongue around the skin surrounding the peak as she looked down at me.

"Let me taste you just this once." Her breathing was heavy with need.

I stopped biting and looked up at her. "Babe, if you only knew how badly I wanted you to but, fuck, I don't know if I can."

She kissed me lightly never opening her eyes. "We can do it. I'll wear the blindfold if it makes it easier." Her lips stayed against mine as she continued the movement up and down my swollen dick.

Did I trust her enough to allow it? No girl had ever had my dick in their mouth. My imagination ran wild with the thought of sliding it over her tongue hitting the back of her throat. Would she let me come in her mouth? Hell, if she didn't, it still had to be the best feeling ever knowing she wanted to suck me off.

She would never use it against me. I knew she would understand. We'd used the blinders and ropes a lot now and not once had she balked when I brought them out. Surely we could advance to something more intimate, and we'd both enjoy it. Shit, I'd be in deep-throat heaven for the first time ever. Oh, hell, yeah.

"Noelle, let's go to my room." She pulled back and looked at me.

"You're going to let me?" she barely said it loud enough for me to hear her.

"Yeah, I'm willing to try."

She jumped up and took off down the hall.

"Who's more excited about this?"

"Me," she yelled enthusiastically, and I laughed. My dick smiled so much, he spat a little extra precum as I walked.

She sprawled naked in the middle of the bed as though she waited for me to give her directions. "What the hell are you doing?"

"Waiting."

"Okay?"

She rolled on her side, and I pulled the box out from under the bed. "I'm willing to try this however you want to do it, Blue. I'm waiting for you to tell me, sir."

I whipped my head around and looked at her. "I am not a sir, babe. That's not the kind of thing this is, and you know it."

She laughed. "I know. I was being funny."

"Ha ha. No sirs around here."

"Got it, master."

"Very funny." I rolled over toward her with the blindfold and the rope. "So I guess I'll put this on you, and then I'll tie your hands behind your back. You can sit up that way." I looked at her judging the way she'd take those directions. "Wait, are you sure you're okay with this?"

"Yes, Blue. I told you. However you want to try it, I'm good. I don't mind the bindings."

"This seems staged, but my dick thinks it's fine with staged. What about you?"

"I already told you I'm good. However, let's just do it."

She turned around and clasped her hands together so I could wrap them in the satin ribbon. Next, I picked up the blinder and pulled it down over her head covering her eyes.

I kissed her hard bringing the desire we'd started on the couch back to the both of us. When I pulled back and broke the kiss, I wrapped my arms around her. "I'm gonna pick you up and sit you on the floor by the bed. Should have thought of this before."

"Okay. You know you'll have to put it in my mouth, right?"

"Not a problem, babe. God, you look so good sitting there in front of me." With my bed as tall as it was, she was at a perfect height on her knees. I leaned down and kissed her again while I ran my hands down to her perfect nipples, tweaking them earning me a moan into my mouth from deep in her throat. All I could think about was how that would feel on my dick.

I broke the kiss, wrapping my hand around the hard shaft stroking it a few times before I tapped it on her lips. Her pink tongue tip slipped out and ran around across the top. With me in charge until she took it all in, I ran it across her tongue several more times. She took it upon herself to slip it across the slit where a bead had formed.

"Oh, yeah," she said, and again I tweaked the other nipple. She slipped the head into her mouth and ran her tongue around it.

"No, oh fuck. That feels so damn good, babe. You don't know how long I've dreamed of this happening."

Her entire body bowed over my hard cock, and she took it as far as she could down her throat. She worked it over, sucking, licking, and a little scraping until I pulled it out of her mouth.

"What's wrong?" she asked in a thick voice.

"Not a fucking thing, babe. I want you to do it some more, but I want to take your blindfold off. I need you to tell me I can do that and you'll keep your eyes on mine. Can you promise to do this? Can you only keep your beautiful eyes locked on mine? Tell me you can do it."

She nodded. "I promise I can do it. Please take the blindfold off, Blue. Please?"

I tapped the head against her lips again, and she opened up and sucked me back in. I slowly pulled the blindfold off her, and her gray eyes had a bright silver look to them.

"Oh fuck, babe. You look, damn… I can't even describe how this looks with your pink lips closed around my dick." She blinked her eyes quickly, and I saw tears pool up in them.

I pulled back. “Shit, did I push too far?” She slowly shook her head a little from side to side before she sucked it back down, and I felt her swallow it into her throat. Who knew she could do this? Damn, why had we waited so long?

I wrapped my fingers through her soft hair and pulled her back before pushing the length back in. She took charge and pushed the shaft further in hitting the back of her throat again before swallowing again. Over and over she did it.

“Babe, that feels so fucking good.” I tweaked on her nipple again all while keeping her eyes locked on mine. She moaned from the pleasure.

“Oh fuck, babe! I’m gonna come if you do that again.” She did it again without pulling back. “I’ll come in your throat.” She did it again, and I bucked forward from the intensity of it.

“I’m coming, babe. Right fucking now. Fuck, fuck, fuck, babe. Oh fuuuccckkk…” Each word sounded strained as my body pumped ropes of liquid down her throat.

The feeling was like nothing I’d ever had before. I dropped down on my knees directly in front of her and wrapped my arms around her. My labored breathing continued, and I couldn’t do anything but hold her close to me.

When we both could finally talk, I leaned back, and tears ran down her cheeks.

"Noelle? Did I hurt you?" She didn't answer. "Babe? Are you okay? What's wrong?"

Did I hurt her?

Did I fuck this perfect moment up somehow?

"Blue. Don't you see how much I trust you? Don't you see how important you are to me from this? I would never do anything to hurt you in any way. What we did here should prove that to you. Untie my hands and let me touch you. Let me touch you everywhere. Let me show you it's okay."

I looked at her. I'd never let anyone get this close to me. I didn't know if I could. I knew what she said was true. She'd just blown me, and it obviously meant a lot to her to swallow my come with her hands tied behind her back.

I'd moved down in front of her to keep her from seeing my deformity. I knew she'd guessed why I did it.

Would she laugh at me?

Would she think it was so weird that she wouldn't want to have sex again?

Would she find it gross or creepy?

"Blue, look at me." I pulled back, so we stared at each other. "No matter what it is you're afraid of, we can get through this together, remember? Together. Don't keep us apart over whatever this is."

"I know you're right, Noelle. I'm just..." I took a deep breath. "I'm afraid of how you'll see me. What if I creep you out?"

"Blue. What if you don't? Look at all the great sex we could have. Shower sex, spontaneous sex against the wall. Sixty-nining. We could do it all without anything between us. Hell, I'm on birth control. We could do it with nothing physical or mental between us."

"Damn... when you put it that way." I smiled at her. "But really, babe. I'm afraid. That's the honest truth."

"Then you're silly because nothing you show me could bother me enough to be creeped or grossed out about your body. You're beautiful inside and out, Blue. Let me know you... all of you... the good and the bad, the beautiful and the ugly. Whatever it is between us will be out in the open forever."

Her words were true and kind. I knew she spoke the truth to me. I knew she was trustworthy to allow me to be myself with her.

Finally, I nodded. "Okay. I can do it."

I reached behind her and untied the ribbon. I rubbed her wrists to restore all the feeling. I'd never kept her tied this long and knew the rush of feeling tingled in her hands. When I thought she was good, I took her hand and brought it around in front of her between us. Her fingers wrapped around my dick. If I'd been hard, I might have nutted right then from the sheer pleasure of having her hand touch me in such an intimate way. I moaned instead, and I felt it start to harden in her small grip.

She continued to rub a small amount up and down. I knew she felt nothing unusual since the movement stayed on my growing length.

"Blue?"

"Yeah, babe?"

"I don't understand. This feels normal."

"Thank God. There's nothing wrong with my dick, babe."

"Oh. Okay."

This was one strange conversation to have after sex, but she hadn't found the problem yet.

Did I help her find it?

Let her reach down and touch my nut and know?

Shit, this was weird to me, and I knew what was wrong.

She continued rubbing making me harder and harder until she brought the other hand around and double fisted my length causing me to bow over some.

"Fuck, babe. That feels so good. This is a first, too."

"Are you saying a girl's never touched you before? I get the honor of being first? This is like a virgin thing."

"Uh, no. I'm not a virgin."

"Not like that," she snickered at me. "Oops, sorry. I said I wouldn't laugh, but this isn't the same thing."

"Right, so get the giggles out of your mind right now, or we're done." The light mood made it better in some ways.

"I'm good. Promise." She stroked a few more times and then one hand ventured further down. Shit. Here it comes. Face the truth, Blue.

Her warm hand cupped my sac, and a gentle squeeze caused it to draw up because I fought the orgasm trying to happen from her touch. Concentration on too many things at once had my brain firing in all kinds of strange directions.

I had a gorgeous naked woman in my arms with one hand stroking my hard cock while the other carefully kneaded my nut sac with only one nut inside, with the other half somewhat shriveled up from lack of substance. This should be enjoyable to have female hands on my nut for the first time, my dick for the first time, and her hardened nipples scraping across my chest. I couldn't decide whether to be excited, petrified, or shooting my load.

"Blue?"

"Yeah, babe?" Shit, here it comes. She's freaked out.

"Do you only have one?" Her voice was still soft and deep from before.

"Uh, yes. Only one nut down there all lonely by itself, but he's excited to have your warm hand saying hello for the first time." Humor was the only way I could stand this.

"Did you lose it?"

"Uh, well, yeah in a way. I guess you could say I lost it."

"Were you born this way? I mean like it didn't drop or something?"

"No, babe. I had two in the beginning."

"Where did it go?" Her soft sound still deep.

"I had a football injury in my freshmen year of high school. They had to remove it, or I might have died."

"Thank God they did the surgery. How scary for you." She continued to cup the sac making it harder to talk with each light squeeze. This had to be the strangest sex I'd ever had. Her asking questions while fondling my nut and jacking me with her other hand. Damn, I'd been missing out for years on this feeling.

I leaned down and kissed her. "Babe, can we get in the bed? You're about to make me come all over your hand the way you're handling me down there, and as good as it feels I'd rather not."

"No, Blue, I'm so horny now. I'd rather you be fucking my brains out while I get to touch your body for the very first time. I may have an orgasm thinking about it."

I eased up the side of the bed taking her with me. She still hadn't seen it, but I couldn't worry about it. We rolled onto the bed barely able to keep our hands off all parts of each other's bodies. Fuck, this had to be the best sex in the history of sex.

I'd never had sex bareback before. I pushed inside her wet channel, and she wrapped her legs around my thighs holding me inside before she reached down with both hands and grabbed my ass cheeks pulling me in a little more. Oh, shit, I thought I was in fuck heaven. This was fucking as it should be. This was truth and trust, and maybe this was love.

NOELLE

The morning light managed to shine directly into my eyes. A giant arm across my stomach held me down. Ugh. I couldn't move. The weight of said arm felt like a brick, but when I turned and saw hair covering Blue's tanned face with scruff that I know left marks in divine places on me, my lips turned up in a smile. We'd rounded a huge corner last night.

I snuck a finger under the hair moving it back so I could get a few minutes to look at him while he slept. Damn, how did I get so lucky to find this guy when I wasn't even looking? The question now was where do we go from here. A quiet sigh escaped as I decided I didn't care at this point. Happiness was all that mattered and damn, finding words to express my happiness this very minute fell under the category of 'Not Available.'

He looked so peaceful sleeping on his stomach. The sheet covered those perfect ass cheeks that I sunk my fingers and nails into more than once last night. I think I remembered sinking my teeth into one of them, too. We slept off and on, but once we'd truly found each other, it was as though we couldn't get enough of exploring each other's body. My mind continued to replay last night's revelations.

Blue tried to put up a fuss when I kissed across his hard pecs and ran my tongue and nails over all the perfectly formed peaks and valleys of his abs, but I decided if we were going to break the ice on his hot body, it would be a total reveal. No more secrets, and, wow, he had kept some.

As my tongue circled his navel dipping in to offer an added zing to his hard length begging for my attention, I left open-mouth kisses down the light blond hair that led to the base of the massive erection standing proud and tall before me. I first wrapped my hand around it, my fingers being too short to cover the circumference. I could almost make it all the way around, though, so when I pulled up to the head, he felt the friction all over.

Kneeling beside him, I had total access, but so did he which made it awesome for us both. We both explored with hands and fingers, but my mouth got the best of the deal. I ran my tongue down the thick, engorged vein running the entire length from tip to base, but when I moved lower, he pulled my head back.

"No, babe. That's far enough."

"No, Blue. It's not anywhere close." He pulled my hair forming a curtain across his body back, so I captured his hooded eyes as I kissed closer to the prize. I knew his desire for what I wanted outweighed his fear because he never stopped my progress.

The bedside lamp glowed with a low soft beam. With my eyes still holding his captive, I grazed my tongue down and across the sac he worried over. It didn't feel different than any of the others I'd had my mouth before. My palm cupped the soft, smooth skin. Being blond, he had basically no hair anyway, so it didn't get in my way as I rolled the ball around in my fingers.

He bowed off the bed. "Oh, mother… Noelle. You cannot imagine how that feels."

"No, I can't, but I know how I feel when you use your lips and tongue on me, and if it's half as good as that, you probably feel like cloud nine isn't high enough."

He had a brief chuckle. "Yeah, you do know then."

Finally, I licked around the orb before putting it in my mouth.

"Ho-ly shiiittt, babe." He sat straight up and then leaned back on one hand. "I gotta watch. I don't think I can stand much of this."

As I easily tongued the single nut around, I decided one might be a good thing. Lots easier to handle in my mouth. I slid my finger down behind the sac and lightly rubbed the space back toward his entry.

"Oh no. One strange thing a night, and I'm not sure we'll ever go there anyway."

I smiled looking up at him before sliding the spit covered ball out of my mouth. "Not a problem, just teasing you." My lips kissed a path back up to the swollen pink head before I climbed on him and rubbed up and down his length.

"Girl you are going to be the death of me. My headstone will read: Died from the best head ever."

I laughed out loud until he pulled me forward to kiss me slow and deep. His forehead rested against mine. "Thank you, babe. Thank you so much."

"For?"

"For being you. For understanding. For not making this weird." His sincere words marked my heart with something new and perfect.

In one move, I was under him, and he kissed me softly as his head breached my opening. He slowly filled me inch by inch, his pelvis rubbing my clit with every move. This sex was different. It was slow and magical. It wasn't sex, it was sharing love. The love we made to each other with him kissing my lips and holding eyes to his until we both found the peak we sought, spoke volumes.

"You're awake." He smiled at me.

"Yeah, but I didn't want to wake you. You were sleeping so soundly, and I knew you were spent from the game."

"That was fun and games all right. Had to rate up there with the top." He grinned again.

"Top five, huh? That's it?" I tried to glare at him, but nothing would ruin our night.

"Well, there was my little league super bowl where I scored the winning touchdown, then when we won the state championship in high school two times, and then there was the first touchdown I scored here at TAU my freshmen year. Yeah, those were all great games. So this one is in the top five."

"You're a devil. Our night was perfection, and you damn well know it." I punched his arm.

"Owww. You hurt me."

"You big pussy. Get this monster arm off me. I swear it's caving in my stomach. How much does that thing weigh?"

He rolled over and flexed his bicep. "That, babe?" He flexes it again. "Pure muscle, and muscle weighs more." He stretched his arm out and caused other muscles to pop out along with veins.

"Quit making nurse porn with your arms. It's kinda gross." I scrunched up my nose.

"What? That's blasphemy, woman. Bite your tongue."

"You bite my tongue!" Instead, he reached over and sucked it into his mouth, and I immediately pulled it out.

"Ewww. No. I have morning breath." I jumped out of bed and headed to my bathroom to brush with him laughing.

"Yeah, but you have a pretty sweet ass staring at me with a couple of bite marks that weren't there yesterday." His laugh died off as he went into his bathroom.

"Why didn't you join me in the shower?" I asked as I walked through the kitchen doorway.

"First, I figured you might be a little sore, and second, I needed to eat something."

"Right, you're starving." I shook my head. When would I ever learn?

"Yeah, and I want to go see what's happening with Timms as soon as I'm done."

"Good idea. I know he'd probably like to see all y'all. He's probably sick of parents and doctors.

"I'm sure you're right." He placed two plates of eggs and toast on the table, so I joined him.

"What kind of plans do you have for the day?" he asked after his first bite.

"I've gotta finish my paper that's due tomorrow."

"K." He'd already finished before I'd taken two bites. He stood and threw away his paper plate. "I'll see you back here later then."

"Sounds good." He kissed me on the top of the head before heading out. As he opened the door, he turned. "Hey. Last night was the best, babe. You know that, right?"

I smiled at him. "I do."

He smiled back and shut the door. Now, how was I supposed to think about anything else after those parting words?

I finished eating and gathered my materials when the door opened. Quinn stuck her head inside. "Hey."

"Oh, hey. What's going on?" I started spreading out my notes.

"Not much. You know... Sunday fun day, and all that fucking stuff."

"Right. I've got a paper due tomorrow. What's fun about that?"

"My thoughts exactly. The old bitch that's teaching my psych class expects us to memorize the entire damn reading selection for each class. I've been working on it." She held her book up.

"Where's Gerrod?"

"Same place Blue is, the hospital."

"Yep. The whole damn team's probably there."

"Truth. Most of them are a bunch of little bitches. Can't piss without each other."

We both laughed at her comment. "Now that's the truth."

"Looks like someone's been dining at the Y." Quinn leveled her eyes on my thigh. "Bite marks makes me think it must have been tasty."

"You're so nasty."

"Me? Cover that shit up if you don't want people to see it then."

I pulled my running shorts down a little. "I can't pull these down anymore. Besides, I'm in my house so uh, take that." I poked her with my pen.

"Stop. Hey, does this mean you've been doing a little reciprocating on his fine body?"

"Not talking about this, Quinn." I scrolled around through my emails since I'd opened my laptop.

"Why? I'm your best friend. If you can't talk about sex with me, who the hell will you talk about it with."

"No one. It's private."

"Don't be such a prude. It's just sex."

"No, it's not just sex. It's between my boyfriend and me."

She mocked me in a sing-song voice. "Between my boyfriend and me."

I slapped at her. "Stop. I don't ask you about sex with Gerrod."

"What do you want to know? I'm an open book. He's got a ten incher that's the size of his forearm and damn, it's like getting fucked by a tree trunk."

"Enough!" I yelled at her. "I do not want to know this information. Lalalala." I started singing, and she started laughing at me.

"Such a little goodie-two-shoes."

"Lalala."

"Okay, I get the message." She opened her book as she sat back in Blue's big chair. "One question then I'll stop, and this is pertinent info."

"What?" I looked over at her.

"Y'all do the deed in this chair?" I glared at her. "Shit. I was afraid of that. Where haven't y'all buried the hot dog?" Again I glared at her. "Well, hell. I'm getting a towel to sit on. Don't need any of his spooge touching me."

"You are so gross. There's nothing like that on our furniture. Just sit down and read."

She jumped up and ran to the hall closet returning with a giant beach towel. "A girl can never be too careful."

I shook my head. "Shut up, Quinn, and read."

Gerrod and Blue walked in the apartment together laughing about something sometime later.

"Hey, babe." He kissed me hard on the lips. Good thing I was finished with my paper because I could see there would be no more working now.

"Hey, yourself. How'd it go?"

"Not good. Surgery's tomorrow morning. He's out for the rest of the season."

"Oh no. What about the draft?" I had to ask. After all, Timms had told anyone who'd listen about it.

"Yeah, that's up in the air. He might not ever get to play again. No one would say it around him, but we all know what kind of rehab this takes, and he's not even eligible to sign yet."

Quinn joined us. "That's just shit. Players need to have a backup plan and knowing that asshat, he doesn't. He can't sit out there on the fucking porch in his lawn chair the rest of his life."

"No, he can't. We might have to take turns with school and keeping him entertained for a while. He'll be on those damn crutches for six full weeks or longer. Hell, he might be on them past Christmas." Gerrod looked down shaking his head as though he was thinking the worst-case scenarios.

Blue handed him a beer. "Let's not count him out yet. He's tough. He might come back strong."

"Yeah, but you heard what he said, nine months to a year," Gerrod continued.

"That's a long fucking time," Quinn commented.

"Sure as hell is," Blue added. "We need to make a plan as to what we're going to do to help."

"Right, a plan's good." I knew they were both grasping at anything to keep from thinking the worst.

"As soon as they say he can come home, we'll make a schedule, and everyone can sign up for their times when they don't have class."

Timms was ready to come home a week later, but that presented a problem. All those guys at the XOX house were barely able to take care of themselves much less him, too. We met and decided the best thing, in the beginning at least, was for him to stay with Blue and me. We were the only ones with a downstairs apartment and an empty bedroom if Blue and I moved into one room.

"Babe, are you okay with us moving in together?" Blue asked as we picked up my things and walked down to his room with them. My room was closer to the den so we thought it would save Timms a few steps on the crutches.

"Sure. I mean if you are?"

"We sleep in the same room together every night anyway, so it's not that much different, right?"

"Yeah, but now, there's no place to go if you piss me off," I said jokingly, but deep down I knew there was a hint of truth to it. We were mostly living together, but I still had my own place to go if I needed to ignore him.

"If we have a fight, I'll go to the XOX house. Hey, does this mean we can have some wild make-up sex when I come home."

"Oh, yeah, with Timms in the room across the hall. How'll that be?"

"It's not like he doesn't know we have sex, babe."

"No, but that doesn't mean I want him listening to us."

"You'll just have to learn to howl a little quieter if you don't want him hearing you."

"What? I don't howl."

"Okay, beg quieter." He smiled at me.

"I don't beg."

This time he raised an eyebrow questioning my comment. "Oh… let me think about this. I seem to remember a few nights ago when I kept stopping with you so close to the edge. 'Oh, Blue, please. Please let me come.' That sounds like begging to me, babe."

"Don't be a dick. You knew what I meant."

"A dick? Me? Babe, I'm the best boyfriend ever." He threw down the controller to the Nintendo and stalked over to me as if he was a lion on the prowl. "I use an arsenal of things to make sure you have multiple orgasms every time we fuck, and you're calling me a dick? I'll show you dick." He roared at me as I ran around the other side of the bed from him and skirted the corner to make it down the hall. He caught me as I rounded the couch and picked me up.

"I'll show you a dick, right after I spank your perfect little ass for calling me names."

"Do not spank me."

"You should have thought about that before you called me names. As a matter of fact, I think I'll tie you up to the headboard and footboard and spank you with that crop I have. Hadn't ever used it on this fine ass of yours." He popped my ass with a loud noise about the time the door opened.

"Oh, hey Timms and Mr. and Mrs. Timms," I called to them from my position over Blue's shoulder. "Come on in."

Blue swung around and then stood me up in front of him. "Hey." Blue's cheeks turned a little pink, and I wanted to laugh so badly. He'd embarrassed himself with his words, and all I could do was smile.

NOELLE

"Let me help," Blue told them when he saw their hands full of moving boxes. "We were uh, uh..."

"Finishing up on moving my things, and we're almost done. Blue, go help get boxes, and I'll take the last of my clothes from the closet."

Timms moved slowly to Blue's big chair to sit down. "These damn things are driving me fucking crazy. They hurt my underarms like a son of a bitch."

His mom just stared in horror. My sympathetic look helped take some of the sting out of his words. No matter how often parents heard that kind of language, most of them hated it coming from their own child's mouth.

"Let me show you his room, Mrs. Timms. You can decide where his clothes will go."

"Thank you, Noelle."

We walked down the hall. "We appreciate you and Blue offering to help out with Theo. It's been extremely difficult for him. We wanted him to come home, but he won't hear of it."

"I'm sure it has, and we're happy to help him. He'd do the same for Blue."

"Yes, he would. He speaks highly of his teammate. They seem to have a good connection."

"Being on a team does that." I turned on the ceiling light, and she looked around. "I know it's not as big as his room at the house, but it'll be okay for a while, won't it?"

"Absolutely. His dad and I are thrilled he's getting away from the horrid house. The things that go on there are a mother's worst nightmare." She tried to smile to cover her true feelings.

"Yeah, that place has quite the reputation. I've been out there a few times, and Blue had a room there until he moved in here as my roommate."

"Oh, I uh... well, Theo said y'all lived together. I assumed you were more than roommates."

"We are now but not in the beginning. We started out barely friends because of the things that I saw go on at the house. I wanted nothing to do with what went on out there even though I was a cheerleader.

The head cheerleader, Madelyn, required us to attend events for the team at the house."

"Oh yes, we've had the pleasure of meeting Madelyn." I wanted to laugh because her statement told me she'd seen the real Madelyn and saw right through her pretenses. "She told us that she'd invited Theo to stay at her place, but I'm afraid I'd have put my foot down and told her no. That girl is trouble waiting to happen. I hope Theo sees her for what she is."

"He's got it covered, I'm sure, Mrs. Timms." In more ways than one, I wanted to add but kept it to myself.

She gave me a strange look. "Let's hope so, Noelle."

Or maybe we were on the same page. Either way, I didn't reply. "Let me check on Timms, and I'll help you unbox his clothes."

"I'm sure I can take care of this. You probably have more important business to take care of today."

"No, I'm good." I walked out to the den. Timms' leg extended off the end of the recliner's footrest in its huge dressing and immobilizer. "You comfortable?"

"Hell, no. I can't get comfortable. My leg's throbbing. I wonder if I can have another pain pill already. They don't do shit, but they make me think they do."

I chuckled at his comment. "I'm sure the meds are doing more than you think they are. How would you be if you had nothing but ibuprofen?"

"Yeah, it'd be worse than a mother—" He stopped when his mom breezed through to go back to the car.

"Good play, Timms." I laughed out loud this time. "You need anything? Water? Soft drink?"

"Yeah, I need some good shit to knock out the pain and a beer to wash it down."

"I'm thinking those two things don't mix, dude."

"Okay, Mom." He grinned at me. "Is this how's it's going to be?"

"Afraid so."

"Fuck. I figured the two of you might cut me some slack. I might as well move my shit back to the house. At least there, the freshmen will let me drink or take whatever I want."

"Not going to happen. You need rest, recuperation and eventually physical therapy.

"I'm praying for a hot little PT to waltz in daily to relieve some of my pain." He wiggled his eyebrows.

"Such a manwhore. The injury didn't take that away from you."

"Nope. She can climb on right here. Perfect chair for it. The only thing that would make this shit any better is if it rocked. Rock me all night long," he sang to me.

"You're sick. And no sex in Blue's favorite chair. He'd have to burn it when you left."

"I ain't leaving. Didn't Mom tell you? I'm staying until graduation." He grinned at me. "This chair will be so broken in by the time I'm done with it, it'll be dumpster material."

Blue walked in, arms loaded with boxes and heard him finish the statement. "Like hell, it will be. Buy your own damn recliner. I carry that one everywhere I move."

"Mom, Dad..." Timms yelled.

"What, son?" His dad walked in with more boxes. Maybe he was moving in until graduation. We didn't bargain for a full-time roomie.

"I need a recliner like this one. My leg can stay elevated all the time, and Blue's not willing to be a sharing roommate." He cut his eyes at Blue. What a manipulator.

"Blue doesn't need to share anything with you. We'll get you one of your own, but this room's a little small for two big recliners and a couch. Maybe we'll get a love seat to exchange for it if you're okay with that, Noelle."

Timms had his parents wrapped up tight. I sat back and watched as they did everything. They continued to his bedroom as Blue came back from putting his boxes down.

"You're such a dick, Timms," he commented as he went to the fridge for water. "Your parents are good people. What happened to you?"

"They love me," he said with a smile. "You know they're leaving me here to fucking fend for myself?

They wanted me to move home, and when I said no, they told me to deal with my damn problems."

"Good. You're an adult. You don't need to depend on them." I had to put my thoughts out there. We didn't plan to baby him either. Home health was going to provide all he needed, and the coach wanted the sports doctors to oversee his PT, so he'd eventually be going there when he could manage. "We've got a copy of all your info on the fridge, so there's no pulling dumb shit on us."

"Damn, I can't catch a break. Can I at least get some of my groupies to make house calls to take care of me? You know sponge baths, emotional help, quick releases?"

"Yeah, in your room. Neither of us wants to walk in on your naked ass boning some chick," Blue told him with me nodding in agreement.

"I see how it's gonna be. I get to listen and see the two of you go at it like rabbits, but I've gotta go to my room."

Blue jumped in. "That's something you'll never be doing. I don't share." He pulled me to his side and kissed my head. "We're not into the sick stuff you and Madelyn are into with your public sex."

"Fuck, that chick's down for whatever I give her." He grinned at me. Timms knew we'd seen their towel sex at the beginning of the semester. "I was hoping your girl here would be more like Maddie, but dammit, she made it clear right up front she wasn't."

"You got that right." I stopped with that when his parents returned.

"Theo, we're all done. Everything you'll need is in your room now. We're going to buy some groceries because God knows he'll eat y'all out of house and home."

"Just buy me some beer, please."

"You don't need beer. You're an athlete, and you have too many drugs in your system right now."

"Right, Dad… an athlete. When you gonna see that's never going to happen now? That dream has gone to shit in one bad play."

I felt the air in the room lose all the oxygen in one sentence. I didn't want to be around for this conversation. Blue and I had already had it before he moved in.

"Son."

"Stop, Dad. You heard the ortho doctor and Coach both say it. A full fucking year of recovery, and then I'll still probably never play another down of football. The dream's dead. I want to concentrate on getting to walk so I can make smooth steps across the stage in May."

No words were spoken until Mrs. Timms stood up. "Let's go get groceries, honey."

"Yeah. If there's anything you want special, text me, and we'll get it, Theo," his dad said as he closed the door behind them.

"That's fucking hilarious. They both think I'm still going to be drafted into the pros. Don't they see this shit for what it is? I'm done. Gotta move on to plan B."

"Yeah, and what's plan B, dude?" Blue asked.

"Don't know yet. Going to explore my options." He moved forward in his chair and picked up his crutches to stand. We watched him struggle but didn't try to help. Timms needed to see what he could do on his own, and he did. Good thing his upper body strength and other leg were in excellent shape.

"I'm tired from all the moving. I'm going to get in bed for a while." He crutched off down the hallway. "No free play in the den. The parents will be back soon. Oh, yeah, but that's Blue's specialty isn't it, being a minute man?" He laughed to himself as he finally made it to his doorway.

"Shut up, dickhead. I'm good for at least five." We smiled at each other. This might've been a bad idea, but we'd deal with it.

"You about ready to take off, babe? Class is in twenty minutes."

"Yeah, you think we should check on him? Make sure he's okay?" I worried when no noise came from his room.

"I'll go in and check." He knocked easy on the door and went in. I heard some talking and then Blue stepped out.

"Well?"

"He's fine. Home health is coming over to get things organized for now. He's going to be temporarily doing his assignments online. His laptop's on his nightstand."

"Good. That makes me feel better."

"Me, too. I won't be back until this evening after practice, so it'll be the two of you for a while. You okay with that, right?"

"Sure. I'm cooking dinner, as usual, so he'll be eating with us, and I'll be busy."

We walked out locking the door behind us. I felt better but not great about leaving him. It would be his first day alone for a while.

"I'll see ya at the Coffee Bean?" Blue slipped an easy kiss across my lips when we reached our parting place.

"I'll be there, big guy. Now go be big jock on campus." I smiled at him. I liked to tease him about it.

"Will do." He took off in a jog since his class was further away than mine.

After a full day, I headed for home. Before I turned the corner of the building at the apartment, I heard a loud noise. Someone was playing music way too loud. They'd be getting a notice from management. Not good. Walking to the sidewalk, I saw people hanging out the door of our apartment. What the fuck?

Timms sat on the little porch in a lawn chair that rocked back with his leg elevated. People surrounded him, mostly females. Oh no. We weren't having this shit. This place would never be a miniature version of the XOX house.

I walked up trying to remain calm especially when I saw who was sitting straddled across him on that chair. I think I was about to fail our first test on roommate etiquette.

"Timms, what's going on?" I asked standing beside Madelyn on top of him.

"A few friends came by to check on me. They like knowing I'm still the fucking best at the XOX house."

"I'm sure they do, but the music needs to be turned down. We'll get in trouble if someone complains."

"Who's going to complain, Noelle? It's only a few friends and a little music in the afternoon," Madelyn said as she rolled her hips over an obvious boner.

"Anyone can complain, Madelyn. And sex on the porch isn't going to fly either." Bitch. I wanted to snatch her up and send her flying over the hedge onto the sidewalk.

"Calm down, Noelle." Timms thought he could placate me with his easy going speech. "Sweets, get up. We'll have to let this one go to waste." He glanced down at his tented sweat pants.

"Thanks for that cockblocker," Madelyn said to me.

“Anytime, now take your skank ass and all its ho friends and leave, please.” I could give as good as I got. She had to know this by now. Madelyn glared at me like she wanted to say more, but then leaned down and whispered in Timms’ ear before kissing him and walking away.

“Now, ‘elle, there was no reason for name calling.” He grinned as though this scene was all a big joke, but I refused to play into his bullshit.

“Did home health come today?”

“Sure did. She gave me a bath, too. That little thing they sent left here plenty wet, too.” He wiggled his eyebrows.

“Maybe next time it’ll be a fifty-year-old hairy man.”

“Nah, I called them and said I’d like them to assign this one to me.”

“Like that’s even possible.”

“Didn’t hurt to ask.”

“Right. What about classes? Did you get any work done? You’re a week behind.”

“Okay, Mom. Yes, I got some work done, and you know being the injured star quarterback has its perks. Profs are gonna forgive all my assignments before today. All my grades were good and current up until the game.”

“You are one lucky bastard.”

“Don’t I know it.”

"I gotta start dinner. Your parents bought a variety of things for us to eat."

"Does this mean you're cooking? I can't remember a woman cooking for me since Mom."

"Yeah, I cook when Blue's at practice, and he cooks when he's not." I forgot Timms wasn't at practice and felt bad for bringing it up. "When are you going to go over to the field and watch them?"

"I don't know. Standing on the sideline watching that kid play in my position might be too damn hard to do."

"But he could probably use your help, Timms." I watched his eyes to see how he took the suggestion.

"Yeah, maybe. I can't drive, though. How would I get there?"

"I'll take you. We could take your truck so you could get in and out easier. I could come back and pick you up."

"Let me think about it." I could see the wheels turning. He did want to do this. Timms wasn't a slacker. He liked helping other people get better on the field. I'd heard the guys talking about how good he worked with the new team members. Better players made a better team, and that goal stood above egos.

Blue walked in as I finished setting the table.

"Hmmm. Cozy little dinner tonight?"

"Yeah, it's our first dinner with Timms, and I thought we'd sit down together. I asked him if he could sit up that way, and he said sure. He'll use the other chair to prop up his leg."

He moved up behind me at the stove and slipped his arms around my middle. "Thanks, babe. I know you didn't plan to take on another mouth to feed. I appreciate you helping him."

"It's not a problem. I cook for five now. Still easier than cooking for one." I stirred the macaroni and cheese, courtesy of Mrs. Timms. Apparently, he didn't eat as healthy as we did so this was a treat for us.

"Five? Who else is coming?"

"No one, but you eat twice as much as me, so I figure he will, too. That's five servings."

"How'd you get so smart?"

I tapped my temple. "I'm just good like that." I turned in his arms. "Now give me my reward for being so good." He kissed me softly at first, but it heated up quickly when his tongue connected with mine. He pulled my leg up on his hip so he could put his hardness in the best place to feel him where I needed it.

We didn't hear Timms' crutches being preoccupied so when he made a throat-clearing noise, we finally broke apart.

"Sorry guys. I can take mine to my room." He picked up his plate.

"No. We were warming up. The real fun can wait. It'll be better thinking about what's to come." I grinned at my comment. "I swear y'alls fourteenness is rubbing off on me."

"Yeah, I promise I won't be coming like a fourteen-year-old, babe." He grabbed my ass cheeks and pulled me hard against him.

"Stop. We have dinner and a known voyeur in our midst."

"That's right, 'babe,'" he mocked Blue. "I'm willing to help y'all out any damn time you need to spice things up."

"Dude, we don't need spice. We got plenty."

"Let's eat before y'all get into a pissing contest. I swear two pubescent boys live here now." They both laughed as Blue and I carried the dishes to the table.

I walked into a quiet apartment the next day. Timms was gone which scared me until I found a note on the table saying he had found a ride to physical therapy, and he might stay for practice. I prayed he did. Not that him being there bothered me, but him leaving with a friend sounded like progress and going to practice was a huge bonus.

His life would never be the same without playing ball, but being around the team gave him more to think about than what new trash TV show he might binge on today.

Blue kept me awake for half the night. He was so worked up from practice. We barely got the door closed before he started stripping my clothes off. He'd apparently thought shower sex would keep our lovemaking noises down, so we gave it a shot. His magical dick powers grew to full force as I snuggled in next to him and round two happened in our bed—Timms be damned. He woke me sometime in the middle of the night when his tongue slid over my clit, and I cried out from the sheer pleasure of it.

Him getting over his body image problems made for a lot of make-up sex. That's what he called it anyway. He wanted to make-up for all the lost time he spent looking for girls who were willing to be tied up.

On Friday evening, I asked Timms if he would be attending the game on Saturday. He'd gone to practice every day. They got him a golf cart he could drive around on the field on the second day. So far, he loved going to practice. Mrs. Timms called me to tell me how thrilled they were about him not wallowing around in self-pity for long. She thanked me for all we'd done to help him realize he needed to get back out there.

"It's all him, Mrs. Timms. He hated sitting around here while he knew the team worked hard each day. We talked about it, and the next day he went, even found his own ride."

"His dad and I are so thankful. We feel like this will help in making it a speedy recovery."

"I don't know about that. We don't talk about PT much. I know he goes daily before practice. He did tell me that much."

"If there is anything y'all need or we can do to help you and Blue, please let us know. We're willing to do whatever to help out."

"Thanks, but we're good for now."

We hung up about the time Blue and Timms walked in from the field. "Hey, guys. Are we ready for tomorrow? It's a big game."

"Don't you fucking know it. That damn kid, Devillier, has worked his ass off. He's going to be a great quarterback when he gets a little more game time under his belt," Timms was quick to point out.

"Good. So we'll be winning tomorrow."

Blue kissed me. "That's the plan, babe. That's always the plan."

"Right. Can I have a kiss if I agree with you, too?"

"Hell, no, you can't. You keep your lips off my woman. Find your own. Where is your endless supply of women anyway? I expected to be constantly waking up to women in our house."

"After the first day when 'babe' here came home to the impromptu party and wasn't too damn happy about it, I decided I would wait a while before inviting that shit back here."

Blue turned and looked at me. I'd never mentioned it to him. "What the hell is he talking about, Noelle?"

"I forgot all about it. Yeah, the first day a loud party was going on, and my favorite cheerleader was riding Timms in the lawn chair like it was a bull at Rodeo's Bar. She left pretty quickly after I got home."

"Really? Any other secrets you two are keeping from me?" Blue didn't sound mad, but the look on his face told me he wasn't happy either.

"No, Blue. We don't have any secrets."

Then Timms popped up with, "Well there was that time in my recliner," he said it with a perfectly straight face when he knew it would only add fuel to the fire.

"He's lying straight up, Blue."

Timms started laughing unable to hold it in any longer. "Dude, I'd never mess with babe here. She's yours through and through."

Blue laughed, too, but I had an uneasy feeling about it. Why did he want to plant that idea in Blue's mind? I'd never cheat on him. He knew that, didn't he?

BLUE

Timms living with us sounded like a great plan in the beginning, but when he made that comment, I couldn't get it out of my mind. I knew Noelle wouldn't cheat on me, but him saying that might mean he's thinking about trying something with her. He'd find his ass out of this house so fast his brains would be swimming in his empty head.

I needed to forget about it and didn't have time to waste on his bullshit. I needed to be concentrating on playing my best game tomorrow. This team held the number one position in the polls, and our goal was to knock them down to number two so we could claim that coveted position. Our freshman quarterback held his own in last week's game. The win wasn't a pretty one, but once again, we pulled it out without Timms.

The Rams ran on the field with Timms on the sideline in his jersey. Him standing there pumped the team up with much-needed bravery. We faced this team like all the others. Play like winners, and winners we would be.

By half-time, doubt began to creep into my head. I hated myself for it. Timms came up to me in the locker room and tugged one handed until we were in a training room alone.

"Dude, what the fuck's going on?"

"I know man. I'm playing like shit out there."

"Right, so pull your head out of your ass and do it right. You know what it's going to take to win, and the shit you're doing now isn't it."

"I know. Play like a winner. I can do it."

"Then start now and begin by going out there and leading this team to victory. I can't do it for you this time. It's on you." He pulled me in until our foreheads met. "Do it for me. Do it for the team. Hell, do it for your babe."

"Leave my babe out of this."

"I know man, I was joking with you. And about earlier. I was only fucking with you. You know that, right? What y'all have is special, even a dumbass like me can see it. I'd never do anything to come between you."

"Glad to hear you say that, dude. It might have left a little doubt in my mind."

"Well, drive that shit out. No secrets between y'all. Now get your ass on that field and play your fucking ball game."

"Hell, yeah. Right now."

We moved back into the locker room, and the coaches were finished telling us how bad we looked.

I stepped up. "Hey, guys. I want to say something. Timms over there just gave me the ass chewing that I deserved. He set me straight, though. I'm returning to this field to play one hundred and ten percent. Who's with me?"

The locker room erupted into mayhem, and we took off for the field. We fought the next two quarters for every inch on the field, but we did it. We won like we should have all along. Someone needed to remind me what I did on the field, and I was damn glad he did. Having him on the sideline to help us fight, gave us what we needed.

Quinn and Noelle decided to take Timms out to the house right before the game ended so he wouldn't get hurt in the crush on the field or locker room. When I came off the field and into the locker room, I shot her a text.

> **Me:** *Going by apartment. Picking up Timms' private stock of booze and condoms*

Noelle: *Just come on to the party. He can drink beer like everyone else*
Me: *He's planning on getting laid tonight*
Noelle: *Then hurry. You know I hate this place*
Me: *It'll only take a second, and I'll be there to party with everyone*

I went to unlock the door, but it wasn't locked. Noelle must have forgotten to do it again. The porch light shined all the way to the kitchen, so I didn't bother to turn on a light. As I rounded the corner, something was stuck on my face, and I couldn't get it off me.

I fought, but more than one person spun me around, and whatever was on my face made it hard for me to breathe. I felt myself going down. I couldn't stop it. "Fuckkk…"

My head hurt like I'd been hit with a two by four. When I opened my eyes, I couldn't see anything.

What the hell?

I tried to talk, but it caused more pain. I raised my hand to my face and figured out I had night blinders on, the kind I used on Noelle. I tried to peel it off, but a hand popped me with something that stung. My crop.

"Leave it alone, Blue boy." I'd heard this voice before. My arms were pulled above my head, and I had no strength to fight it. "I found your toy box."

"Noelle? Is this a joke, babe."

"Babe isn't here. She'll never want to come here again after what we've been doing. By the way, you've got some interesting things going on in your package, Blue. A little secret you've been hiding from all of us. Now everyone will know why you use these shitty little masks and ribbons to tie the dumb fucks up."

"Who are you?" I asked.

"I'm wounded you can't figure out who I am, Blue. I thought you'd recognize me faster."

"Then enlighten me." I felt a hand on my stomach. I laid there naked for all to see. More than one person was in the room if the movements were an indicator.

"Y'all want to help me?" Hands touched me all over. Someone had a hold on my dick, too, then a mouth closed over my softness. Hands rubbed my skin from head to toe.

"Poor Blue. The chloroform we stole from the lab must have warped your cock. And down here, this one poor nut all alone. How long has this been like that, Blue?"

"I'm not telling you anything. How long have I been out?"

"Long enough to take some awesome photos. We had to keep covering your nose with the rag. You woke up faster than we thought you would from it. The drowsy look was awesome for the pics, though. Your little babe is going to love it. We're sending them from your phone, too. She'll know it's true."

"Bitch, what have you done?" I felt my dick getting hard even though I didn't want it to.

"We figured this would happen, so we crushed a little blue pill and got you to drink it down when you were coming to. This chloroform's the shizz. In and out of consciousness. Cool, huh?"

"This is crazy. Let me go." My arms and legs were tied down. "You're fucking crazy, Madelyn."

"So you do recognize me, but we can't take off your blinder because we want to play like you do with the girls you tie up."

"Let me the fuck go, Madelyn."

"No can do, Blue boy. We're not through playing. Don't want to waste that little blue pill now, do we?"

"This is rape, Madelyn."

"Oh really, 'cause the pics make it look like you're enjoying the hell out of it. The two of you thought you were so smart moving Timms here. He refused to let me come over after that horrid ho you're shacking up with told him to. I knew that girl was trouble from the moment she stepped on the field and tried to call herself a cheerleader. Are they fucking, too?"

"Wait. That's what this is. You're both doing her. What a selfish fucking pig she is. Not only does she want you off the market, she wanted both of you." I felt her climb on me and rub my dick with some lube before she slid down on it.

"Take my picture riding him with the crop. It'll look great. Smile, Blue." I didn't know if flashes were going off or the lights were on full bright, but from the noises she made, she was giving them a good show.

"I know. Let's do a porno video, and we'll wipe my face out on the screen. That'll be our finale. Give me one of those masks. I'll wear one, too. Target his nut so everyone can see it. How great will that be? Everyone will know why he's Half sac. His little ho will hate him. Timms can come live with me. It's the perfect storm for me."

She rode me, but I wasn't coming anytime soon and from the feel of it, not going soft either. Dammit. What a shit show. She finally got tired of doing all the work and stopped, climbing off the bed and me.

"Untie me, Madelyn."

"Not going to happen, Blue boy. Not until I'm done. Okay, who's next? Got a whole bottle of lube here, girls."

A voice I didn't recognize yelled across the room, "It's my turn, but I'm putting on a condom. I don't want your germs."

"Very funny. I'm clean, bitch, but whatever. Let's just get pics."

This girl came on my dick in no time at all.

"Anyone else?" Madelyn asked. "What a bunch of pussies. Oops, guess we all are."

She leaned over my face and whispered, "We're all done, Blue boy. Was it good for you like it was for us?" She started laughing. "Here, you're sweating. Take a drink." She held a bottle to my lips, and I gulped down the liquid.

"Guess we're out, Blue boy. Enjoy your nap."

"Yeah, I won't be sleeping anytime soon."

"Oh, yes you will."

Shit. What was in the water? It didn't take long, and I felt myself drifting off. *Bye, bye Blue boy*, was the last thing I heard.

"Blue? Blue. What's going on?"

My arms felt like they each weighed a ton. I couldn't move them, but they were tied anyway so what difference did it make. Slap, slap.

"Dude. Open your eyes."

"Can't, covered." My speech was garbled.

"No, they aren't. Open up big guy."

It took all my strength to stretch them to slightly open. Jenko and Gerrod stood over me.

"Dude. What the hell are you doing?"

I couldn't answer. My tongue felt like it was three inches thick. "Thirsty."

"Here, there's a water bottle right here." He held it up to my lips.

"Nooo. Wrong."

"What do you mean wrong. There's something wrong with it?" I nodded once.

"You were drugged?" Again, I nodded.

"No way. Is that how the videos were made? I knew something wasn't right."

"Cops."

"Are you sure you want to do that?"

"Yeah." I couldn't hold my eyes open any longer. "Madelyn."

The smell of cleaner assaulted my nose before I opened my eyes. My mom and dad were in the hospital room with me.

"Dad?" They both appeared quickly beside my bed. "What happened? How did I get here?"

"Jenko called an ambulance. Thank God you're okay." My mom told me this through teary eyes as she reached for my hand to hold.

I looked around the room. "Where's Noelle?"

"She went home to her parents' house."

"Why? I need to talk to her."

"A lot's happened, Blue. She felt it would be better to get away for a day or two."

"Shit. Better for who?"

"Better for both of you, son. The videos and pictures are floating around, and the gossip and all associated with that is vicious."

"Vicious? How? Tell me what's going on Dad."

"Blue. Someone drugged you. Well, maybe more than one drugged you and made some horrid videos and pictures of you with other women. You don't look drugged in the pics, though. They sent them to her from your phone with some awful messages about her and Timms."

"Yeah, and then the other pictures," Mom added.

"What other pictures?" I had to know it all.

"There are pictures of your problem, Blue, with an erection, so it looks unusual," Dad informed me with a tortured look on his face.

"Dammit. I'll kill that bitch."

"Blue. Don't say that about Noelle."

My mom didn't get it.

"Not Noelle, Madelyn. I'll kill her for doing this."

"You know who did this to you?"

"Yes, it was Madelyn and some of her friends. I woke up some and tried to talk her out of it. She kept letting me come to from chloroform they stole from the chem lab at school."

"But you were out, son. They gave you that date rape drug." The sad look on my dad's face made me mad.

"Yeah. After she fucked me, sorry Mom." I glanced at her. "After we had sex for what seemed like forever, I was dying for water. I didn't know she'd put something in it, so I drank it down like a dying man. Then she told me. Must have been at the end of the ordeal. Guess she needed me out for a while."

"Did she give you anything else?" he asked me. I knew he prayed not, but I had to tell the truth.

"Yeah, she gave me Viagra. They crushed it up and stuck it in my throat while I was out on the chloroform. They knew that wouldn't last. Whoever was helping her knew some stuff. They stole the chloroform from the chem lab, knew how long it would last, helped get the Viagra down me, and then had GHB."

"These are very serious accusations."

"Shit. You don't know the half of it. The rape is a whole other matter."

"Rape!" My mom gasped on a cry.

"Yeah, it was rape. They tied me up, blindfolded me, used a crop on me, drugged me, and raped me. You don't think I'd go through that willingly, do you?"

My mom sat down and shook her head before she laid her head beside my hands on the bed. "Oh, Blue, I'm so sorry. I never realized sending you to college would end in this."

"End? My college hasn't ended. We'll put her ass in jail, and I'll move on with my life. She's sick, Mom. Psycho. She needs help."

"You can't mean to stay here." She looked at me as if I spoke another language.

"Hell, yeah. I've got football to play. I've got to get my girl back here. If you think this is going to keep me down, you're wrong. I've dealt with a lot of shit. This is nothing."

"But what about all the videos and pictures? They've been pulled down now but who knows how many people had them saved."

"I don't give a shit about that. I'm stronger than a few pictures and videos, guys. Compared to losing my nut, this is small time." I knew they were upset. "Yeah, I'm not excited about people seeing my junk, but I'm kinda glad it's out. Now there's no hiding it from anyone. Now get my girl on the phone. I want to talk to her."

BLUE

I tried for hours with no luck. With her phone off, I had no way to get in touch with her. Jenko, Gerrod, and Timms came to see me in the afternoon.

"Dude. You're looking a whole lot better than when we saw you in the middle of the night."

"Right. Thanks for that. Hey, did I still have a boner then?"

"Uh. I don't remember," Jenko said. I knew this would be uncomfortable talking about it, so I wanted to get it out in the open.

"Look guys. The girl is a psycho. They did some weird sex stuff to me, but it's not the end of the world.

I don't even remember most of it, so it's done and over. Now a big boner or not?"

Jenko grinned. "Yeah, dude. You did. You were buck naked on the bed with your dick pointing to the sky." He gave me a strange look and rubbed his eyes. "I hope to God to never see that shit again. We covered your naked ass up before we called the ambulance. No one else needed to bleach their eyes."

We all laughed at that comment, and I knew we'd be all right.

"Next thing. Where's Quinn?" Quinn could get me to Noelle.

"She's out on the porch. She didn't know if you'd want her in here or not."

"Are you telling me we found something to embarrass her? Well, fuck that. Get her ass in here. I need her."

Gerrod's eyebrows shot up like they were attached to his hairline. "What?"

"Just get her, please."

He opened the door and motioned for her to come in.

She peeked around the door at me. "Oh, hey, Blue." I'd never seen Quinn look so meek. It wasn't her.

"Quinn. It's okay. I'm okay. Everything's going to be fine, but we have a problem that I need you for."

She looked down at my dick. "Uh." I started laughing so hard, I thought I would cry. "I'm not sure where the hell you're going with this, Blue, but I'm not doing anything that'll help you with the monster I heard these two douche waffles making jealous comments about."

The three of us were howling over her comment. I swore this woman should be a stand-up comedian. "No, it has nothing to do with my awesome body. I need to talk to Noelle. How can I get her?"

She dropped her eyes to the floor. Something was wrong, very wrong. "What's going on Quinn? Talk to me."

"She went home, Blue. I haven't talked to her since she left."

"What the fuck's going on, Quinn?"

"She's confused and upset about the pictures and all the publicity that came with them, Blue. Those pictures were damaging evidence for someone. You need to look at this from her standpoint. She turned on her phone long enough to make sure you were okay, but she wouldn't allow me to tell her any of the story. All she asked was if you were all right. I said yes, and she said thanks, hung up and turned off her phone. I tried to call her right back, but it went straight to voicemail."

"So, she doesn't want anything to do with me? This wasn't my fault. Can't she see that?"

"All she knows is that you were with other girls. It looked like you were fucking them in the video and the pics. The girls were blacked out, you weren't. You look like you're having a great time."

"I was fucked up, Quinn. They drugged me with several things."

She looked point blank at me almost as if she's accusing me. "Your flag pole is at full staff, Blue."

"They gave me Viagra. I had no control over it."

"They did what? They poked a little blue bill down your throat?"

"Sure did, along with GHB, and that all happened after they chloroformed me. What could I do?" I pleaded for her understanding.

"Well, shit. This is bad, dude." She finally understood.

"Right. So, get my girl here and let me tell her the truth about the damn pictures. How could she think I would do something like that? Maybe I'm the one who should be angry."

"No, we've had enough anger, misunderstandings, and misinformation to last forever," Gerrod spoke up. "Let's get this shit behind us. Call her, Quinn."

"I can't call her. I don't know how. What's her parents' name? Maybe they have an old-time landline."

"Her parents' names are Tom and Janna." I knew this much even though I had only met them once. "Tom and Janna Jeffries." She did a search on her phone and found a number.

"You want me to call? She might talk to me first," Quinn volunteered for the task.

"Yeah, good plan." The more I thought about this, I had some mixed feelings about it all. What had I done wrong? We'd deal with my feelings later. Right now finding her and talking to her was all that mattered.

Quinn stepped into the hallway to make the necessary calls. It seemed like forever, but the door opened quietly, and Quinn had the phone to her ear. We could only hear her half. She must have been afraid to put it on speaker phone.

"Listen, Noelle. None of this is Blue's fault."

"Yeah, I know it looks bad. Those videos and pictures are pretty damning, but you need to take a breath, chica. Think about who this is, it's Blue lying in the hospital bed. He was drugged several different ways and used."

"No, they haven't said when he can go home, but there's nothing medically wrong now that the drugs have worn off, so I'm sure it'll be this evening sometime."

"Do you want to talk to him, at least?"

"Okay, here he is."

Finally, she handed me the phone.

"Noelle, babe. Come home." The pleading in my voice must have told the others what I felt since they all got up and left the room.

"I'm sorry this happened to you, Blue. I truly am, but I don't know if I can continue putting up with all this bullshit. Between Madelyn, football, the house, and now the videos and pictures, I think it would be better for me to live alone for a while. I think I might see if the university will allow me to finish the semester online."

"Babe. What about what I need? If you run, Madelyn wins. We can't let her win."

"Hopefully, she'll be in jail after you tell them all they need to know."

"Yes, I feel like she will be. I want you here with me, though."

"I'm not sure about it at this point. My parents and I are going to talk about it again later and make a firm decision."

"So you don't plan to let me tell my side of this?"

"It's not about sides, Blue. It's about shit happening time and time again. I'm so tired of it.

"All I want to do is go to school, graduate, and get a job. This needs to be done with."

"It will be done with when she's in jail. It'll be done with when we are back together as we should be. Please come home, Noelle."

"I don't know. I'll call you after our talk."

"Okay, babe. I get it. Talk to them. They'll surely make you see what I'm talking about."

"Maybe. We'll see."

"Noelle?"

"Yeah?"

"I love you, babe."

With no reply, I heard the phone disconnect. "Well, shit." I threw the phone across the room.

The noise caused the group to return to my room. "Tell me that was not my phone you threw across the damn room."

"Sorry, I'll buy you a new one. She hates me. I told her I love her, and she didn't say shit."

No one said a word. Telling her I loved her was something new for me, and I knew they all understood my raw reaction. I'd never told another woman I loved them. Probably Gerrod was the only one in the room that had said it.

Timms stood from the chair. "Look, dude, this is bad, real bad. Maybe we need to go get her. We can all drive up there and bring her home to you. She can't turn us all down when we are staring at her."

"No. She might not come back at all this semester, and if she does, she's not going to stay in the apartment. She's going to talk to her parents and make a decision this evening, but I already know what it'll be. She's done."

"Like hell, she is," Quinn spoke up. "We started together, and we'll end together. I'll move back home."

"And where will I move to?" Timms asked. "I mean, I guess I can move back to the house."

"No, we'll share a room, and you can live in the other until the end of the semester. Then we'll decide. That'll give us six weeks to convince her to stay."

Jenko leaned in to join the conversation. "I feel like we're all playing musical beds. Where can I sleep tonight?"

"Dumbshit, you're not moving. Just me," Quinn told him.

"Oh, okay. Thought I was moving this time. Isn't it my turn?"

We all looked at him and shook our heads.

The hospital sent me home in the evening because the effects of the drugs had worn off. My first stop was the police station. I'd only given them the bare necessities when they came to my room, but I filled out a complete report with all of my lab results and the doctor's report.

They issued a warrant for her arrest, and the police left to go pick her up. My parents had contacted a lawyer who advised us on what needed to happen. This shit needed to be over as soon as possible.

To my surprise, Noelle drove up to the apartment the next morning. She left me hanging all night. The door opened, and Timms and I both looked up at her. She walked in, and Timms stood up.

"I think there's some new music on my phone I need to listen to. I'll talk to y'all later." He went to his room, shut the door, and cranked up his Bluetooth speaker.

"Hey," she said as she sat on the couch alone.

"Hello, babe." I wanted to move over beside her but was afraid I'd cause her to run.

"My parents convinced me that I needed to listen to your story before I made any decisions."

I smiled. I couldn't help myself. I wanted to jump up and kiss her, but again, didn't want to scare her off. "Good. I think you need to hear the real story that I told to police this morning. They should have Madelyn in custody by now."

Her head jerked up to look at me. "She's being arrested?"

"I tried to tell you this wasn't my fault, babe. She attacked me. The girl needs psychiatric help. She's lost her ability to think rationally."

"But what if they let her come back to school?" I couldn't stand it any longer. I moved over beside her but sat far enough away not to touch bodies.

"My lawyer spoke to the president of the university and their lawyers this morning. She's done here." A slight smile formed on my lips. I wanted her to see that we'd be fine now.

"I guess that's a good thing, but you should know, I've decided to finish out the semester at my house. I'm here to load my stuff and head back home today."

"What? Why would you want to do that?"

"I can't do this anymore, Blue. I need to regroup. I've been getting horrible messages. The videos keep appearing everywhere I look. It kills me inside to see them. Seeing you fucking her with that blindfold on, it wrecks me every single time. We finally got past your problems, and now every time I see that, it throws them in my face over and over. I don't want to do it anymore."

"Is this forever? Like you're not planning to return?" I prayed she'd say no.

"I don't know yet. When the holidays are over, I'll make a decision."

At least it wasn't a yes.

"I'd hoped you'd come back for the remaining time so we could spend time together while you decided."

She sat with her back against the couch. I wanted to reach out to her. Touch her. Hold her. Assure her it would be over, but every move I made scared me. The longer we sat without talking, the angrier I became at the situation. I finally had to speak, but my words grew louder with each sentence.

"You know, Noelle. I'm the victim here, too. They did this to me. They put all my private business out for the world to see. I was raped, Noelle. Did you even think about the effect this had on me? Did it matter to you that I'm the one who took all the abuse, had all my shit broadcasted across the world? And yet, I'm still the one punished by it? You leave me to deal with the aftermath alone."

She turned her head and looked at me maybe actually seeing me for the first time since she walked in. "You're right, Blue, and for your sake, I'm getting out of the picture. There'll be no reason for others to add to the story by seeing us together on campus. It'll just be you. You and the team. You and your friends. There'll be no more stories about us. It'll be better this way." She stood up and walked to the doorway. When she opened it, I saw boxes on the porch. She'd never planned to stay just like she said. There was no talking her out of leaving.

Well, shit.

NOELLE

I drove to Quinn's apartment to tell her goodbye before I left for home. More tears formed than the ones I shed while I packed my things in Blue's and my room. This sadness had to stop. I wasn't this person. I thrived on being happy and loving life until this fall.

"So you're really going?" she asked when she opened the door.

"Yeah, I have to."

"But you're coming back for spring semester."

I looked away down the sidewalk into the bright sun that heated the cement. It might be fall, but this was Texas, and fall was only a frame of mind and a few good cool days before winter. This mimicked my life. What I pictured happening away at college appeared on a few good days, the rest cold and unfriendly.

"I don't think I will, Quinn, but we'll see." Tears ran down my face as I said it. "I'll miss you."

She stepped forward and hugged me tightly. "I'll miss you, too, chicka. We'll talk on the phone, though. You're not getting off this easy."

"And you'll keep deleting the videos and giving the gossipers hell for me?"

"You fucking know it."

We hugged again, and I turned and jogged to my car. Gerrod and Jenko sat in the den watching. They must have been afraid to say anything to me.

Before I could drive away, Jenko walked up and stood next to my window. I pushed the button lowering it with the understanding this conversation could go either way.

"You know you're running, right, Noelle?" I considered his comment for a moment. His words were correct, but I didn't want to think about the move that way.

"Yeah, probably, but I have to take care of me at the moment, and it won't happen here at school. There's too much shit going on to concentrate on what's necessary."

"And what about taking care of Blue? Who do you expect will do that? Doesn't he deserve your time and effort to see him through this?" When he decided to speak up, his comments cut straight to the jugular. He wanted to see me bleed.

I took a deep breath choosing my words carefully. "Yes, he does deserve help, but I'm not sure I'm the person he wants it from."

"That's bullshit, and you know it. Don't you get how this is not his fault? Don't you understand he has feelings for you?" His anger rose with each question.

"I get it, Jenko. I do, but I'm not sure I can be the one. I'm not sure our feelings are the same." I inhaled deeply trying to find the courage to continue. "I need time. We both need time. Me leaving will give it to us. If I stay here, I'm not sure if I can move forward. He doesn't need me keeping him from doing that."

"Keep telling yourself that, but know this, Noelle, he could move on without you when it's all said and done. Where will that leave you?"

"That's a risk I'll have to take, Jenko. We'll see if we were meant to be." I rolled my window up. This conversation was over. I backed out leaving him watching me from the same spot.

It took longer than usual to get home because I had to stop a few times from all the crying I did. I knew I'd made the best decision possible for me, but it still hurt. It seemed like I remembered doing this once before only not with all my belongings.

My parents stood at the door when I drove up. I'd texted when I stopped the last time so they'd know when I'd arrive. The last thing I wanted was to come home to an empty house. I supposed I needed to get used to it because they ran the roads all the time now since I'd left. They had no reason to stick around anymore.

"Glad you're here, honey." Mom pulled me in for a tight hug.

"Yeah, I guess I am, too."

She leaned back and looked at me. "You didn't have to move home, Noelle. You could have stayed and stuck it out. You know we'd support whatever decision you made."

"Yeah, I know. This is the decision, though, so I'm going with it."

Dad walked up behind us and wrapped his arms around both of us—family hugs offered so much love.

The semester dragged by slowly. My classes were Skyped, and my assignments turned in online. I stayed so far ahead since I had no life at home. All my friends worked or were off at school having fun. The idea of looking at other schools turned my stomach. I'd considered enrolling in an online university and finishing out my degree. Home life offered no exposure to drama. I felt like I'd had enough drama to last a lifetime.

While I scrolled through the courses of one school, my mom came in and sat beside me.

"Courses for the spring?" She watched as I moved up and down through the listing.

"Yeah, at Texas College."

"That online university?"

"Yep, that's the one. They have a lot of interesting courses."

She reached out and took my laptop from me and set it on the floor. "No. Absolutely not. You are not going to finish college online. You'll go back to school in January. We've let this go on long enough."

"You can't make me go back there." We stared each other down.

"No, we can't make you go back there, but you will go somewhere. You can't let a few bad experiences ruin your life, Noelle. Okay, so you had a bad run with one guy. There's a lot more to choose from. You had a bad experience with cheerleading. Find a new passion. You dealt with a nut case. Let me tell you, little girl, you're going to deal with lots of them in your lifetime. You learn to take the good with the bad.

"Do you think when you take a job, you won't deal with people who have problems? If that's the case, you need to reconsider. Everyone has problems, Noelle. Every workplace has crazy people. Some people deal with their problems better than others, and you'll need to learn to work with these people.

"It's the same thing with Blue. Guys make mistakes. It's the way they're built. What'd he do that was so bad you can't get passed it? Was he involved with another woman? Did he lie to you? Was he sleeping around behind you back? Tell me what he did that makes you hate him."

"I don't hate him, Mom, but he did have sex with another woman when he was with me." From her reaction, I knew my comment made her angry.

"Oh, please, Noelle. It was not of his choosing. Damn, give the guy a break here. It wasn't what he wanted. It's not like he went out looking for a quick hookup with another woman. What if the shoe were on the other foot? What if you'd been drugged, tied up, and raped? Would you have wanted Blue to ditch you?"

I looked at her a long time before I answered. "No, I wouldn't, but would he ever want me again anyway?"

"Do you want him any less because he's been raped?"

"No."

"Then what's the holdup here? You need to get your shit together and do what's right. Our Noelle was never a quitter. What happened to that person we sent off to college? First, it's cheer and now this. You need to suck it up, buttercup, and start being an adult. Where are your big girl panties because now is the time to put them on and be one?" I stared at my mom as she walked out my door without looking back. Her speech shocked me. She'd never spoken like that to me.

I rolled over and wrapped around my pillow. Maybe she was right. I missed Blue horribly. I cried so often at night when I rolled over, and his big warm body didn't take up more than half my bed. I knew I'd done him wrong. He told me how he felt about being the victim. I never treated him like the victim. In my mind, I was. That was so wrong.

I tossed and turned for most of the night trying to decide how to take back control. If I went back to school, would Blue forgive me for leaving? What could I do to make him see my apologies were sincere? Gerrod was right. This was bullshit. I needed to woman up and do what I knew was the right thing.

I punched in my phone code. This required reinforcements. I prayed they'd agree to help me find my way back.

I drove in the parking lot of the apartments and parked down by the second building where I could still see the front door. I knew my two roomies would be home from practice by now. I'd called Quinn the night before and told her my plan for today, happy to hear she was completely on board with the idea. I had a lot to make up for with Blue.

She needed to get Timms out of the apartment for me. She and Gerrod passed by my car and then whipped a U-turn and parked in front of Blue's place.

Gerrod went in and came back out with Timms still hobbling along on his crutches. They must've told him the plan, too, because he looked my way and did a little head tip toward me. When they drove away, I picked up the hot pizza and put on my pizza boy hat. I looked ridiculous in it, but it was part of the act.

I knocked on the door and disguised my voice. "Pizza."

"Not mine. Go away."

I knocked again. "Pizza for Blue."

"It's not my damn pizza, so leave."

I knocked a third time. "Pizza."

He jerked the door open this time, and his pissed-off expression dropped immediately. He stared at me but said nothing. "Pizza for Blue."

He leaned against the doorway. "Don't want your pizza."

"It was made special for you." I smiled at him but never received one in return.

"Special doesn't matter anymore. Apparently, I never mattered enough to be treated special by anyone, especially a girlfriend." He shut the door in my face. I wanted to cry so badly, but I sucked it up and sat down against the door.

"I'm not leaving till you talk to me, Blue." He made an ugh noise.

I felt the door give a little when he sat with his back to me against the door. The déjà vu effect I felt sent a shiver up my spine.

"I don't know what to tell the pizza girl. I said all I had to say, and she didn't want to listen to me."

So we were doing this in the third person?

"She's had a long time to think about everything you said and wants to listen better this time, and this pizza smells so good. She knows you're hungry all the time." I tried to laugh, but couldn't pull it off. No noise came from the other side either.

"Not anymore. The girl took away my appetite for pizza and a lot of other stuff, too."

"Like the girl?" I asked afraid of the answer.

"Both pizza and the girl. You see, this girl didn't care enough to find out the whole story about events that happened. She ran at the first sign of trouble. She gave up without a fight, which is weird because this girl had a lot of fight in her when she got here. She stood up to people who tried to give her shit. She didn't back down when times got a little tough. Hell, she even agreed to take in an invalid so he could get better."

I couldn't help it. The lump in my throat caused the tears to well up in my eyes and spill over down my cheeks. "You're r-right, she d-did," I stuttered.

"That, right there, is what I don't get about this girl. She bucked up for everyone except the person who she claimed was her one. The guy who did it for her.

The guy who was ready to give her everything. Hell, this guy even gave up his needs for her and settled on being her friend so he could be close to her. What does she give him? Nothing. Nada. Not a damn thing."

"She knows and is so sorry for that. Sorrier than she knows how to express in words, but it took a mom to show her the way. Guess this girl still has a lot to learn about life. Maybe she needs a lot more practice at it."

"Yeah, maybe she does, but I'm not sure this guy is the one who needs to be her guinea pig. He needs someone who is willing to go the hundred yards and under the uprights with him. This girl might turn around and run the wrong way with the ball."

"But what if she was willing to let the guy lead her to a touchdown at the right end zone? Would he be there every step of the way?"

"Don't know if he can. The other team puts a lot of obstacles in the way. Would she be willing to let me run beside her knocking the problems out of the way?"

"Yeah, she would." I smiled to myself. How did we get onto football euphemisms? It didn't matter, though. We needed to see each other now.

"Maybe if you opened the door and tried seeing how far this girl would fight to get to where she needed to be, your opinion would change. And there is still this yummy pizza to consider. Your appetite might return for the girl and pizza."

"Why should I try? Would this pizza girl care if I tried?"

"This pizza girl would so care if you did."

"Why?"

"Because this pizza girl happens to love you and doesn't want to see you starve. And she's tired of being sad without you."

"Oh yeah? She thinks she loves me, huh?"

"No, she knows she loves you, and she knows you used to love her and pizza. Maybe if you ate some, you'd learn to love them both again."

I heard him stand, and I popped up, too. The door swung open. "That's faulty logic, pizza girl." He pulled me to him, taking the crazy cap off my head letting my hair fall down around my face.

"It's my faulty logic, and I'm sorry."

"I happen to enjoy finding faulty logic and straightening it out." He tugged me into him tighter and kissed me. Taking the pizza box, he threw it on the floor before he picked me up, and I wrapped my legs around his waist.

He pulled back. "Pizza's bad for my waistline."

"Hot sex will work it off." I kissed him as he headed for our bedroom.

BLUE

Before the kick-off, I looked in the student section of the stands to make sure my biggest fan sat in her seat. She waved and smiled and then stood and shook her #1 fan foam finger with my name running across the palm. She looked ridiculous with that huge hand sticking up off her arm, but it was okay with me. I wanted to be her number one choice.

This would be our last game before playoffs. The Rams were going to a bowl no matter what the outcome of this game was. Winning would get us a step closer to playing in the championship bowl and being national champs.

Timms rolled by on his golf cart as the kicking team lined up on the field. "See your fan's got a finger up for you." He smiled when he said it.

"Yeah, got my name right there in the palm, too."

"That third finger gonna have a ring on it anytime soon?" He waited for my answer, but I simply stared and smiled.

"We'll see. Too soon to tell, but it's looking good for next year at this time. We're going to practice being adults for a while longer."

"Practice, huh? I like to practice a lot of adult things." He started laughing. "That's the best thing about moving back to the house. I get to practice all the damn time. This thing..." he pointed to his immobilized leg, "... it's good for attracting females to practice with. Getting me the best rides of my life. Funny how some females feel the need to do whatever it takes to make me feel better." Seeing him back to his old self helped ease the pain of him not being out there behind the line ready to lead us to another victory.

He spent a lot of time working with Crew. The kid took instruction and performed like a pro. With Timms coaching him, he might see a Heisman in his future. Too bad we'd all have moved on to the next phase of our lives.

Gerrod came up behind me. "You see my girl standing beside that crazy finger in the air with your name plastered on it?"

"Yeah. Looks good, doesn't it?"

His big body rumbled with laughter. "The only thing that looks good is the one wearing it and the hot girl beside it."

"You're probably right, but I was thinking about how I could use that to my advantage. Is she sending me a message, like where she would like this finger and palm to go? Or maybe, we could use it somehow to create a little friction where we need it."

"Dude, you're sick. Where do you come up with this shit?" He walked off shaking his head. I knew it would get to him.

Jenko and I ran out to the huddle together. "We ready to do this, Half sac?"

"Hell, yeah. I think my jersey next year's gonna have it printed on there. No more secrets about me around here. Might as well embrace it," I yelled out to their quarterback, "Hey, Twelve, I'm coming for you." I pointed to him. "Yeah, me, Half sac's coming. For. You."

The entire offensive line started laughing just before he snapped the ball.

SPRING SEMESTER

"Lots of changes going to be happening around here this spring leading into our season in the fall. As you know, with Timms graduating in a couple of months, we will be looking to replace our starting quarterback. Crew Devillier certainly showed us his capabilities by stepping up to lead the team to the championship bowl, so he'll be the number one contender to beat out of that position." Coach informed the team.

Crew did an outstanding job. Timms became his personal coach for the remainder of the season, and Crew's performance couldn't be beaten. The team got behind the kid one hundred percent which only added to the confidence he already possessed. It seemed like the kid was born to be in the spotlight.

We were careful to keep his ego in check, though. When he got a little too full of himself, we'd pull some prank on him to knock his ass back to reality. He learned the hard way that the upperclassmen weren't going to put up with his cockiness. We even invited his dad down one weekend to help us out. None of us knew until that weekend that his dad wrote most of the music for Assured Distraction, and those men showed up sometimes to give him and Tucker hell at every turn.

Coach continued, "We wanted to announce today that Theo Timms has been added to the coaching staff for the fall semester. He will be working with the quarterbacks." The locker room erupted in applause. "Timms has agreed to volunteer his services during the spring in an internship here on the coaching staff. You will treat him with the respect a coach deserves from here on out. Is that understood?"

"You want us to call him Coach Timms?" I had to ask.

"No, you cannot call him that until he's officially employed by TAU, but that doesn't mean you won't treat him any differently than the rest of the coaches."

"But Coach, he lives in the XOX house. How are we going to treat him differently out there?"

"Okay," Timms spoke up. "When we're at the frat house, you can treat me normally. You know, like royalty while I'm the president. I'm looking for my replacement recommendations as we speak for that important leadership role. Keep that in mind when you address me at the house."

"Well, fuck. He's turned into a coach already," Jenko commented quietly to me.

"Yep, sounds like it."

Coach let us go after all the announcements. Spring training officially started tomorrow. Timms' dream of going pro in the draft was replaced with coaching. Those of us who knew him knew it's where he needed to be. After watching him work with Crew and the other backups, the guy seemed born to it. His quiet style had a lot of punch to it.

Gerrod, Jenko, and I were glad because he would be around for our senior year. He might not be on the playing field, but he'd be there for us when we needed him.

His year got better when Madelyn was dismissed from the university before Thanksgiving. With charges filed against her, the campus banned her from stepping foot on the grounds. We would be going to trial if her lawyer hadn't convinced her to take a deal. Part of it involved a stay in a psychiatric facility for a year, so we didn't have to worry about her anyway.

I walked into the apartment, and there were candles lit everywhere. Noelle didn't have classes on Mondays this semester. I liked where this was going already. Rose petals were sprinkled down the hall leading to our bedroom. I peeked in the doorway, and there she lay in black lace. She had a blindfold over her eyes and those black furry handcuffs locking her to the headboard.

Even though I never required these things anymore, we liked to play from time to time with them. Guess today was that time, and who was I to question playing?

"Blue?"

"No, it's Jenko."

"What!"

I leaned over and ran my tongue around her nipple hiding under that lace causing it to make hardened pebble that I nipped at lightly with my teeth. "No, babe. No one else has a key to our house but me."

"I was waiting for you." She smiled.

I ran my tongue to the other perfect peak and skimmed my teeth over it causing her to arch off the bed.

"Hmmm. Does that feel good?"

"You know it does."

I dropped my clothes before moving to the foot of the bed and picking up her smooth leg kissing her ankle bone on my way up the soft skin of her calf. I climbed on the bed.

"If that feels good, wait 'til you feel this..."

UP NEXT

Theo Timms' dreams of making the pro draft died the day he took a bad hit, but he knew he'd found his calling with the Rams as a coach for the quarterbacks. He loved working with the kids who came to campus full of hopes and dreams of leading the Rams to the National Championships.

Now that he had a life at TAU that didn't include coeds, his personal life needed to move on, but how did he resist all the females who flocked to him at every opportunity? The rules stated no teacher-student relationships would be tolerated.

Damn, so many hot chicks under his nose, and they were off limits.

Life had challenges, and he loved a challenge.

On a more serious note:

This book is a work of fiction but some situations discussed here are of a sensitive nature, specifically the rape scene. I didn't start out to have an event so life changing or serious. Madelyn's character is a vile individual and the scene took on a life of its own.

Rape is rape, no matter if it's female or male and a serious issue. Men are less likely to report it or even admit to it or talk about it. If you or anyone you know has been a victim of rape, please seek help or assist them in getting help. Reporting the crime could possibly prevent another incident.

Crisis hotlines exist everywhere, so please don't hesitate.

RAINN- 1-800-656-HOPE, if you live in the U.S., calling this number will connect you to a rape crisis center near you. If is free and confidential.
From Canada call 1.888.407.4747 for help
Internationally call +1 202.501.4444
The Samaritans UK 116 123
Lifeline Australia 13 11 14

Beginning a different sub-genre in romance has been more challenging that I thought. It's been a lot of fun playing around with football and the players on the Rams. I'm glad I went through with it because I love college football. The new adult section to publish in excites me, too. It's some of the best days of our lives so writing for them is rewarding.

I'd like to thank a few people who helped along the way.

I'll start with my husband, Steve, for putting up with me writing while we're supposed to be on vacation. He never complained about it like I figured he would.

I'd like to thank Theresa, Mayas, and Julie for beta reading my newest baby. I appreciate their help more than I can ever say.

Thank you, Jason Anderson, for the beautiful cover design. We are getting better with each one. Old friends we can rely on are the best and you've been around forever! Makes me happy that we met so long ago and renewed the friendship recently.

The author and readers who have encouraged me to continue in this adventure even on the days I want to throw in the towel. Mayas Sanders, Dale Gardiner, Theresa Talbot, Julie LaFrance and many others I'm sure I've left off.

Thanks to Wander Photography for the gorgeous picture of Jamie Walker for the cover. I can always count on Wander's team to make my covers look the best! Thank you all.

Thank you to the great people in Finn's Freaks who answer when I call out for help! It's awesome to know I can count on many of you to come running when I need you the most.

Goodreads Links

Check out the books below and add to your TBR list.

Assured Distraction Series

Assure Her (Assured Distraction Book One) –
Keeton's Story

His Distraction Assurance Distraction Book Two) –
Ryan's Story

His Assurance (Assured Distraction Book Three) –
Gunner's Story

Distracted No More (Assured Distraction Book Four) –
Carter's Story

Hayden's Timbre (Companion Book to Assured Distraction
Series) Hayden's Story

Website

http://www.thiafinn.com

Email

author@thiafinn.com

Facebook

https://www.facebook.com/ThiaFinn/?fref=ts

Goodreads

https://www.goodreads.com/author/show/14206242.Thia_Finn

Growing up in small town Texas, **Thia Finn** discovered life outside of it by attending The University of Texas, only to return home and marry her high school sweetheart. They raised two successful and beautiful daughters while she taught middle school Language Arts and eventually became a middle school librarian. After thirty-four years, she retired to do her favorite things, like travel, spend time off-roading with family and friends, hanging out at the Frio River, reading, and writing.

She currently lives in the same small town where she grew up, with her husband and the boss, Titan, the Chihuahua. She can often be found stalking on social media, watching Outlanders, Vikings or Game of Thrones to name a few on Netflix.